# THE WORLD AFTER

## By D.L. Gore

Thanks to everyone who believed in me and helped me,
in any way large or small, to make this book happen.

You know who you are.

# PREFACE

On September 26th 1983, Lieutenant Colonel Stanislav Petrov was the commanding officer on duty at Oko, the Soviet early warning system, located in a bunker just south of Moscow. Shortly after midnight, five intercontinental missiles were detected, apparently inbound from the USA. The equipment was new and Petrov's gut feeling told him that it was just a glitch, but he had only his instinct to rely on. He had no way of knowing for sure whether his country was under attack or not until after it would have been too late to respond.

He should have immediately reported the incident to his superiors, who may have then decided on a retaliatory strike. Fortunately for the entire world, Petrov took a unilateral decision to ignore protocol and he did nothing. It turned out that he was right and it was a false alarm after all, but what if he had followed the correct procedure?

The above is true. The fictional story that follows is based on just that one deviation, from a history that could have been...

# CHAPTER 1

I was born three years after the end of the world and the world ended twenty years ago.

This life holds so few opportunities, surely Gill could not deny me this one. I remember the day that he sent for me to break the news. Although there was no longer any real navy, Admiral Gill would always be Admiral Gill, to everyone; both the ex-crew of HMS Sedbergh and also what remained of the Islanders themselves. If anyone was in charge it was Gill. Every community needs a leader and Gill had slotted right into the job. I suppose having a nuclear aircraft carrier and a small air force at his command had helped there. People had appreciated the need for structure and discipline that Gill could offer when the ship arrived, and the protection he could provide.

The Sedbergh brought with her a second chance of life to the Island back then. The Islanders would have been foolish to turn her away. The ship gave the people a chance to live in a way that better resembled that of the world before. It had been their only choice for a civilised future.

As I walked down the hills, through the town and then down the old Victorian pier towards the ship and his office within, I did not know why Gill would have sent for me, but I knew it must be important. You did not just walk into Admiral Gill's office to say hello; it was strictly invitation only, even to those of us who lived aboard the ship. Gill was a very reclusive man, more so since the war, almost certainly exacerbated by his blindness; he had lost his sight to the intense glare of a nuclear flash. I knew that if Gill wanted to talk to me he must have good reason, especially if it was urgent enough for him to interrupt my working day. So I was rather nervous as I made my way down from the fields I had been helping to harvest on that summer morning. As I was soon to discover, nothing I could have imagined at the time would have prepared me for what he had to say to me that day.

I knocked politely on his door and I went inside. The office was a cold grey painted cube, sparsely decorated and barely changed from its active military days. There were two doors, the one I entered through was in a corner and the other was half way along the wall to my left. Gill's desk and seat stood in front of the other door, which I knew led to his personal quarters. Opposite was a leather sofa, cracked with age, and above that was a picture of the ship in an embossed wooden frame. Apart from a single additional chair, every other part of the room was bare of decoration or furniture.

Gill was sat behind the desk in his high backed leather chair. He was dictating food supply rotas to his assistant, Helen. She and her adopted son Edward also lived on the ship and, though five years younger than me, he and I had been at our small school together for a while. She smiled briefly at me and pointed to the sofa with the back of her pencil, indicating for me to take a seat, before continuing to take notes. I sat and waited as patiently as I could, anxious to hear what Gill had to say, given the rarity of a visit to his office. A few minutes passed and Gill finished what he was doing.

He asked Helen to go and fetch a pot of tea, then for the first time since I had entered the room, he turned his attention towards me.

I was still feeling very apprehensive, wondering what he would have to say and desperately trying to remember if there was anything I could have been caught doing that I might now be in trouble for.

"How are you doing, kid? I presume that's you, Badger," he asked me in a friendly manner.

"I'm fine thank you, Sir." Everybody called Gill 'Sir', even those that had not been crew of the ship, or like me were born after the war.

"I suppose you're wondering why I have requested that you come here," he said and then he carried on without waiting for a reply. "You're going to hear this one way or another and I think it will be better if you hear it from me, rather than from the rumour mill."

He paused, apparently thinking how best to continue and my mind raced, wondering just what he was going to say next, relieved at least that I did not seem to be in any trouble after all.

"I'm going to ask you to promise not to do anything rash or stupid, absolutely promise me," he said.

"Sir? Yes, Sir." I was starting to wish he would just tell me what it was he had to say, rather than continuing to tread delicately around whatever the issue was.

"Okay well," again he paused, "well we've had a small amount of radio traffic from the mainland. Your friend Shiel picked it up." He seemed hesitant, waiting for a moment before he continued. "Just a few seconds, you understand. If I could trust Shiel not to tell you...," his voice trailed off to nothing and he seemed reluctant to tell me more. This was out of character for a man who was usually so very confident; he was obviously uncomfortable with the news.

After he had paused, "And, you see, it might have had your father's call sign and a part of his serial number in it."

"What...?" I sat dumbfounded, unable to speak, my mind racing. My Father had been missing for ten years after disappearing over the mainland when I was seven, and despite the searches neither he nor his plane were ever found. What did Gill mean by 'might have had'?

"Either it did or it didn't," I thought to myself. Then he told me everything, the very last thing I had expected to hear, the most elating, the most disappointing and the most unexpected all at the same time. Firstly my Father could still be alive on the mainland, but most shocking of all, Admiral Gill was not going to do anything about it.

Well I certainly would do something and I did not care if he thought it was rash or otherwise.

"Listen to me," he said, "the chances of it being him are negligible."

"But there *is* a chance?" I could not suppress the hope and excitement that was welling up inside me.

"No, listen. We received his plane's call sign and the first four digits from his serial number, that's it. The message cut off and we've had nothing else since. We tried to reply and we've got nothing back."

"It has to be him!" I said. "Who else would send that?"

"Look, stop and think about it for a moment. There are lots of explanations why we could have received it. Some kids could have found his plane and played with the radio for instance, pressing the mic."

"After ten years the battery would be dead," I started to raise my voice, "and why would they send his call sign and serial number? Explain that!" Under normal circumstances I would not have got away with talking to the admiral like that, but at that moment I could not help myself.

"It was written on the plane and on the front of his flight suit," he said in a cold, matter-of-fact tone, waiting for me to realise what that meant. "There could be any number of people waiting to ambush any rescue party sent for him. Frankly, kid, that's much more likely don't you think?"

I had a moment to calm down and think as Helen re-entered with the tray of drinks, laid it out and left again discreetly, leaving us alone to talk. With my hands trembling, I poured and passed Gill his cup. We talked on for a while and I was glad on that one occasion that he could not see my face. I could keep my voice as monotone as possible, but the expression of anger and outrage on my face would have been impossible to hide.

The way that he explained it to me, it seemed that it was simply maths that prevented him sending people to look for my Father, just maths. The odds of him surviving for so long were too low. The cost in resources of going looking was too high. I did not care about any of that.

Gill just sat there, drinking tea from an Isle of Man souvenir mug, an almost surreal relic of a past age, telling me that he was not going to give my Father any chance at all. Still I tried to argue with him.

"People do survive out there, Sir," I pleaded. "We see them on the coast every time we fly over, or sail near."

"None of them crash landed or came down with a parachute," he tried to reason with me. "Your father would have been of great interest to the locals, even if he survived the landing he would not have gone in unnoticed."

"He *could* still be alive, you know he could!"

"It's been ten years, why would he stay out there for ten years before trying to get in touch. That doesn't make sense." Gill might have had a point, but I was not ready to believe it. "We looked for him for days afterwards, you remember that, don't you? How your mother was?"

"Of course I do, Sir, I remember she cried for weeks." I also knew that she would have done anything it took to get him back, however slim a chance it might have been. "Surely, if not for me, you owe it to her memory to try."

"Don't put yourself through it all again. Accept it, he's gone." Gill put down his cup, feeling for the table first. "I'm sorry, Badger," he said, "but that's my decision, I'm not prepared to risk losing any more lives to the mainland, for such a short piece of radio traffic and that's final, do you understand?"

"Yes, Sir," I replied sullenly. I had been given my cue to leave. I felt a whole range of emotions as I stood and walked towards the door. Overflowing with joy and hope at the prospect that my Father could be alive; incredulous and angry that he was being abandoned all over again.

"Of course, if we do pick up any more properly identifiable transmissions then we wouldn't hesitate to go looking," he said as I walked out through the doorway. I did not reply.

I slammed his door behind me, furious, confused and immersed in my thoughts. How could he give up on him like that when there had been a clear signal that he was still alive? Gill and my Father had at one time been through so much together, the war and the early years on the Island. They had been much more than

mere colleagues. I remembered clearly the two of them
laughing together once on the hangar deck. I had been
a child, held by my Father, laughing along with them
without properly understanding their joke.

I was almost at my own room before I realised that I
had forgotten to leave the mug behind. Still half full, it
shattered against the wall and I made up my mind there
and then. The rest of the harvesting would have to be
done without me, I had plans to make.

I could never give up on my Father.

# CHAPTER 2

I went to see Shiel and I caught up with him on his way home from his shift in the wireless room at the heart of the ship. He and I had been best friends for years. Shiel's great passion was technology. He tried to recreate, repair or bodge together any equipment from before the war. Despite the damaging effects of the electromagnetic pulses of the atomic bombs, when he was eight years old he had managed to get an old record player working. He had only found the one record, but that did not bother Shiel; he had only wanted to watch it spin round and round, marvelling at the workings of the machine. He had played it over and over again until he drove everybody mad and they were forced to go and find him some more for variety. Now, amongst other responsibilities, he was part of the team who listened for radio traffic in the hope of picking up signals - either friendly or otherwise, from remaining civilisations or reformed governments, or anyone who might be using radios to co-ordinate an attack on our people.

It was not Shiel's technical skills I was interested in then though. Shiel also had access to a boat and equally importantly, he was on the roster to take it out every two days. He ferried food out to an oil rig that was located between our Island and the coast of the mainland, for the men that worked out there. Maybe Shiel could get me to the mainland... if I could persuade him.

"I know what you're going to ask and the answer is no, absolutely not," he said flatly as soon as he saw me. "You wouldn't last ten minutes out there. They would eat you alive, Badge, literally".

As we walked through Ramsey, I did not say anything at first. He knew me well enough to know that I would have already determined to go. Likewise, I knew he would try to stop me and that he would feel duty bound to talk me out of it.

"They're animals over there, Badger. Honestly, it's suicide. I've seen them on the coast, painted with tribal colours and wrapped in rags," he pleaded. "They're not like the people here on the Island, you know. They would hack you to bits and gnaw on your bones. If you're lucky, they'll kill you first."

"Where did it come from?" I asked, ignoring his concerns. "I know you triangulate from the other receiver at Port Erin. Where did the signal he sent come from, Shiel?"

"Manchester, near the centre. You'd never make it to there would you?" He almost looked hopeful, as if that would change my mind. It was wishful thinking on his part.

"Oh, I'm going," I told him, "and you're going to take me to the mainland."

"I've already told you, no. There's no way I'm taking you to die in that wasteland."

"Come on, Shiel," I tried to cajole him, "they won't see me, won't even know I'm there. I can hide during the day, move at night."

"You'd be lost in less than an hour." He was right of course and I had no intention of hiding all day, but I thought I might be able to persuade him it sounded safer. It was time to try a different plan of attack, coercion had not worked and I had nothing to blackmail or bribe him with, so I had only my last resort: guilt.

"Shiel, it's my Dad. I'm going. One way or another, I'm going to Manchester." I would never forget where my Father had crashed and if the signal had come from there, then he had to be alive. That had to be the best place to start looking.

"I'm not taking you to the mainland," he repeated. "You want to kill yourself? Fine, but find somebody else to help you do it."

"Look, Shiel, if you don't take me I'll find another way, I'll swim across if I have to." I meant that and he knew it. "If it was your dad out there and there was a chance he was alive you'd have to go, wouldn't you?" He looked less firm in his resolve. "Or would you leave your dad out there to die?" With that I thought I had him.

He looked at me quizzically. "Do you think he'd expect it? Would he expect or want you to mount a solo rescue mission and maybe get yourself killed, on the slim chance you might find and save him?"

I looked him in the eyes and said, "Nobody else is going to do it. He might not want it but he should be able to rely on it. He knows nothing should stop a rescue and you know it too. You either help me or I'll just steal a boat and I'll go on my own, Shiel, your choice."

Shiel knew it was no idle threat since there were plenty of boats around the Island and I could be stubborn when I set my mind to something. He also knew that I was not a good sailor and would likely come to a bad end much sooner without his assistance.

"Okay, I'll help you, but don't you dare get yourself killed you idiot," he rolled his eyes, "or I'll be in it up to my neck won't I?"

That was settled then. He was due out again the next morning, so I had ample time left that day to prepare.

"I'll be round to yours later then okay?" I said to him.

"Whatever. Come round if you like. I'm not happy about this, Badger, I'm really not."

"See you later, Shiel," I said as I walked off excitedly back towards the ship.

I grabbed a late lunch of stew and bread in the ship's canteen, glad that it was empty, sitting on my own and talking to no one before heading back to my room. Although most people lived in the town, this was the closest thing to home and family that I had. After my Mum died I had begged to be allowed to stay and, although I was only twelve at the time, Gill had relented.

I immediately dug around under my bunk and pulled out my backpack, it had a frame of aluminium tubing and when empty it weighed hardly anything at all. I threw it onto my bed and piled up beside it all of the other stuff I would be taking with me on my trip.

I had a waterproof poncho which used to belong to my Father; it was a dark green square and six feet long down each side. The hood in the centre could be pulled shut with a drawstring. Like my pack, it was made from heavy water-proofed nylon. In each corner it had metal rings pressed through the material and it had been designed to double up as a small tent in addition to its primary function as outerwear. I rolled it up and put it in one of the rucksack's side pockets. Refusing to accept that my mission might be anything other than straightforward, I had decided that I should only be out there for a few days and I hoped that would be all the weather protection I should need in the summer.

From my cupboard I dug out a camping stove and the alcohol that fuelled it. I often used it when I went on long hunting trips to the centre of the Island and it folded up quite small and compact. I tossed it onto the bunk along with the thin walled metal bottle that the fuel was stored in. My Dad had taken me on my first hunting trip and I often thought of him when I had been out there, trying to sleep in my tent in the rain. Right then I had no time for such nostalgia. A small box filled with candles joined the pile on my mattress. To stop them rattling around I filled the rest of the box with string, which was always handy when living and sleeping outdoors.

I had a pair of binoculars, only small and not very powerful, but they were perfect for travelling light. I put them in the other side pocket of the rucksack, along with an old Ordnance Survey map of the Manchester area that I had kept ever since my Mum had given it to me as a small child. She had used it to show me the last known position of my Father's plane and I had always felt a strange sense of comfort looking at it, as if he was not missing if I knew where he was. I felt such nervous excitement to be going to see the places marked on the map but it was tinged with fear about the prospect too.

My compass and the stub of a pencil joined the map. Again I remembered my Father; he had given me the compass on my first camping trip in the hills with him. I tried not to get carried away with the memories, but it was difficult. Growing up without him and then later on without my Mother had made me self reliant and strong, but I had missed out on so much with them. I think that was why I was so determined to go through with my mission to find him, clutching at the hope of getting one of them back.

I then turned my attention to an item that was extremely rare and precious to me, so long after almost all but the most basic of manufacturing had ceased. I took it out from a drawer, where it was wrapped in cloth and stored in a tin. A small red plastic gas lighter, still half full, the word 'Bic' was embossed on its side. I had kept it for years and I had never used it except for once to make sure it worked. I had a traditional fire-making flint and steel that I packed too, but the lighter was such a convenient thing to have and I could not think of a more fitting circumstance in which to finally use it.

Next I took my bow down from its hooks over the bed and put it into the semicircular bow bag I usually carried it in, leaning it against the wall. I put the quiver of arrows next to it, having taken them down off the top of the cupboard where I stored them. I took each arrow out, one at a time and I checked the keenness of each lethal broadhead. I inspected each shaft too and the fletchings at the rear; those arrows could mean life or death the next day and I could not afford for them to be less than perfect.

Then I pulled out my archery repair kit and re-glued one of the arrow's fletchings that was a little damaged. When I had finished I took a few of the more essential bits of the kit and packed them too: glue, a few spare fletchings and points, a good long length of bow string and a block of lubricating wax, amongst other things.

The next part of my preparations would be a little more difficult. I left my room, carrying a large empty canvas zipped bag, and I made my way through the bowels of the ship to its food stores. I had to go past the reactors as I walked. The heat was tremendous in that part of the ship, steam from the cooling water leaked out sometimes and it was a hellish place to work. There was a team of three attempting to plug a leak with a temporary patch until that section could be switched out and a full repair could be made. I walked through without incident or comment, stopping only at the condensers for a quick drink from the fountain there.

The stores were not usually guarded, but it was a busy place and I had no valid excuse for being there. I would have to sneak in to steal the provisions that I would need to take with me the next day. I waited down the corridor from the entrance for a while and this in itself would have appeared suspicious. People did not usually have time to just hang around during the middle of the day in our community. After a while I had counted the legitimate visitors to the stores in and out and I was confident that the rooms were empty.

I trotted down the corridor and made my way in through the heavy steel door, closing it behind me. Surveying the shelves quickly, I headed straight towards the preserved foods. I did not have much time to be choosy and I took the first suitable items I came across. Five jars, all filled with cooked mincemeat and stored with airtight lids were placed into the bag, along with a large quantity of ship's biscuit, a kind of salty dough baked to seemingly last forever. As I finished filling my bag, the door swung inwards and I had only an instant to move to the back of the stores and hide from sight. I took refuge behind some sacks that were piled up against the wall.

I did not see who came in and was relieved when they stayed inside the store for only a minute before leaving without noticing me. I followed as closely as I dared and as I left and walked away down the corridor towards the deck of the ship, I saw one of the duty chefs coming towards me. I had got out just in time.

I walked along the deck, taking a detour on the way

back to my room, to try to cover my tracks in case my theft was discovered before I left the next morning. The weather was warm and I lingered to look off the edge of the ship towards Ramsey itself. The small town with the huge Nimitz class warship moored off its old Victorian pier had been my home for all of my life. Aware that this could be my last chance to look out across it, I savoured the opportunity.

"Don't forget you promised him, Badger." I jumped, slightly startled by the voice, I had thought that I was alone.

I turned around and saw it was Helen, standing behind me. She must have seen me from across the runway.

"Do you think it's fair to make me promise before he would tell me the news?" I asked her.

"I don't think it makes the slightest bit of difference. You'd get yourself killed out there if you went to try and find him." Her opinion was not reassuring, but nothing she said could have dissuaded me from carrying out my plan and I was careful not to give anything away. I tried to change the subject, as subtly as I could, away from myself.

"I think Gill should be sending a rescue party," I told her flatly.

"I know you do, Badger, but that's how your dad got into trouble in the first place. It's been ten years now, I know you've no one else but haven't the rest of us here been like a family for you?”

“You know my Dad could still be alive, our helicopters could be there and back in a few hours,” I said.

“And another pilot could be shot by some barbarian hiding on the ground in less than a second,” she told me. “Gill has to think of the lives of others, his job isn’t easy you know.”

I knew that she was right and I could not deny it was risky to fly over the mainland. Any rescue would indeed put the lives of additional people in danger. I remained silent, unable to think of any rational argument and not wanting to risk saying the wrong thing and arousing her suspicion. The strong sea breeze whipped across the runway, blowing her auburn hair across her face.

“Listen,” she told me, while moving her hair out of her eyes, “if Gill knew for certain that he was alive, I know he’d send a team. It’s the uncertainty that’s preventing him.”

I did not want to hear any more of her defence of him, no matter how rational it was, it did nothing to calm my anger or weaken my resolve.

“I’ve got to go back to the harvest, I’ll see you later,” I said to her sharply, before moving off.

“Don’t forget your promise, Badger,” she called after me. “You promised him!”

I went back to my room, using a route that could have led off the ship to the pier, until I was sure that I was out of her sight. Then I went back down below deck and through the hangar. I walked past the fighter jet that I knew my Father used to fly and its four metre high twin tail fins towered over me as I stopped to look at it for a moment. Nearby was the helicopter that my Mother had piloted, a narrow lethal Cobra attack helicopter with weapons bristling all over it. Seeing them just spurred me on and I hurried on back to my cabin.

When I got back there I packed the food that I had acquired and tested the rucksack's weight afterwards. It was not too heavy, even fully loaded. Next I laid out the clothes I would wear the next day, selecting them from my meagre wardrobe with care. Most of my clothing was practical and durable attire and I did not have much to choose from.

I then realised that in my haste I had packed but I had not yet planned out any of my journey. I grabbed the map back out of my pack again and went out through the door, locking it behind me. I left the ship carrying the map in the waistband of my trousers, hidden by my shirt. I walked down the pier to the shore and headed across town to Shiel's small flat. I banged on his door a few minutes later.

# CHAPTER 3

Shiel answered the door on my third loud insistent knock. He stood aside and let me in. He looked like he had just woken up, wearing only a pair of trousers and scratching at a mop of 'bed head' hair.

"I was up at four, did a shift on the radios and then three hours in the fields grubbing up turnips. Don't I deserve to have a nap in the afternoon any more?" he asked rhetorically.

"Not today, I need to have a look at your maps," I said as I swept by him into the flat.

"Put the kettle on. Have a drink of something and wake yourself up," I told him as I reached his small kitchen. I looked at his table in there and shuddered at the filth he lived in, a stark difference from the almost clinical cleanliness I was used to on the ship. I cleared everything off it, either into the sink or piled it up on top of his already overflowing bin. I then spread out my own map on the surface, hoping it was not too sticky.

"I've got this one of Manchester and its outskirts, but I'm missing the first half of the route, from the coast," I said to him. "I can't really go and ask anyone else. I'm not risking the library and I doubt Gill would lend me his, but I thought you would probably be able to help anyway."

While the kettle was boiling on the wood stove, he went into the other room and came back with what I needed.

"You live like a pig, Shiel."

"So?" was his only reply as he measured out roasted and powdered dandelion root into two mugs and added the water. He passed me a cup of the 'coffee' and blew on his own.

"Where are you going to drop me off?" I asked.

"I'm not, I'm going to shoot you in the head and dump your body overboard as soon as we're out to sea," he said straight-faced. "Same end result but I save myself a bit of fuel for the boat."

"Now is not an appropriate or indeed a helpful time for you to be a complete pain in my rear, okay?"

"Okay," he said, "let's pick somewhere for you to get killed then." He looked at the map. "If you want it over with quickly I would recommend Liverpool or Southport. I've seen loads of vicious looking killers hanging round on the shore there."

"Shiel, don't," I implored him.

"Okay, so you want it a bit slower, more drawn out. In that case I think perhaps here, between Formby Point and Southport. I don't think I've seen any ravenous bloodthirsty mobs on that bit of coast for a while."

I punched his arm as hard as I thought I could get away with.

"Ouch!" he cried. Then, "Right, okay, dumped in the sea it is."

"Shiel," I said in a warning tone, lowering my voice. I gave him a stern look over the rim of my mug, blowing on the hot liquid before I took a sip of it.

"What? You choose then. I'm only being realistic." He sounded genuinely agitated and I knew that behind all his jokes he was worried about what might happen to me.

"Right then," I said, "here, amongst those dunes." I pointed at the map.

"If you want," he said grumpily, putting his mug down on the map, leaving a stained ring around Chorley.

"How long do you reckon it will take, I'm thinking three, maybe four days to walk there?"

"Yeah about that long, don't forget, you'll be moving slowly due to being stone dead."

"If you don't start being serious for a while, I'm going to have to give you a proper good kicking, Shiel." I stared straight at him.

"Alright, alright." He put his hands up in supplication. "You win, as usual. I know that look well enough."

Finally he looked at the map with sincerity, moving his drink off it. Shiel was my closest friend and he had been for years, but he really knew how to annoy me if he wanted to.

"Yes, I'd say three days is about right," he said. "It's around forty-five miles and I guess you won't be hanging around to enjoy the scenery too much. Even at a slow pace, you should easily clear fifteen to twenty miles a day."

"What time do you think we'll get to the coast tomorrow?" I asked him.

"Around late morning I'd expect, maybe a little earlier, but not much," he said and looked back down at the maps. "Stay away from the towns, Badge, they're bound to be trouble."

"I'm not planning on doing any sightseeing," I said. "I'll go straight across country, swerve round any towns I see and I'll try to get to the motorway by the end of tomorrow."

"That might be a bit ambitious," he said. "I'm not sure you'll move that fast."

He pointed at the map again. "Look," he said, "if you're going to go ashore here, and I do think that is about the safest place by the way, go slightly southwards of true east towards this place, Skelmersdale. Follow the old motorways after that, here and here." He indicated at the blue lines on the map. "You won't get lost following them, all you've got to do is find the first one and then you're on a winner."

"I've got a map and compass, I won't get lost."

"If I'm right about how dangerous it is out there, Badger, you're not going to have time to stop and look at your map. And never mind the days, what do you think you'll do at night?"

"Well, I'm taking my old poncho, you know, the old army thing of my Dad's. I thought it would be best to find somewhere in the open, either to camp or just wrap myself up in it," I told him.

"Probably for the best, maybe find a dip or a ditch first if you can," he said. "Don't forget to keep to the lower sections, don't go along the skyline anywhere will you."

"Shiel, you're stating the obvious now. I've been in all the same 'inconspicuous movement' lessons as you have at school," I said. "I'm probably better at it than you are."

"You probably are, but, well, I'm going to worry about you, that's all."

"I suppose I'll have to see how it goes once I'm out there, but I'll be careful. You know I'll be careful," I said pondering on his words. "By the way your coffee's awful."

"I assume you won't want to try my cooking then," he quipped. "Where to for dinner then, mate?"

"Oh, so we have a choice now, has a restaurant opened near here recently?" I joked.

"Ship's slop house as usual then, I hear Gill's upping the penalty to death for any of the chefs caught cooking anything that's actually edible."

"None of them need lose any sleep," I replied. "Get dressed then and let's go eat."

We walked together towards the ship, talking as we normally would about the inconsequential and the mundane, not concentrating on the next day. Along the sea front, first towards the pier, then down it and onto the Sedbergh herself. Shiel knew his way round the ship's interior as well as I did and we took the shortest route to the canteen almost subconsciously.

Seal was on the short canteen menu that afternoon, it had never really been a favourite of mine but it made a change, it came with a selection of steamed vegetables and I chose that. Shiel had a bowl of the same stew I had eaten for lunch. We ate quietly, the canteen was not very full but it would have been too easy to be overheard.

"I've got some beer stashed in my room, we can pick it up on the way back to yours," I said as we finished eating.

"We can drink them on the promenade, if you want. I think it'll be a nice evening," Shiel suggested.

"It's a good idea, but I've left the maps on your table," I said.

"Badge, you can't forget things like that after today," he hissed at me.

"Don't start again, Shiel. Gill's over in that corner, I don't want him to hear anything."

"Maybe I should go over and tell him everything anyway," he whispered back to me.

"Firstly you'd lose your best friend and secondly, hunting accidents happen." I gave him a threatening look as I whispered back.

"Let's go and pick up the booze," he said, standing up and leaving the table.

Shiel's concern was understandable and as we walked I thought back to the classes at school that we had been talking about. Our education was basic in academic terms, but rich in the more important skills that we need to live. At school they had taught us to read and to write, along with mathematics and science, but in other ways it had been more like army cadet training. Not that I complained, that type of syllabus did not suit everyone, but I had loved it. There were plenty of books on the Island, in the houses or in our library and I used to read all I could in the evenings. We had been taught from an early age the benefits of knowledge and I was always thirsty for it. The practical stuff though, the running through the assault courses and the tactical exercises, for me those were the most fun parts of our learning.

'Inconspicuous Movement' was not the only

survival skill we learned. 'Improvised Munitions' and 'Hand to Hand Combat' were also on the curriculum. 'Devising Defensive Objects' was another favourite subject of mine, and 'Primitive Projectile Weapons' in which we mostly studied archery. All of us could field strip the most common rifles and pistols that we would encounter, oil them and reassemble them correctly.

When we reach twelve years old, that is the end of school for us and we start work as apprentices to one of the many Island trades, but before that our graduation involved a three day escape and evade manoeuvre. The teachers dropped the blindfolded students at an undisclosed location on the Island. From that moment we had three full days to get back to Ramsey and aboard the Sedbergh without being caught. All of the Islanders were part of the game and tried to find and stop us. The closer you got to the ship the more kudos you earned. I had made it right up to the pier, few people had ever got closer than that and only once had someone ever made it aboard. The equipment they left us with was minimal and did not include food or water, we had to find or appropriate whatever we needed. It had been one of the most fun experiences of my life so far, the best game in the world I had thought. We were trained well from a very early age and I hoped that training was going to pay off; it was not going to be a game on the mainland.

"Hey, Shiel," I said out loud, "remember our 'Escape and Evade'?"

"How could I ever forget it?" he said. "How you didn't get spotted on the beach I will never know."

"Who said I went down the beach?" I asked, winking at him. The truth was that nobody knew how I had got so close to the ship, I had never told anyone.

"Come on, Badge, it must have been the beach, you popped up onto the pier from underneath."

We reached my cabin and I went inside, Shiel leant against the door frame waiting for me; my tiny room always felt cramped with two in it. I fetched the beer, passing half for him to carry.

"We came over the mountain still as one group and the others went down through the plantations. You and me went towards the coast but that doesn't mean I went to the beach after we parted," I teased him.

"Go on then tell me how you did it?" he pleaded.

"No," I said stubbornly, "it's a secret."

"Well after tomorrow you might not get the opportunity to share your secret. How did you do it, Badge? I won't tell anyone else," he assured me.

We had walked back out again, through the bowels of the ship, eventually breaking out to the evening sunlight above.

"Okay," I told him, "but you won't like it."

"Go on, how did you do it?"

"I... well, I used all available resources," I revealed subtly.

"Meaning?" he asked me.

"Well, have you noticed I never asked you which way *you* went to try and get on board?"

He looked confused for a moment as it dawned on him. "It was you!" he shouted. Everyone on the deck looked up at him and he lowered his voice, "You sold me out."

"I used all of my available resources. You made a great distraction." I could not help smiling a little.

"You followed me and then you sold me out to them!" he accused me, incredulously.

"You panicked is all. Just because someone shouts 'look there's one of them over there!' doesn't always mean someone's actually seen you," I said. "You bolting off like that was a perfect distraction and I used that opportunity to sneak under the pier while the guards chased after you."

"You used to be my friend," he said despondently.

We had reached the pier by then. Its hundred year-old frame was as well maintained as we could manage. Replacement planking seemed to appear every time we walked along it, the repair crews working tirelessly at their job. Power cables and pipes snaked along the pier's length, connecting the ship with the Island and distributing power and water to the town.

"I was trying to hang onto the bottom of it till it went dark," I told him. "How had you planned to get aboard anyway?" I tried to change the subject.

"I was just about to make up my mind on that when my ex-best friend sold me out." His bottom lip extended out comically in mock contempt.

"Come on, mate, it was five years ago," I said. "You can have an extra beer to make up for it."

"Traitor."

"That's harsh, Shiel, very harsh."

We reached the end of the pier and turned right, towards his flat again. I knew his sulk would not last long and as we walked together along the sea front the sun sank. He had been right; it was indeed a nice evening in Ramsey.

A few minutes later as we approached the swing bridge he spoke again. "So how did they catch you then, after you had handed them my head on a plate for your own convenience?"

"I wasn't the first person to try to get on board from under the pier," I said. "It was greased for a start. Then there was the newly installed barbed wire."

"I'm sure Gill invented the escape and evades to test his own security measures," Shiel mused.

"I'm sure it helps at least," I agreed. "He cheats though too."

"What do you mean?" he asked.

"Do you remember seeing the guard dogs on the pier at any other time prior to that year? It was one of the dogs that sniffed me out, five minutes later and I'd have climbed along the power cable and been inside," I said. "I was planning on walking right into Gill's office if I could have got on board."

"He wouldn't have liked that," Shiel said.

"That was kind of my point."

That night we sat together, Shiel and I, sharing a few beers together in his lounge before the challenge ahead. The packing was done, the plans were made and we just chatted, like old friends do. Talking of the things I was likely to see on the mainland and later on as we relaxed more, of some of the things I was rather less likely to encounter there.

"Do you think they'll all be mutants?" Shiel joked. "Loads of weird arms and things growing from unusual places?"

"Be serious," I told him, throwing a cushion at his head. I spluttered out beer, laughing through clenched lips as the cushion hit him in the face and he spilled some of his own drink into his lap.

"I am being serious," he insisted as he wiped himself down. "Don't you remember that freaky priest that came over here when we were kids?"

"He wasn't a mutant, Shiel, you idiot." Although as I remembered, I could not deny he had been a bit strange.

"He was far too scary to be normal and too hairy, way too hairy," said Shiel, starting to giggle. "I'm sure he was a big hairy scary mutant."

I realised that we should probably make those beers our last, if we were to have clear heads for our early start the next day.

"Edward should be glad your mutant brought him here," I said. "He'd have been dead a day or two later if he hadn't. Helen told me so herself."

"I didn't say he was a bad mutant." Giggling again he added, "Why did that guy leave anyway? Why did he go back to live on the mainland, when he could have had such a better life here?"

"I was seven, how would I know what he was thinking."

"Do you remember what he said when he left? You should look him up, Badge." He had stopped giggling and was more solemn again. Our mockery had not been meant to be cruel, but was merely a reflection of the way we had seen things when we were younger, in that slightly altered perception of reality that young children often observe; not helped by the fact that we were by then a little drunk too.

"Why, what did he say?" I asked, calming down. I had no recollection at all of his leaving, though I remembered the tall, wild haired priest clearly.

"He told everyone that he owed them a debt and said something about how he would help the people of Manx if we ever needed him. You should go to his peculiar church, Badge. I really mean it, it's a great idea and hopefully he might be able to help you stay alive a bit longer."

"What church?" I asked him. "I don't remember him saying anything like that."

As Shiel spoke he lowered his voice to a rumble, impersonating the priest. "'Go to the church at Ormskirk, the only one with a tower and a spire. Sit by the altar and say Sedbergh loudly, and I'll give any of you what aid I can.' Surely you must remember that. Everyone remembers that."

"No. No recollection at all, but I don't doubt you. Where's that map gone?" I asked him. "Maybe I should look him up. Do you really think he might help me?"

As he rummaged around he replied, "If he's still alive he might. He seemed pretty serious when he said it. What have you got to lose, it's almost on your way." He pointed out the location to me, on the now unfolded map. "There it is."

He was right, what did I have to lose. "Okay, I'll go look for your mutant priest then, Shiel. At least he'll probably know his way around out there by now I suppose."

"Right," he said abruptly, sitting upright, "early start in the morning. Are you sleeping here?"

"Someone will have to drag you from your stinking bed at five a.m. Get me a pillow and I'll crash on your couch. Oh, don't forget I'll be needing the alarm clock. It never wakes you and I'm taking no chances."

He disappeared briefly into his bedroom, returning a moment later.

"Okay, okay. It's set and wound already." He turned, throwing the clock to me from his left hand. As I caught the clock, the pillow he threw just after it with his right hand hit me full in the face and I fell backwards onto the sofa, trying not to drop the clock.

"Ha, vengeance!" cried Shiel, closing the door behind him.

I settled down to sleep on his couch, trying to remember everything I could of the time that selfless old eccentric had visited our Island, on his mission of mercy. My last thought, while drifting to sleep, was to wonder if he would remember me.

I did not sleep very soundly that night. The tension, apprehension and nervous excitement led me to toss and turn, dreaming of the things that worried me most about my upcoming trip. There were so many unknowns to face. Apart from fly-overs, as far as I knew, nobody in our community had ever really been out to the mainland since the end of the war, though most of them had theories and horror stories about the conditions.

We all have to grow up fast on the Island and the older ones who grew up in the world before seem to think of that as a bad thing, but as one of the first of the post war generation I have not had to adapt to our life. For me the world has always been like this and so I had nothing to miss. We have to work hard, but that is still better than being amongst the scattering of uncivilised people that exist elsewhere. I know that everyone on the Island now appreciates how lucky we are compared to how things could be... how things are elsewhere.

One thing that was certain was that the mainland was still home to some. We did not really know how many. There were not the millions that there had once been, possibly not even thousands, but a minority of people had lived through the war and lived there still to this day, scavenging an existence any way they could. How they had survived for so long and in what conditions however, was mostly pure speculation as far as I was aware.

We had been given lectures in school; teachers had stood and told us scare stories about the cannibalism and the barbarous behaviour of those left alive. Looking back I could see that in some regards we were being taught to enjoy our lives on the Island and not to think of going to the mainland. At the time it had not occurred to me to wonder where our teachers had gleaned this information from.

The children from the world before might have been taught about the myth of the Bogey Man and maybe told that he would come and get them if they were naughty. The 'Bogey Men' of our childhood nightmares were the mainlanders - and they were real enough.

However, although it is clear that they were only trying to protect us by instilling those prejudices in us from such a young age, in some ways they were trying too hard and as I got older it sometimes did just feel like they were only fairy stories.

# CHAPTER 4

The next morning I awoke at the first ring of the alarm clock's bell and went straight in to rouse Shiel. To my surprise he was already awake.

"You get ready and I'll go fetch my stuff," I told him. "I'll meet you at your mooring."

"Right," he said to my back as I left, "try not to attract any unwanted attention."

I headed straight out, not pausing to reply, only to grab the maps. I was excited and my head was filled with thoughts of the adventure on which I was about to embark. I tried to focus on the positives of finding my Father and bringing him back, rather than dwelling on any fears.

It was raining as I crossed the town and ran down the pier to the ship and my own room. I ran, partly to avoid getting too wet and partly to shake off the last of the night's sleep.

I was relieved to get on board unquestioned. The guards knew all too well that people were likely to come and go at odd hours of the day and night. There were plenty of jobs that needed twenty four hour attention and, in the summer, early starts on others to take advantage of the natural light of the longer days. I waved to them as I went past and they waved back. I hoped that Gill had not asked them to keep an eye on me and I reached my room still thinking about that possibility.

First I changed my clothes, putting on those that I had selected the day before and left on my bed ready: lightweight military issue trousers in an urban camouflage pattern of white and greys, with a long sleeved grey t-shirt. Over the top I wore a leather jacket, which dated back to before the war when one of the things the Island had been famous for was motorcycle racing. The leather was thick and armoured in places, some of which I had added to with inserts at the front and the shoulders. Originally black, the jacket was now battered and faded, having been well worn over the years; as with everything else on the Island I was not its first owner.

Like almost all of our apparel my boots were also pre-war, they were many years older than I was, but I had looked after them carefully, savouring them. Good footwear was very hard to find and my boots were about the best that was left. They came up over my ankles giving good support, but were light enough to run in easily.

Next I strapped my quiver of arrows around my waist, buckling the leather belt, complete with hunting knife in its scabbard. The quiver swung at my side with the tip reaching down to knee level. My rucksack was waiting where I had left it, packed and ready. I stuffed my map back into it along with Shiel's and then hoisted it onto my back. Lastly I picked up my bow, leaving it in its bag - I was planning to leave the bag on the boat with Shiel, but I would have looked a little conspicuous walking through town with the lethal compound bow on show.

I took a deep breath. That was it then, time to go. I took a thoughtful look round, wondering if I would ever see my home again. Walking back out of my room I locked the door and slipped the key into my bow bag. I saw no one as I departed, until I passed the guards again, leaning on the rail at the landward end of the pier.

"Hello again, Badger," one of them called to me. "What are you setting off to catch then?"

He obviously thought I was going hunting, which suited me perfectly.

"Wallabies, Kev, those little pests have been at the carrots again," I called back. Then to be polite I added, "Morning, Judy," to his fellow guard.

Judy called back to me, "Wallaby steaks, lovely. Good luck, bag a few." She indicated towards my pack.

"Don't worry, I'll do my best," I lied unashamedly.

I waved again and made my way ashore, heading to the mooring where Shiel kept his small boat. Again I ran, slower this time under the weight of my equipment and I soon got to the spot. I arrived before Shiel and so I stowed my rucksack and bow on the starboard side, away from the dock in case anyone walked past. He arrived a few minutes later carrying a hamper.

"Big day, bigger breakfast," he said, passing it aboard to me.

"Perfect, that's just what I need, Shiel, thanks." In all of my haste and excitement I had not even thought about food since I had woken and should have known better than to set off on an empty stomach. Nourishment was going to be hard to come by soon enough.

"Shall we eat after we leave the harbour?" I asked. "Best if we can get away quickly and avoid anyone seeing me with you. Plus, I want as much daylight as I can get for my first day over there?"

"Sure, as long as you don't get seasick, there's nothing in there that can't wait," he answered. "Let's go and load up then and we'll set off ASAP." He always liked to pronounce an acronym as a word.

I untied the small craft from the harbour wall while he started its smelly diesel engine. We put-putted off down the harbour to the dockside stores. It took us half an hour to load up the boat with the food for the oil rig. Then we were off, out of the harbour mouth and onto the longest journey of my life. We headed out to sea and after turning starboard we soon passed the huge leviathan of the Sedbergh, the little engine of Shiel's boat echoed back at us off the steel walls. The aircraft carrier sat proudly at the end of the long pier. Her mountainous grey hull soon towered over us. The rear of her flight deck over our heads shielded us from the rain for a few moments, as our boat passed underneath it, miniature by comparison. We continued farther out to sea, towards the east and the breaking dawn.

We had a couple of hours then to eat and talk as the

Island got smaller behind us and the mainland grew. It felt strangely like the world moved under us, rather than us travelling over its surface. The boat bobbed around on the waves and the sea was calm enough for us to pick our bearing and leave the controls unattended.

We opened Shiel's breakfast hamper and ate together for what we both realised could be the last time.

"You're still sure about doing this?" he finally asked after five minutes of silence.

"You know I am, Shiel. How long have we been friends? You know I don't change my mind."

"I won't think any less of you if you do. You're probably going to get yourself killed and I'll blame myself for aiding and abetting you," he said as he picked out a thick sandwich from the box.

"Anyone who tries to kill me, I'll ask them if they wouldn't mind not doing then, just to save your conscience," I snapped at him. "It's my Dad, I'm going and that really is final. If I need to swim from here, I will."

He said nothing, just sat there and chewed.

"Do we need to part on an argument, Shiel?" I tried to keep calm as I spoke. "I'm very grateful for your help and support and I know that you wouldn't be doing this if you didn't believe I could make it."

"It's not a case of believing in you or otherwise, I'm

just trying to minimise the damage that's all. You've always been a head case, I don't know why I bother." He leant back on the hull of the boat as he spoke and took another bite from his sandwich. "You know I'll be listening out for you, on the radio."

"Okay, I'll try to send you a message as soon as I can."

"Here," he said reaching into his jacket pocket, "take this, it will help you to fulfil what I now regard to be a promise."

He passed me a book, wrapped in clear plastic. "What's a 'Spark gap transmitter' then?" I asked sardonically. "You know I'm not into all this stuff."

"Listen to me, Badge, you fool. It's the easiest way for you to get a message to us. If there was still access to a working radio your dad would have got in touch again, so forget about two way radios, they're too complex anyway, but this," he pointed at the book, "this you can make. Even you could do this." I moved towards him to punch his arm. "Make it powerful and use Morse code. Gill would send a rescue if he was sure the two of you were still alive. I'd make him if I had to."

"How would I get it on the right frequency for you to hear it?" I asked him. I was unconvinced.

"That's the point," he was getting excited, "this just makes a noise on all frequencies. It interferes with any other transmissions, but it's not like we get much anyway. That's why you'd have to use Morse code, but we'd hear your message for sure. I've stuck a page on Morse at the back."

"Okay," I told him resignedly, "I'll take it with me."

"And I'll be listening, all the time that you're out there. That's the beauty of this, I don't need any of the specialised equipment in the radio room, I can just take a little portable radio out and about with me."

Eventually we spotted the oil rig and Shiel packed away the remains of our breakfast, before bringing us around towards its small docking platform.

The platform was a lot larger close up than I had expected and it towered over us on its huge stilts. It had been located by the Sedbergh just after the war. When found, it had still been full of half starved rig workers and they had been given food in return for their promise of cooperation. Gill knew that oil would be essential in any attempt at trying to maintain a civilised life. The Sedbergh carried enough reserves to keep its planes fuelled for a while but it was not enough to last indefinitely and Gill was the type of man to plan ahead. He had left behind a crew to keep it ticking over and to defend it if necessary. Oil was still a valuable resource, probably more so after the war when there were fewer alternatives.

Shiel's boat ran on it and there were numerous other uses for it on the Island. We distilled it in our small refinery. We needed to be able to work the land far more efficiently than we could by hand; not to mention how essential Sedbergh's helicopters and fighter jets could be for protection, if the Island was ever attacked. Usually though, we did not even need them to fire a shot, the threat alone was enough of a deterrent.

Shiel told me to hide out of sight while he docked and unloaded his cargo, but I could not resist peeking out. Finding a way to step production back up to full capacity had been Admiral Gill's priority project for many years. The ageing nuclear reactors on the Sedbergh had a long but limited lifespan and using them to provide energy to the Island was not ideal in the long term. He knew that like oil, electricity was vital for the ongoing quality of life on the Island and he was right of course, so he already had the Selby hydroelectric power plant up and running again. However, there was also an oil fired power station at Peel on the west of the Island and the other part of his plan was to try and work out a way to get that operational again too. One of the problems was getting the oil back to the Island. Diverting the pipes that ran across the seabed to the mainland was beyond us at that time, so boats had to be used for the time being.

After unloading his cargo of food, Shiel took aboard a dozen or so barrels of oil to take back to the Island with him after our detour. I listened as the rig workers unloaded the boat.

"Have you got the meat this time?" one of them asked Shiel in a gruff voice.

"I only forgot it *once*," said Shiel. "You lot never forget anything, do you?"

"I ain't a rabbit," Gruff Voice replied, "I can't live off of just carrots."

"You've got your meat, it's over there. And the beer Gill promised you. It's all here," I heard Shiel say.

"You'd better not be skimming some off and watering it down again, you little thief," Gruff Voice told him, solving the mystery of Shiel's long standing 'extra beer ration'.

"Would I do that to you guys?" he protested. "My friends on the rig, I wouldn't do that to you."

"Shut up and help us load the barrels of oil, thief," Gruff Voice said.

I sat hunched up in the prow of the boat, listening to them grunt and groan. The barrels clanged as they were pushed together and then roped down for the return journey.

"No point going back empty," he had told me earlier. After the boat was loaded we set straight off again, however, that time Shiel did not head back to Ramsey, at least not immediately.

The sea was a little rougher then, so Shiel steered the course as we proceeded on.

"What are you going to tell them when you get back?" I asked him.

"I'm just going to have to tell them the truth straight away," he said. "There's no point in me lying."

"I could rough you up a bit, give you a good old beating so you can pretend I forced you to do it," I offered as warmly as I could.

"Thank you, that's really thoughtful of you," he said joining the joke. "I could just tell them you pointed that at me all the way here." His head moved towards my bow, now out of its bag and across my lap.

"Ah, but not at the rig," I pointed out.

"There was no bruising on me at the rig either," Shiel retorted, "I'd best stick to the truth then I suppose."

"Okay."

"If, or rather when, Gill gets angry with me," he reasoned, "I'll just point out that it's his fault you've gone. What did he expect you to do? You're not one for sitting passively by. Gill knows that. Everyone knows that."

"Hey, watch it or I will be pointing this at you," I threatened, patting my weapon.

"Don't do that, I might lose my concentration and accidentally go back to the Island instead of dropping you off for your rescue mission," he threatened.

"Do you *really* think I'm being stupid?"

"Honestly? No, I understand why you've got to go. Do I think you've got a good chance of making it back, also no." He sighed. "I wish you would change your mind, but I know you won't. There's a very good chance I won't see you again after this morning."

"No going mushy on me now."

"Be serious, Badge, do you really think that it's going to be easy to walk to Manchester from the coast? Everyone out there will be after you for one thing or another. Just look at your boots," he said, "they look practically new. Someone could try to kill you just because they want to have comfortable feet."

I looked downwards considering what he had said and I knew he was right.

"Look I'm not trying to upset you or start an argument with you. I know what you're like, how driven you are. I know you're good in a fight and that you can take a fly out of the air with that damn compound bow of yours." He let go of the wheel for a moment and came over to me, crouching down. "Here and now, this is my last chance to change your mind. To save your life even, come back to the Island with me, Badger, please."

I did not say anything for a minute or more and eventually he went back to the boat's small wheel, holding it steady once again.

"I *will* come back, Shiel, I will. There's nothing and no one out there that's going to stop me getting my

Dad back."

"I've changed my mind, you are being stupid," he barked at me and we sailed on for a while in silence.

I tried again to make him understand, "You know I won't settle for anything other than bringing him back, I'm not going to fail him, Shiel. Gill might have abandoned him, but not me. I'm going to walk across that land and I *will* kill whoever gets in my way, nobody will stop me, Shiel, nobody. You listen out for my signal, you'll hear it, and then send those choppers. Make sure that Gill orders them to come because I *am* going to get him back."

"Have you finished? You really are a complete headcase, I knew it all along. I do hope for your sake that it is as easy as you think, but real life isn't like that and you need to prepare yourself for that possibility – and it's a possibility that might well leave you dead."

It took us two more hours before we stopped, near to the coast.

"Here we are," he said simply.

"Thank you, Shiel, thank you for doing this for me."

"Don't," he said. "Don't thank me for bringing you here. Thank me when you get back alive."

"See you, Shiel," I said as I slipped over the side of the boat.

He did not answer me as he passed me my things.


59

Shiel had dropped me off a short swim from the coast, just to the south of a place called Ainsdale. My pack had been tied onto an inflatable raft, along with my boots and clothes, and I had strapped my bow and quiver to the top. I pushed the raft in front of me as I swam to the shore. The water was so cold that my limbs started to go numb despite it being a warm summer day and I was glad not to be in the water for long.

It was a very barren area, chosen carefully so that there would be little chance of anyone else being around. I quickly climbed through the waves, abandoned the raft and carried my possessions ashore. I ran over the hard packed beach to the sand dunes beyond. There was a strong breeze and I was freezing cold. I was scared too, now that I was facing the harsh reality of the situation and I admitted to myself I did not really know what lay in store for me. Perhaps Shiel had been right, but I did not want to deliberate on that.

I waited until I was in the seclusion of the dunes before I dressed and organised myself – hiding not out of modesty, but out of apprehension for that unfamiliar territory and its inhabitants. Once I was clothed, and more importantly properly armed again, as quickly as I could I moved onwards. I tried to lose myself between the drifts of sand, heading inland but also trying to make myself difficult to follow. The dunes were part covered in sharp, reed like grass and I kept to that as much as possible, to disguise any tracks I left.

I stopped and waited for a while amongst the many dunes, to see if my landing had been spotted and in case anyone came. Then, when I was sure I had not been seen coming ashore, I set off again further inland. Almost immediately I saw the first buildings ahead of me, just slightly off to my left. They were all identical; squat, grey and two stories high, made of concrete, with flat roofs, all set out in a regimented pattern. On their sides were external staircases with decaying wooden banisters which gave access to the upper floors. Curious, I walked towards them, passing a wall also of concrete but not as hardy as the buildings themselves. The slabs of wall lay flat on the ground and as I crossed it, I was careful to avoid the rusty barbed wire at one end. It was hidden by nettles and I took care not to be stung. I wanted to have a quick look round and see what sort of condition the buildings left on the mainland would be in, hoping it would give me an insight and help me to understand what I might expect on the rest of my journey.

As I made my way towards the buildings, I had no idea initially what they could be as I looked round them. They were arranged in blocks to form four sides of a misshaped square, the squares fitting together to form a huge circle of accommodation blocks. Towards the far side was a tower, perhaps for guards I thought. I wondered if it had been some sort of prison or internment camp until I discovered its true purpose.

I pushed a warped, rotten door open to look inside one of the blocks. The hinge creaked as I did so. The door moved reluctantly, jamming against the floor. As I pushed slightly harder it came away from the frame at the top and swivelled around the bottom hinge, hanging off it and giving me access to the small room beyond. As I stepped into the room, over the lower corner of the door, I looked around at a dingy little living area.

In one corner of this room was a kitchen area and in another the shell of a TV set. Facing the TV was a low sodden sofa, the whole room was damp and the air thick with the smell of mould. Another door stood open revealing a bed and beyond that was a small bathroom. There was nothing of any use to me in there, so I left the residence and walked on around the complex.

A short while later I found an old brochure inside one of the other buildings and I was surprised to discover that where I stood had once been a holiday village. I looked around me at the devastated site, the smashed windows and the burned out frames where doors had once stood and I tried to imagine happy crowds playing games, sunbathing on bright days, or running after their children. I thought of all the cheerful smiling people that had once been here. I did not think often about life before the war, but I did then. How pleasant it must have been for those families, to come to this place, secure and relaxed, without the need for weapons to ensure their own safety.

I did not hang around at that place too long to envy those who had holidayed there, now probably all long dead. I took a look inside one or two more of those buildings and I walked on, across a tarmacked area off to one side, marked out with painted lines for football games. I decided at that point to leave any other buildings well alone. There was not going to be any point investigating others on my journey, they might only contain danger. I had already learned everything I could from that place and I reminded myself that my curiosity should not be allowed to put me in danger, nor could I afford to waste the time either.

Heading onwards out of the camp, in front of me I could see the larger ruins of the town and decided against crossing straight through them, instead skirting round the edge. I hoped to avoid contact with anyone, worried about how they might react or what they might do. I wondered if there was any truth in the stories about the mainlanders I had been told as a child, I hoped not.

Leaving the holiday camp behind me, it was hard not to think of my own childhood and the holidays I could have had if that world had not been destroyed. I knew that at one time our Island had been a tourist destination too, we still had relics of that age, but it was a concept I struggled to really grasp. The only way of life I had ever known was by necessity very functional, although I knew that my life was much better than other survivors elsewhere. The comparative utopia of a world where you could just leave all of your responsibilities behind, and visit new places without fear, seemed almost surreal.

It took quite some effort to walk further inland from the coast. The dunes stretched off into the distance beyond the camp. I did not look for a road or any easier path and I would not have used one if it had been going exactly the right way. Walking along a road there in that alien environment I would have been too exposed and an obvious target. I walked in between the dunes for the mile they covered, so I had to refer to my compass at regular intervals. It would have been easy to lose my bearings on the rolling sand without it. For a while it felt like the whole country could be like this, the high dunes rolled out as far as I could see, at times blocking anything else from sight. It was a very barren and lonely place and I had no option other than to trudge across it as well as I could.

I crossed a railway line as it ran along a raised platform of earth across the sand dunes. Hugging the earth, I crawled the couple of metres to cross over the top of it, to avoid standing out with the sky behind me. I had learned as a child that movement attracts the eye and any movement on the horizon can be seen for miles around.

Beyond the railway the land grew flatter and easy to walk over and my pace picked up. Waist high grass surrounded me and nothing moved but the vegetation, blowing in waves around me by the wind.

Soon afterwards I was hiding in a small pine wood with my back to a ridge of earth and to the coast. I had a drink from my bottle, then remembering Shiel's comments I covered my boots with handfuls of mud, rubbing it all over them so that my prized possessions became less conspicuous. A squirrel startled me for an instant as it climbed down the back of the tree next to me, though I suspect it was equally surprised to see me too. I tried to catch it as soon as I saw it, but it ran back up the tree and out of reach at lightning speed; I was not hungry yet, still full from Shiel's breakfast, but I knew that I needed to make the most of any opportunity. Taking my bearings and leaving the wood, I continued slowly inland heading south-east, around the edge of the small town. I was heading towards Ormskirk and its unusual church, as I had been advised to.

In front of me as I walked through the long grass I could see a long strip, a runway still almost intact. In places there were patches of grass growing though and a few small saplings here and there. Compared to the runway on the ship it was vast, needing no arrestor wires to stop the planes at the end. I saw another strip crossing the first and on this lay the ruins of a small plane, mostly hidden by the long grass, stranded on its belly with the wheels having collapsed long ago. It had been picked over thoroughly by the look of it and almost anything of use seemed to have been taken off it. I kept away from both the runways and the plane, preferring instead the cover provided by the long grass on the open areas.

On the other side of the airfield I came to my next obstacle: a wide, open stretch of road, running parallel to the coast. I was nervous about crossing it, as I would be visible for at least a mile in either direction, but there was no detour so I had to risk sprinting across, vaulting the rust covered barrier in the centre with ease. The surface was breaking up at the edges and on the far side it was much worse than where I had started to cross. The frost must have got into it, in winter after winter.

Scrambling down the embankment on the other side, I quickly set off again into another wood. Again I paused for a while to see if anyone was following me. Still there was no one to be seen.

As I crossed the countryside in that desolate area I kept to the hedgerows. I could still make out the pattern of the fields around me, though they all looked to contain little but the deep grass, young trees and the occasional wild flower. I was surprised by how much had survived and it felt good to have available cover all around me, all I needed to do to hide in that countryside was drop to the ground.

I noticed in the corner of one field that someone, or something, had been digging and took a small detour to look. It had indeed been people; there were recent tool marks in the soil and the stalks of some wild growing vegetables were spread around, trodden into the mud. There was evidence of a fire so I presumed that they must have taken the time to cook them. I looked around but there were none left growing so I resumed my journey and for the first time doubt set in and I hoped I had brought enough food with me.

I made good time as there was little to do other than keep a wary eye out for any other people. The land was still flat and easy to traverse. Any buildings that were more than rubble were easy to avoid. Apart from a very thin looking cat, I saw no other sign of life until much later that day.

The later part of that morning brought rain with it, but it was only a brief summer downpour and it quickly subsided. I had decided to wrap the bow in some cloth I had picked up; I was concerned that if anyone saw such a quality weapon with the kind of power and range my bow had, they might try to take it from me. It was a valuable item, so I did not want to flaunt it. It was a dilemma because it would make me appear more vulnerable if I was not so obviously armed, but it might also remove a reason for someone to take an interest in me.

I walked cross-country as much as I could, the roads were not direct and the grasslands were easy to cover. I was forced to reconsider when I saw a canal ahead. I had to cross the water somewhere and so I walked along parallel to the bank, a few metres away from it, until I came to a road, intending to cross over the canal using the bridge that the road ran over. The bridge was old, stone and hump-backed, when I got there I saw a set of steps going down to the canal.

I decided to take a look underneath and see if it was secluded enough to stop there and rest for a short while. The steps were quite steep and oddly mismatched, with only a few of them showing any uniformity. I went down them with little difficulty but taking care, since they were slippery with no hand rail and I did not want to lose my footing. At the bottom there was a tow path that ran alongside the canal and under the bridge.

Once down I followed the path and sat on the canal side, within the short tunnel. It was an isolated spot that I hoped would offer me some protection for a brief respite. On the canal itself floated general debris. Its surface was littered with rubbish, almost hiding the stagnant water completely. As I sat I looked out across the water and along the length of the canal. A few feet out from the bridge I saw a face in the water. Dead, empty eyes stared up at the sky. His flesh was bloated and quite rotten; he must have been in the water for a long time. The dead man's arms could be made out, now that I had noticed him floating there. They were spread wide, supplicated, as if he was asking the sky a question to which he could never receive an answer.

It was around noon and a long time since my early breakfast. Ignoring the dead man I ate some of my biscuits down there and reviewed my position on the map. I had already covered several miles without incident and reassured myself that if I continued at my current pace I would easily reach Manchester in three days as I had planned. I took a short while to check on my equipment before going back on up the steps to the road.

I wondered how things were going back on the Island once my disappearance had become apparent. I knew that they would have definitely missed me by then. That morning I had been supposed to be going to the town of Laxey to work, with a load of fish from the docks for the freezers. There is a water wheel there that has been adapted to generate electricity, to keep the nearby industrial sized freezers running. The water wheel very rarely stops and that makes it ideal to power them and store food all year round.

The journey there is undertaken in a cart, pulled behind a tractor. When I did not show up, they would have sent someone to look for me.

I wondered about Gill's reaction, he would know

where I had gone, of that I was in little doubt. He could order the helicopters to search for me but that was unlikely. I would be able to hide from them with little difficulty. If they saw me at a distance, they would not know if it was me with any degree of certainty and they could not land unless they knew for sure that it was safe.

I hoped that Shiel did not get too badly treated by Gill. He was the obvious accomplice for me. Shiel would not lie if asked a direct question by Gill; nobody on the Island would. It was one of our laws and the punishment for that would be worse than the punishment for helping me.

Gill had learned long ago that our Island was no place for a democracy. Benevolent dictatorship was needed; it allowed a quick response to problems that arose, but also meant that mistakes could be made without accountability. This allowed Gill the flexibility to run our Island in the best interests of the group as a whole. We are taught and understood this from a very early age, our teachers educate us to follow orders and to work for the interests of the many. There is little resistance since no one wants a return to the way things were just after the war.

I thought of Laxey. It would have been a hard morning's work filling the freezers, and cold too. The only thing to have looked forward to was seeing an old friend. There was a refrigeration operator and guard called Samantha who I knew. She lived in Laxey now, but we had been to school together. Although she was two years younger than me we were quite friendly. I wondered if she would miss seeing me come across the hills on that rattling smelly old cart.

I continued on my journey and crossed over the canal on the bridge, keeping to the right-hand side. There were some houses on the left - or rather, the ruins of houses, burnt out. Ahead was a farmhouse and I avoided that too. As soon as I could I went cross-country again, still keeping off the roads.

For a while the terrain opened out again and became very exposed, very flat like a huge overgrown meadow. Then after a while, as I moved further inland, the landscape started to become somewhat more sculpted as small hill rolled into small hill. I walked on for hours keeping as well hidden as I possibly could.

It felt very strange to walk alone like that, having been taught those horror stories about the people from the mainland since I was a child and since then repeating them myself to other children. Thinking that around me those same people could be lurking anywhere, I was on edge as I walked along, more than a little apprehensive.

A short distance to the south I saw a square building, topped with many aerials and a tall mast. It looked like it might still be in use by someone. It was surrounded by grey metal fencing, which seemed to include a small compound and maybe a generator house. Written in paint on the walls, two stories high, were warnings to keep away. Through my binoculars I could see the remains of what looked like two bodies hanging from the fence at the sides of the gates. I needed no encouragement to take heed of the warnings and I continued on my way.

This seemed in some way to confirm the opinion I held about those native to that land. Displaying the bodies of the dead as a warning, while effective, was not something that I felt was acceptable whatever the circumstances. The smell and the danger of disease must both have been considerable. I wondered for a moment what the conditions inside the building would be like for those living within, without the power and clean water we had on the Island.

I walked on for several more miles across the land and very little caught my attention. It was very calm and quiet, the only sounds were the wind and the inane chattering of the birds. I saw a flock of starlings swoop around one another in the far distance through my binoculars. At another point I saw a strange building that I guessed must have been a water tower. A large bulbous disc, shaped like a classic UFO that I had seen in old books from the fifties, it was supported on a slim pillar. Whilst that was unusual in itself, there was nothing of any real interest to be seen though.

I continued on my way for the whole of the afternoon. My attention to security occasionally deviated; I knew this was dangerous but nothing untoward had happened so far and I found it difficult to concentrate for hours at a time. Sometimes I would find myself staring at a cloud that resembled something, or I would be thinking of my Father as I walked on in a world of my own. Whenever I realised that my diligence had waned, I would bring myself to the present with a start and look around again quickly, using the binoculars that I was carrying around my neck.

In the distance above the tall grass and the trees I saw a pair of gulls swooping across the sky together. I let myself watch the two birds spinning around each other as I walked along. I was miles inland now and was surprised to see seabirds this far from the coast. On the Island we were never very far from the sea and now I realised that it had never occurred to me that seagulls might travel further inland if they had the opportunity to.

I could not help but let my mind drift back to the Island; it would be time for the annual seagull cull soon. We do not have to eat the seagulls very often, only when our other food sources are running dangerously low; their meat is very tough and it does not taste nice. They are sometimes used in the feed for the pigs, mixed in with everything else they will eat.

We need to cull the birds at least once a year as they are a pest, scavenging anything they can to eat. They try to steal any food that is left unattended and the community on the Island has little enough to spare already. Their droppings seem to cover the town sometimes. For a community that relies heavily on its fishing it is best to keep the numbers as low as we can.

Sometimes it feels like we are fighting a losing battle with them. Perhaps they fly in from the mainland or Ireland. Certainly a week or two after our culls it is hard to tell if we have made a difference or not.

The seagull eggs are harvested though and they are delicious, boiled for twenty minutes they make an ideal and filling breakfast. The children of the Island are encouraged to pick half to two thirds of the eggs from each nest. My friends and I had spent many afternoons on the rocky outcrops searching for them, as the gulls swooped around us cawing. We had to candle them after taking them from the nest; the developing gull embryos were clearly visible once you had the knack of it and those went to the pigs too, saving the fresher undeveloped eggs for ourselves.

The gulls did everything they could to stop us taking the eggs. I remembered Shiel once, totally covered in droppings. He claimed that the gulls had dive bombed him. His hair and shirt were covered and the entire town had laughed at him as he walked back, except for me. I admitted to him later that I had struggled to keep my face straight and even out there years later, I smiled thinking back to the sight of him stood there, arms outstretched, dripping and feeling so very sorry for himself.

Eventually I came to the outskirts of Ormskirk and strangely, from the side that I arrived, countryside and fields gave way very suddenly to rubble and the remains of an urban housing estate. To me it seemed an unusually distinct line between the two, but again, as with the gulls, I realised that I had very little experience from which to judge.

I crossed the spilled brickwork and shattered roofing timbers, interspersed with bushes and trees. My progress over that type of terrain was much slower than before.

Anywhere I put my feet the rubble slipped or moved and I could not risk twisting or breaking an ankle. After a few hundred metres, a medium sized scrawny dog started to follow me, barking and whining. I did not know if it was begging for food, or hoping that I would leave something behind that it could eat. It appeared to be used to people, not scared at all and I hoped that those it was familiar with were not around. Its noise was bound to get someone's attention eventually.

I was forced to shoot it as it barked and yapped. There was a good chance I could have broken one of my valuable arrows but I had to take that risk. The noise it was making ended with a brief yelp. I butchered it there on the spot with a great deal of haste, hoping it was not part of a pack, either canine or otherwise. I left the remains of the carcass still steaming, more like an offering to them than a distraction. Just in case.

I took no pleasure in killing the dog, but nor did I feel any sorrow. It was merely a necessary act and it is the way of our world, nothing can go to waste.

There are a few dogs on the Island but they are not usually kept as pets, they are working dogs, fed on scraps and seagull meat. Some of their owners do get attached to them, but I had never really seen the point. They are large dogs usually, kept to guard the ship and our food supplies around the Island. My friend Samantha had one, a large German Shepherd she had called Percy, who she would patrol with. His sense of smell was impressive and his loud bark was only a little less worrying than his low snarls; that was the time to be wary of him.

A few of the farmers keep cats as well, mostly to keep down the rodents, so they are working animals too. A few live in the towns doing the same job and we see them prowling along after their prey. They are not fed often, or rather they are supposed to be kept hungry for the hunt, but I think some of the owners cannot help cheating a little and giving them treats.

Their owners have to take great care with them, the animals need to wear a bright easily noticeable collar, since any feral animal would be hunted and killed. We can ill afford any sentimentality and meat is scarce. There had been a few arguments in the past when mistakes had been made and someone's cat had been caught and killed on the other side of town.

In the late afternoon of that day I saw another person, the first live human being of my trip so far, very briefly. Out of the corner of my eye I noticed a young girl, watching me through a window frame that still stood amongst the rubble. As soon as my head began to turn she bolted and ran. I did not follow. It could have been a lure, using the girl as bait for a trap. If not, what could I have done for her anyway?

The light was fading as I reached the town centre and I was glad to see that the church was still there and easy to locate. I could see it in the distance. It did indeed have both a tower and a spire, although the spire had very little roof left. The tower was at the same end as the spire. For some reason I had expected them to be at opposite ends, I was not sure why.

I was starting to feel a little trepidation about my first night on the mainland. If the priest was no longer there I would have to try to find somewhere to sleep and I did not have enough daylight left to leave the town. On my first day I had already broken my own self imposed rules and here I was in a town, risky territory, but I had promised Shiel I would come here and it had seemed a good idea the night before. I was reminded again that talk is so much easier than cold reality. I put the thought from my mind; it was too late to worry about it then. I would have to do the best that I could.

The church stood in an elevated position. As I approached the base of the hill I passed a pond as I entered the grounds. As I walked uphill the tower and spire seemed to loom over me, the gradient emphasising their size. The long grass of the churchyard swayed in the breeze around me, almost level with the tops of the gravestones. There seemed to be no one around but there were some signs of life here and there. A goat with bulging udders was tethered to a railing on one side of the fenced grounds.

I left it for then, but if there was no one there and nobody looking after that goat, I decided I would be back to take it. I then noticed for the first time that the path I was walking along was made of old gravestones that had presumably once stood in the church yard. I could see from the inscriptions on them that they were hundreds of years old. A little farther towards the church, the stones had been formed into shallow steps to make the incline easier under foot. I took to them, walking on the engraved names of the long dead. My heart was pounding in my chest and adrenaline surged.

If all went to plan I was about to meet my first resident of the mainland and I hoped it was not going to be a serious mistake.

I reached the vestibule of the church. It had iron gates across it, shut but not secured. They had a chain and padlock hanging from them and those showed signs of recent use. Someone locked those gates on a regular basis, that was obvious. They groaned against their hinges as I parted them enough for me to enter.

I was nervous, knowing that I could be walking into a trap. As I had told Shiel, I had no recollection of the priest's speech. If Shiel was wrong, the priest may just see me as an intruder and I thought he would probably deal harshly with those. Even a man of God would have to protect himself and his possessions.

Looking around to see if there was anyone following I went inside, through the inner wooden doors that stood open, appearing to welcome anybody. It was dank in there and smelled of bird droppings, I could hear the culprits in the rafters above me.

# CHAPTER 6

Remembering what I had been told by Shiel, I walked as calmly as I could down the aisle, put down my possessions and sat on the step in front of the altar. I wanted to appear self confident and unafraid. I hoped anyone watching me would take my lack of caution as a warning and not call my bluff.

"Sedbergh," I said loudly and then waited.

A few moments later, just before I was about to say it again, a tall shadow moved in the corner of the church and an enormous man walked out into the aisle. His hair and beard were long, grey and matted. He was clothed in black with a flash of white at his neck. At his side was a hefty staff, not of the ceremonial type but a dual purpose weapon, ideal as a club but also it was topped with a vicious looking blade that was unevenly serrated down both sides.

"You're from the Island. You've grown a bit," he said and I nodded. "You're a long way from home. What do you want from me?"

"Advice," I answered and I realised from my croaky voice how dry my throat was.

"Go home, that's the best advice you will ever hear." His voice boomed off the walls. Then he said, "But I wouldn't try getting to the coast at this time of day, too late. Good swimmer are you? Got any food?"

I wondered for a moment if he was asking me for a

bribe. I opened my pack, now set beside me and took out the portions of dog meat I had cut up earlier. Suddenly his face broke into a huge smile and he walked towards me. I was glad that his attitude was warming; I was going to need somewhere to spend the night and as he had pointed out, it would soon be dark.

"Fresh meat, huh. Don't see that very often. Come on then, kid, let's get it over the fire." Then after a pause he asked, "It's not person is it?"

"No," I told him, "it's not person. See, it's still got a bit of fur on it." I held it out for him to inspect. "We have strict rules on the Island about that."

"Yeah," he said under his breath, walking outside, "These days. You've got rules these days."

Not wanting to know what he was referring to, I pretended not to hear him.

Later, after we had cooked and eaten, he asked about some of the people on the Island and we chatted for a while. I tried to temper my habitual impatience and I let him lead the conversation, rather than trying to push him on my own agenda. I did not want to risk alienating my new ally with my usual straight to the point approach. After I had got to know him a little better, I asked him if he knew much about the war and the history of it.

It was not discussed much on the Island and I only knew the bare facts. On September 26th 1983, a date that I think will always be remembered, the Soviets claimed that their early warning system detected five ballistic missiles inbound from the USA. It was a time of great mistrust and tension between the East and the West. With barely enough time to think, the Soviets retaliated with full force. On seeing hundreds of nuclear missiles headed towards them, the American government ordered exactly the same in return. Within just a few hours those two, once great nations had almost entirely wiped each other out.

Many of those I know who lived through the end tell me they do not really know how it all went so badly wrong. Certainly there were no winners. There was a nuclear war and the world ended, at least the world that went before. Someone once told me that it had all been bound to happen sooner or later, as soon as the first atomic bombs were created, but I have never wanted to believe that and I hope that it is not true. If something like that was so inevitable, such a certainty, what does it say about the human race? I was glad when the priest was more than happy to explain what he remembered of those years.

"The world didn't die swiftly, it was long and drawn out. It took almost eight years in total," he said. "Those Americans that were left alive after the first of it blamed the Russians and o' course the remaining Russians blamed the Yanks."

He spat at the fire and I remained silent waiting for him to go on.

"The Russians claimed they had detected a missile attack launch from the American mainland. So they launched an all out attack back at the Americans, to which America then responded in kind. Europe kept out of it 'cos they weren't being shot at and the NATO agreements were ignored. The Russians didn't target Europe as they hadn't detected any launches from there, so no missiles came anywhere near us, they went over the pole or the Bering Straits. Don't Gill have them teach this stuff at school?"

"No, they don't talk about it much at all," I said. My finger traced the lines of the engravings on the stone step I sat on, the year on it read 1839 but the markings had almost been worn away.

"They were both shattered by the exchange back then, but the Americans definitely got the worst of it," he continued. "Not only did they deny having started it all, but the Americans complained and moaned about what they saw as a betrayal by Europe. Even the British didn't get involved at that time, so the Yanks probably had a point." He paused again, poking at the fire with a stick to encourage the flames.

"You see, Russia still had some of its nuclear arsenal left and nobody wanted the remainder of the enormous Russian tank army sweeping across Western Europe. Nobody trusted anyone any more, so wasn't gonna stick up for anyone else neither."

There was a genuine anger in his voice even so many years later. "Those politicians, they're so cynical, so unhindered by morals. People your age won't know what they were like. I hope the world never sees their kind again. They rationalised the whole thing. They wouldn't shoot their missiles at Russia they said, not because blowing up millions was in some way wrong, oh no, but because there were more people alive here. You'd think they'd be happy with that wouldn't you, but they were perverse in their thinking. See, we had a lot of people in a smaller area, easier to aim at, whereas the Russians were all spread out so less 'value for money' so to speak if they bombed 'em. They reckoned the more they lost the less they had to lose, the worse their vengeance would be. Can you believe that, the arrogance of it? The Russians had a few missiles left, probably about as many as we had in the first place, so if we went toe to toe with them, they'd have an easier target than we'd have. From the standpoint of us mere mortals here, there didn't seem to be any consideration for putting an end to the fighting or trying to preserve what little was left, it was just tactics, statistics and equations. That was their twisted brand of logic, the fools had totally lost the plot. It was like they'd forgotten there were real lives at stake, never mind their own families' lives."

I looked up at a cloud as it drifted serenely in front of a rising moon above us, I kept silent, letting the information sink in.

"So anyway they were at a bit of a stand off, not like it was over, just like no one really knew how to get out of it or what to do next. Everything could have stayed like that, 'cept for the Chinese. They went and invaded Southern Russia for the food reserves. Their people desperately needed it. Russia tried to fight them off, encouraged by Europe to keep to conventional weapons. The Chinese didn't want to poison the land they hoped to steal so they stood down their nukes too. The Russians were secretly aided by Western Europe for years, to try to avoid more damage to the planet as a whole." He looked into the fire again and I think he was back there, reliving those years.

"America was left to descend into anarchy. Anarchy that covered a continent as its refugees tried to escape the radiation and famine. Millions of survivors went walking north to Canada, or south into Mexico and onto the South Americas. When both countries tried to close their borders it was entirely useless. The refugees had had the right to bear arms for years, you see and almost all of them had weapons an' very little left to lose. The border guards didn't stand a chance and neither did the defending armies that came to back them up. Then the anarchy spread, like a virus across the world." He glanced briefly at me as he said those last words, looking straight into my eyes.

"Hungry people don't stay hungry for very long," he said chillingly and paused. "They either die or they get something to eat. Sometimes they'll kill to survive. It feels like him or you if you're hungry enough. At that time no one had the resources to send aid to any of the survivors. Everywhere on the planet, food was becoming more and more scarce. The African countries, those that weren't starving already, their crops failed as all those nuclear blasts affected the atmosphere and they were left to starve wholesale. Nobody sends aid when they're hungry themselves." He stretched out his arms, flexing his shoulders.

"That's when they bought that ship of yours. Did

you know that? Bought by the British government with grain and beef, from what was left of an American government that was starving to death. Don't suppose they needed it more than they needed food. Reckon your lot got it at a cut down price too."

I shuffled a little where I sat, to avoid the pins and needles that I was starting to feel in my legs.

"In '91 it all came to a head, eight years after it started. An American ex-serviceman, Keith Something-or-Other who was living in London at the time, discovered all the secret aid being sent to the Russians. He saw that as a bigger betrayal than standing down the missiles years earlier, so he leaked it. The Chinese didn't appreciate that news too much, I can tell you."

"'Leaked it', what does that mean?" I asked him.

"Told the newspapers, who then told everyone else."

"Right," I said, "causing a controversy, I suppose."

"Caused a lot more than that," he said. "All those years of heavy fighting, they had nearly sapped the strength of the Soviet army by then, and seeing as their foreign aid would probably soon dry up, they had no other choice left to 'em. They used a handful of their remaining nukes to try an' drive back the invading Chinese army. The Chinese didn't take long after that to launch an all out attack, both on Russia and her new European 'Allies'. The Chinese population were starving to death as it was, maybe they believed they could win a war with numbers." He snorted with derision. "Then finally, the British and the rest of Europe had someone with a big enough population to be worth the trouble of nuking. They let them all loose on China, at the same time as the Chinese ones made their way here."

"That were it, eight years after the first nuclear strikes between the Americans and the Russians, there was a final round of missiles swapped, then that was it, it was all over. The world that once was, had ended and wasn't coming back. There were no functional governments left to take control, no armies left, no one other than small pockets of survivors dotted here and there, trying to sustain theirselves as best as they could. The landscapes were ravaged radio-active wastelands, and most of the technology of the last world had been destroyed by the electromagnetic pulses from the nuclear blasts. All that remained of us entered a second dark age, a nightmare of our own making."

"There's an old quote from some clever bloke from somewhere. Damned if I can remember who he was now. 'All it takes for evil to triumph is for good men to do nothing.' Well nobody did anything, bar walking through London with ban the bomb placards. Perhaps we deserve what we got."

I did not follow his point entirely, but not wanting to interrupt I remained silent.

"I don't think anyone knows what happened to the Aussies, but there hasn't been a peep from them since then. It's probable the Chinese launched at them too, thinking them allies of ours."

He fell silent for a while so I tried to prompt him to go on.

"What about the rest?" I asked him. "India, or the Middle East, or South America, what happened to them?"

"Look, at that time someone would invade somewhere else, or they got swamped by refugees. Everywhere got it the same, most people starved. Those as didn't got blown up or shot up in some stupid turf war. It's the way it was all over the world, kid. There ain't anyone left now. Anywhere. At least not that I know of."

We sat outside, on the steps made from gravestones, digesting both the food and his story about the war. The sun had set but the evening was still warm and he seemed relaxed so I presumed we must be relatively safe.

It seemed to me then that none of that really mattered to those of us who are left, history hardly seemed worth talking about. Maybe people are better off not remembering or understanding properly; how is anyone supposed to comprehend such a senseless and futile waste anyway? Sat there that evening I could not even imagine the world such as he described it, let alone grasp its destruction.

Now that he had softened from our initial encounter earlier that day, he asked me what I was doing on the mainland. He nearly choked when I told him I was going to Manchester and about my plans to find my

Father.

"You'll be going to The Castle then," he said after he had finished coughing.

"The Castle?" I did not know what he meant.

"Aye The Castle, you'd know it if you saw it. If he's being held anywhere, then that's the place. Lots of bad people round there, kid. Lots," he told me. "Turn around, go back to your little island sanctuary before you get too dead."

The conversation flagged at that point and we both fell into silence for a while. As I sat there, staring into the fire, a hazy childhood memory of my Mother kept prodding at my conscious mind.

"The Castle? Where had I heard of this castle before," I thought to myself. I pushed it to the back of my mind; I still needed information from him.

"Let's just get one thing straight okay. I am not going back to the Island without my Father," I told him defiantly. "You're not the first person to try to talk me out of it and it's not going to happen."

"Look, kid, I don't care. You wanted advice, so 'ere it is. Go back or someone out here will kill you. You might 'ave your super-duper bow and arrows. Yeah, I saw you shoot the dog with it see. I was only teasing when I asked you if it was human meat, I already knew well enough. And if I'd have wanted it, I'd have had that bow off of you too. You didn't try to catch the little girl, well done, that's why I let you get in here." He carried on, ignoring the look of surprise on my face. "But there's too many others out here who ain't like me. They won't let you just walk on by. They'll want to stop you and say 'ello, not friendly like, but so as you can't say no."

"I can take care of myself," I told him, although I was shocked and rather concerned that he had been watching me that afternoon without me realising. It was certainly a wake-up call for me, but I still could not give in. "I'm still going to go and get him."

"Then you'll get yourself killed," he said simply. He looked as though he had stopped arguing with me about my intentions at least. "Well if you got your mind set on going, which way you headin' then?" he asked.

"I thought I'd pick up the path of the old motorways. Go south-east till I pick up the route of the M58, then go east down it past a place called..."

"Skem!" he said, interrupting me with venom in his voice. "Don't you go anywhere near there, kid. Bad things there. Nasty. Got themselves a little cannibal cult going. Woad covered savages. Heads on sticks, the lot. If you must carry on, head south from here."

He coughed, clearing his throat. "Got a map? I'll show you if you want."

"Here," I said, taking it out of my bag and unfolding it for him to see. His outburst had worried me more than a little. After the revelation that I had been followed that afternoon, what else could I wander into unknowingly? It would not stop me carrying on though, I was still determined to find my Father.

"Go past Rainford to the big road down there." He pointed at the map. "Then follow that east to Manchester. Don't you go near Skem."

"Go here," he instructed, tracing a line with his dirty fingernail. "Down here and then across." For a moment he paused in thought. "When you get to here and the road bends a bit to the left, it gets built up on a banking or a bridge, can't quite remember now. If you're so interested in history, you do a little detour and go to the south of the ridge, off the skyline."

His instructions seemed somewhat cryptic, but I marked the detour on the map with my pencil. I could think about that later, if I made it so far.

He was not the easiest conversationalist to follow sometimes. It seemed that no further advice was coming, as he stood and walked back towards the church.

"Come inside to sleep," he said then. "Safer."

I nestled between the pews to spend the night, making a rough bed from my belongings and the few kneeling cushions that were scattered around. I heard the priest's snores in the distance, above the noise of the cooing pigeons overhead. I reflected on my first day on the mainland as I lay there, I had made good progress so far and achieved my goal for the first day but I could not become complacent. I reminded myself that not everyone on the mainland was going to be like the priest.

I wondered how Shiel was getting on back at the Island. I knew for certain that Gill would want to see him personally for having helped me. There is a small brig on Sedbergh but it is rarely used, community service in the form of extra shifts is a more common and practical punishment. The concept of long periods of incarceration belongs to a different age, it is simply not efficient. Exile on the mainland or execution are the last resort sentences for the most serious crimes.

I thought back to the last criminal case, five years earlier. Neither the trials nor the executions are held in public, but after sentencing those condemned to either of the two more extreme punishments are allowed to speak publicly to anyone who is willing to listen. Shiel and I had been to that last one, it was the first since we had been old enough to attend.

The crowd had been strangely quiet. A man from the west of the Island had badly beaten and almost killed another in a fight over a sheep. It was strange to think of losing your place on our Island or even your life over a sheep, but then hindsight is always razor sharp and the rumour around the Island was that there had been more to it than that. The man had been kept in the ship's brig until the fate of his victim had been confirmed. The other man had survived the attack, so now his attacker faced exile rather than the death penalty.

After his hearing with Gill he was led out to speak.

He did not speak rationally, nor beg for forgiveness as Shiel and I had expected.  He had first ranted against Gill's rationing, blaming Gill for the necessity of his own actions. Then he revealed himself to be involved in a black market, claiming he was being used as a scapegoat and finally he resorted to insulting the onlookers, before being dragged onto a boat to be taken away from the Island.

"Good riddance," Shiel had said as the crowd started to disperse.

"Stupid thing to have done, nearly killing someone over a black market sheep," I had said in return.

I knew that Shiel would not end up in quite that much trouble when Gill caught up with him, but I still did not like to think of him taking a punishment for me. I could have stolen his boat and come to the mainland without his help. At least this way they got the boat back. I hoped he would get away with a lecture and a few extra shifts to work.

"Want to come and help me with the radio monitoring?" Shiel had asked me back then as we turned to leave.

"I can't. Mum's took another downturn and she's back in the hospital. She won't be out again this time, I don't think," I told him. "I'm off work on compassionate leave, I'm going back to see her now."

"Oh... I'm really sorry to hear that... I know you had to expect it, but that can't make it any easier. I'll walk with you, maybe say hello to her myself," he said. "I'm not due on shift for three quarters of an hour yet."

We walked off towards the hospital together. At that time I knew already that she was dying, the doctor had told us she had months at most, so I spent most of my time with her. Sometimes though she insisted I take a break; I know she needed some time on her own but I think she was trying to protect me too. It was an incredibly difficult time for me and although I had so many good friends around me, I felt so alone as if no-matter how hard they tried they could never really understand properly. Shiel helped to keep me sane as best he could, distracting me from thinking too much when I was away from her side.

"What are you doing tonight, when visiting's over?" he had asked me.

"Nothing much, perhaps moving my stuff into the smaller room Gill gave me."

"You don't have to rush that surely. Are you sure you want to keep living on the ship? We could fix you up a flat, there's room in my building," he offered.

"Thanks, but it's my home, you know what I mean? I had enough of an argument with Gill to stay living aboard. I can't give it up now."

"Let me know if you change your mind. Anyway, tonight, come round to my place. I've got a video to work, I'm sure of it this time. It's movie night!" he said. "And if we're lucky, the electric might even last till the end of the film.”

“It’s never going to happen,” I said, going off long experience.

“Don’t doubt me now, Badge, it’s going to work. I’m telling you, tonight’s the night.”

We had walked past the bakery and we reached the old cottage hospital. There were much better equipped medical facilities on the ship, but by that stage it made no difference. The nursing staff on the Island and on the ship were good and they did the very best that they could under the circumstances, but there were few drugs left, hardly any basic medicine at all, certainly nothing as complex as my Mother needed. By that point she had decided she preferred to be away from the ship, where she could look out of the window and see people going by.

“You don’t have to come in you know, I won’t think any less of you,” I said to Shiel. It was hard to do, walk into that place and visit someone you love and who you know is dying. The ordeal of it was draining me to exhaustion.

“Come off it, I like your mum and I’ve not seen her in days,” he said.

We went inside and walked through the corridors of the building. I knew where she would be, they had kept the same bed for her each time, in a side room away from the other patients. She was looking very pale and breathing shallowly. As Shiel and I walked towards her

I saw her smile, trying her hardest to look better than she felt.

"Hello, how are you two? Thank you for coming to see me," she said, welcoming us.

"Hello, Mum, how are you today?"

"Oh, so-so," she said cheerily and then turned to Shiel. "Tim, how's your mum and dad? Tell them I said hello."

"They're okay. My dad mentioned he might be coming to visit this evening."

"That will be nice, I'll look forward to seeing him later."

We sat chatting about things for a while but not really saying anything of consequence, skirting around the obvious. I looked back at that period with regret sometimes; the twelve year-old me did not have the ability to put into words the emotions I experienced while watching her slowly fade away. I doubt I ever would gain that power, whatever my age.

Later that day Shiel and I sat round his old television set, watching white noise, while he twiddled with wires and poked with his insulated screwdriver.

"Come on, work, you swine!" he hissed at it.

I just sat on his sofa watching him, while I sipped at a glass of fruit juice. I remember a single tear rolling down my cheek that I had wiped away quickly before he saw it.

"Laugh and the world laughs with you. Cry and your face just gets wet." That was what my Mother always used to say.

His video player never did work.

As I lay there in that cold church, thinking of my Mother's death, my mind turned to my Father. Missing for a decade, I had never wanted to believe he was dead. Thoughts of my Mother fuelled my determination to find him now, find him and get him back to the Island with me. Eventually, on that more optimistic thought, I managed to get some sleep.

# CHAPTER 7

Iate a quick breakfast with the priest the next morning as soon as the dawn broke and we talked again as we ate.

"What do you do out here, how come you didn't stay on the Island with us?" I asked him.

"I have to stay around here, I look out for my friends, you see," he said to me. "There's plenty of people who need a bit of protection and seemingly no shortage of people to protect them from. Anyone comes around this area and tries to take by force what isn't theirs, well, I look out for my flock. We look out for one another. Wouldn't be right after all these years, me leaving them to fend for themselves."

"I see," I said.

"The way I look at it, there's two types of folk, those who get by as best they can without hurting others and there's those that try to steal an easy ride. Well, I don't like those as steals around here, nor those that try to attack or eat the people who try to just get by," he told me. "All I do is try to even up the odds a bit. I can only make a small difference, but I do what I can."

"What about the Island? We have it pretty good over there, why leave?" I asked again. "Why not take your friends there?"

He snorted down his nose, "Yeah, you have it comfortable enough, but what do you lot do for those left over here without that ship of yours? What about the poor souls your lot abandoned? That ship you think of as yours, once it belonged to everyone in this land. Not just to those lucky enough to be aboard it when the bombs dropped. There's a hospital aboard it, yes? Do you have any idea how useful that would have been just after the blasts? Your medical facilities could have saved hundreds - hundreds of those that I had to put out of their misery with my own hands."

He paused and I felt awash with guilt; it was a perspective I had not considered before. I knew that the ship would have been swamped by the wounded and the dying. I knew that a small community of survivors was a better use of its resources in the long term but I could not argue with him. From his point of view there had been an obligation and that obligation had been long ignored.

I had always been told that they had fled to the Island as a refuge. The missile that was sent to sink the ship missed, they thought it must have malfunctioned since it detonated a few miles away. Many of the vessel's six thousand crew died anyway: in the force of the shock wave from the blast, of radiation, in the fighting that followed, or because they just did not want to live on after the end of that world. Some just could not face it. Nobody talks much about those horrific times, I think partly because they do not want to relive the memories, but mainly to protect those of us who do not have to know. Now, I wondered if perhaps my parents and the others on the Island had been greedy to keep the ship and all of its assets to themselves.

"Don't worry, I don't blame you. You're too young to be held accountable, but that's why I came back to the mainland," he said and then added, "amongst other things."

Again he paused, thinking for a minute as we carried on eating.

"Seems if I think about it, I'm not really one as should be allowed to judge anyway. Spent enough of my life before the war just enjoying living here I suppose, not appreciating what I was taking for granted. I called myself a man o' God, thought I was doin' my bit for humanity, but I left those in the third world to starve to death without thinking too much about 'em," he said.

"Third world, what was that?" I asked. I had never heard the term before.

"It's what we used to call anywhere where people were starving to death while others ate more than they needed," he said. "Back then we threw away enough to keep some others alive. Calling it the third world made them seem further away I think."

"Did that really happen before the war? I had no idea." The priest was changing how I thought of the world before.

"Yeah, it happened. Believe me, it happened," he said. "However civilised you've been taught the world once was, a few bombs haven't changed human nature. I sometimes wonder what it's like there now. They might be doing better than us. Now wouldn't that be ironic, if one day they came to our rescue."

I thought of Shiel and our drunken mocking of the priest from the comfort and safety of his flat and again I felt guilty. This was a good man, a caring man. I could see now that before that morning's conversation I had always imagined the earlier world through rose tinted glasses; it was so hard for those of us born after to truly comprehend what life had been like. I had never thought that the people back then would selfishly leave others to starve while there was an abundance of food. Equally I had never before thought of the people on the mainland needing help from us, perhaps in the same way people had ignored the 'third world' he had told me of.

He did not offer any more of an explanation and I felt in no way qualified to offer an opinion. Time was getting on and the morning was warming up. I stood and offered him my hand to shake.

"I need to get going, thank you for all your help," I said as he grasped and shook my hand firmly.

"Good luck, kid, and thanks for the supper. I'm sorry to sound so bombastic and full of bile," he said. "Too much time in the pulpit." He gave me a broad smile. "Be careful out there and call back in any time, okay. You'll always be welcome here."

"If I'm ever passing by again I'll be glad of a friendly face to say hello to," I told him, but I think we both knew that it was unlikely we would meet again.

I left my host then. I walked out from his church, through the unlocked gates, closing them behind me, and I carried on with my journey.

It took me an hour to get out of the town and into the open country to the south of Ormskirk that morning. During that time I saw nothing but rubble and the discarded detritus of the people long gone. As I walked I reflected on how I used to try to imagine all of the things that were and the things that people took for granted. People who lived through the war sometimes try to describe the world before to those of us born after, or who were too young to remember. It always sounds like a mythical paradise to me, almost too good to have been true. Now it has all gone, destroyed and no one is even really sure why. How could anyone have thrown all of that away?

There were the remains of a shop, spilled out onto the road, that I picked my way over. A blue and white striped plastic bag fluttered in the light breeze, wrapped around the wheel of an upturned shopping trolley.

Later, I saw a partially standing building whose door bore the words 'Retirement Home'. Looking inside through a broken window I saw ranks of high backed arm chairs, all lined up in empty rows and I wondered on the fate of those that had resided there. They were probably amongst the first to die, but I also thought how lucky they had been, to have lived out almost their full natural lifespan at the very peak of human civilisation.

Finally the route I followed came to fields and I

began to feel a little safer again. I walked along in a drainage ditch at the side of a tree lined road for a while, with only my head exposed above the level of the long grass, perfect cover from anyone who might have been looking in my direction.

I noticed a book lying on the road, its pages being turned by the wind. Its condition suggested that it had been discarded fairly recently and it reminded me again that other people still wandered that land. I took the time to retrieve the book from where it lay. It was dirty and looked like it had been thumbed through many times. On the cover a woman swooned in the arms of her lover and I could see that it was romantic fiction and of no interest to me. I discarded it again and carried on my way.

The sun shone and under other circumstances it would have been a nice day. Eventually the road I was following met another running east-west and stopped, but I did not alter my course. I continued in the same direction, across the countryside, sticking to the old field boundaries.

The priest's warnings from the night before reminded me to check behind and around me more often, making sure I was not being followed as I walked. He had unnerved me by tracking me unobserved and I was determined to do my best not to let it happen again.

A few hours into the day I noticed movement in the distance off to my left. I ducked down immediately as soon as I saw it and waited, trying to get a better look and work out what it was, but I had to avoid using my binoculars as the sun was already bright and I could not risk a tell-tale reflection on the glass betraying my position. As they approached I could make out what appeared to be a hunting party. There were twelve of them, ten males and two females, very proficient in their style, running across the landscape like athletes. They advanced closer to me on a vector set to skim my position. I had no option but to simply hide and hope that they would not notice me.

As I crouched, in the long grass at the foot of a tree, there was nothing I could do but watch as they got nearer. They all had long hair, tied back into pony-tails, the men with short trimmed beards. In the warm sun they wore very little and any bare skin was painted in camouflaging colours, topped with a thin sheen of glistening sweat.

They kept their distance from each other, none of them less than five metres from the next, well practiced and spread out in an arrowhead formation. As they went past me with the closest barely metres away, I could see the bows they carried, efficient deadly weapons. One of their pack carried a black rifle slung in the crook of his left arm, with his right hand on its pistol grip ready to fire it; I could see from my hiding place that it was very well maintained.

I felt a shiver of fear run through me when I saw the rifle. I had been hoping that there would not be many firearms left on the mainland. Yet there, during only my third encounter with people, was a well cared for gun. I doubted that he would be carrying it if he had no ammunition for it, their weapons were not for threat or for show, they had clear purpose.

Another of them carried a large crossbow slung on his back. It appeared to have been fabricated from the leaf spring of a truck and I was surprised that he could run under the weight of it. It must have had an enormous range, but would have taken an age to wind back its string before shooting. The bolts for the weapon were tied to it and looked to be at least two and a half feet long.

Eventually they passed me, heading off towards the west. I had always been led to believe that people outside of the Island, although unpleasant and dangerous, were disorganised, incompetent and dysfunctional. If everyone out here on the mainland was as lethal, coordinated and as well disciplined as those dozen, I would have a much more difficult mission than anticipated.

I stayed still until I was sure they had gone on their way and would not be back. The only sound was the wind brushing across the grass and I was confident that I was alone again.

I walked on for another hour and although I saw nothing else of note, I kept a tight grip on my bow. It had been my most treasured possession ever since it had been given to me. Almost everyone on the Island had a bow of one sort or another and each one was hand picked for every archery student by Shiel's father. As soon as we were fully grown and we had demonstrated our level of competence with the training bows, he would take us in turn into his workshop, measure us and set up a bow to suit. It was an unofficial rite of passage in our community, a sign of adulthood. I had been top of the class, a natural archer and my weapon reflected that.

Shiel's parents had owned the archery shop that Gill's men had found on the mainland. Shiel and his family had been brought to the Island by helicopter, along with all of the stock from their shop. Shiel's father had taught us both to shoot bows at a very early age and still did most of the maintenance on the archery equipment in Ramsey, working in the Island's small armoury. There were other workshops dotted around the Island and their craftsmen had mostly been trained by Fred Shiel. Archery is essential to the life we lead, for hunting and for defence. If it was not for that alternative, without Shiel's father and his skills, left to rely on firearms, we would have run out of ammunition for the guns years ago.

Later that morning I consulted my map and altered my course a little to the south east, to take me towards the remains of Rainford as the priest had suggested. I had previously calculated that the best route east would be to follow the route of the old East Lancashire Road, but that was still some way off yet.

I came to the first of the motorways marked on my map and the size of it truly astonished me. I had never seen a road quite so big, or so direct. I tried to imagine being in one of the rusty metal shells that littered everywhere, hurtling down the vast expanse of tarmac. Of course, now you would have to swerve round some of the trees on it. We had a few vehicles on my Island home which were used very sparingly, but no roads like that.

I stood on the road surface looking at the bridges that crossed it in the distance, some still standing, some collapsed on to the highway itself. It must have been a huge undertaking to build something of that size and I wondered how many years it had taken.

The landscape seemed to become flatter again and the fields more windswept as I continued on. I saw some traces of rudimentary agriculture. I assumed that there would be someone keeping guard over their valuable crops, so I gave it a wide berth, worrying that they too might be armed.

I walked on, across the empty land. I was starting to feel very isolated. I had not spent much time in my life so absolutely alone. Though I had no brothers or sisters and no other family at home in Ramsey, it was a very close knit community. To be out there then, with nobody to turn to or rely on but myself, I felt very lonely and exposed indeed.

I came to another railway. It ran along a steep sided embankment that I estimated to be about ten metres tall and I struggled up it as I could not see how far it extended off to either side. I might have found a bridge to pass under it if I had detoured, but there was thick tree coverage. I did not want to lose my bearings and there was no easy way to tell how long a detour might be. It was hot sweaty work pulling myself up and over it, the sides were smooth as well as steep and covered in dry loose soil. I slipped and slid backwards more than once as I made my ascent.

I gasped and huffed as I eventually came to the top and before I slid down the other side, I lay on the ground for a minute to get my breath back, careful to keep my silhouette off the skyline. "Perhaps I should have walked along it and looked for a bridge after all," I thought to myself.

# CHAPTER 8

A short distance after I had left the cover of the trees, on the other side of the railway, I noticed with a start that there was a woman standing openly in the field behind me. She must have been sat or lying down in the long grass for me not to have seen her as I passed by her. Either that or she had started to follow me from the tree line, I never found out. She had obviously seen me. She was looking straight at me and I considered raising my bow to ward her off. She did not move, standing a hundred metres away from me as I turned around. She did not appear to represent any sort of immediately recognisable danger to me at that moment, but I was suspicious of her all the same. I continued onwards, waiting to see what she would do.

As soon as I set off she followed, keeping pace with me. I stopped again and so did she, that time I decided that I did need to ward her off. Raising my bow and drawing it, I took aim at her. She raised her hands but she still stood her ground. I did not want to simply shoot her without having good reason to, but I did need her to believe that I might. As I lowered the bow she lowered her arms, reacting to my movements.

I carried on again across the waving grass. Once again she set off, matching my speed and direction, maintaining her distance. For a third time I stopped and again I turned and drew my bow and yet again her hands rose. I was starting to get anxious about this chain of events.

"Stay there," I called to her, "or I'll shoot you." I

hoped the consistent threat of violence would scare her off.

She remained silent, still with her hands raised and I set off again. Ignoring the threatened consequences, she lowered her arms and continued to follow as I moved on. I was in a dilemma over what I should do about her. She seemed to be no obvious threat to me and yet I could not just let her continue to trail after me across the countryside. I wondered if perhaps she might be part of a larger group and if so, whether she would call for them. Then I dismissed that thought, wondering why she would stay out in the open if that were the case.

I stopped again and once more drew my bow, my fear becoming overwhelmed by my curiosity. I needed to find out what was going on and what she wanted from me.

"Come on then," I called to her, "you obviously want to talk to me, so let's talk then."

She raised her hands again and walked towards me. As she approached I could make out more detail, she was of a medium height and very thin. She wore a brown corduroy dress that was much too large for her and was held in at the waist with string. As she got closer I could see she was also wearing dirty trousers underneath the dress and all of her clothing looked ragged. She appeared to be about thirty years old but it was difficult to judge. As she walked through the grass towards me, I saw that she had badly worn out wellington boots on, they were wrapped at the feet with plastic sheets covering the soles. Her lank blonde hair hung loose and shoulder length. Her hands and face were caked in filth, in a manner than suggested neglect rather than deliberate camouflage.

"What do you want?" I asked her as she got nearer.

"Nothing," she said dourly, looking at the floor. "I'm just walking."

"Turn right the way around and keep your hands up," I told her. I wanted to check for weapons of any sort.

"No need to be unfriendly," she said, whilst following my instructions.

She now stood only a few metres away from me and I could not see any obvious armament.

"Will you leave me alone? Stop following me?" I asked her.

"We're just goin' the same way. Might as well walk together."

"I don't want us to walk together," I said.

"You're not from around here are you? Where are you goin'? I'll 'elp to guide you if you like." Her strong accent was one I was unaccustomed to.

"I don't need a guide," I told her. "I know where I'm going."

"Maybe you do, maybe you don't, but you don't know who's goin' to be along the way though, do you," she said. "Besides I don't think you'd shoot me when I'm unarmed, would you?"

"Yes, I would," I told her, trying to sound convincing, although I do not think she believed me. "And anyway, just because I can't see anything from here, how do I really know that you're unarmed?"

"If you let me put my arms down I could undress myself if you'd like," she offered. "I could shake my clothes out for you while I'm naked."

"No thanks. Just keep your distance away from me, okay." I let the string of the bow down and walked on. "I don't need anything from you."

She followed again, keeping a few metres away. If she came any closer than that I drew my bow and her arms would go up again. This happened frequently and it was immensely frustrating, but I could not just kill her in cold blood for the simple crime of following me when I had said not to.

"Have you got any food?" she asked me. Sometimes I was unsure of her words through the filter of her accent.

"If I have or if I haven't got food is no concern of yours," I told her firmly.

"Well you're a bit of a snapper ain't you? Go on give us a bite to eat, I'm starving," she begged.

I ignored her.

"What's your name?" she asked, and without waiting for a reply said, "I'm Julie."

"What do you want from me, Julie? I'm not going to be giving you any food." I turned towards her emphasising the words. "I'm not going to give you anything. Do you understand me? So you might as well just go."

"Look," she said, changing to a different approach and simpering a little, trying for sympathy, "I'm all on my own out here."

"Not my problem, nothing to do with me." I turned and walked on.

"Don't follow, don't follow," I thought to myself, over and over again. Even if she was alone and not part of a larger group, she was slowing me down and more worryingly, distracting my attention from keeping vigilant to any other dangers. She stood out like a flag, putting us both at risk.

"Let me just come with you for a bit then, that bow of yours will protect two just as easy as one," she said, moving on after me. "You didn't tell me your name, what is it then?" she asked again.

"Badger," I told her sighing, knowing what was coming.

"'Cos you're so timid?" she said sarcastically. Then added, "Just joking, Badger, just joking," as I turned round towards her, staring hard at her and lifting my bow slightly.

"Badger is a very nice name," she mocked.

We continued our reluctant travels together and I really hoped that she would give up on following me soon.

"Are you sure you've got no food?" she asked again five minutes later when we were crossing a narrow side road. "What's in that bag you're carryin'?"

"A nice hot roast beef dinner for two, complete with table and chairs," I said as sarcastically as I could. "Put any thoughts about my pack or its contents out of your head," I told her. "There's nothing in it for you. Do you understand?"

"I've never met anyone quite so charming," she said.

We walked on again for a while in silence. She got a little too close once more and once again I drew back my bow string, pointing the arrow at her until she widened the gap.

"Okay, don't trust me then," she said, "I'm only trying to be friendly."

I did not answer her, I just let the bow down once she had moved further away.

"Whereabouts are you from then?" she asked me.

I ignored her again, still hoping she would leave me alone but of course she did not. I wondered how long she would persist before giving up on me. I still could not allow myself to trust her and I would have to get rid of her one way or another before night fell, preferably much sooner.

"I said whereabouts are you from then?"

I was starting to find, after a while of reluctantly joining in with her banal conversation, that it was easier to just answer her questions. She would simply repeat any inquiry a short while later if I tried to ignore her.

"The Isle of Man," I told her in a deadpan, disinterested voice.

"Where's that then? How did you get over 'ere?" she asked. I was getting increasingly annoyed with her again.

"It's out to sea between here and Ireland. I got here by boat."

She was persistent in her attempt to wear me down. "So what you doing here?" she asked.

"What does it matter? I'm here alright. I'm here, trying to get rid of you," I told her sharply, she was starting to really anger me by then. We walked on again in silence.

Two minutes later we came to a small brook. A hundred metres ahead, a row of electricity pylons stretched off into the distance, left to right. As I jumped across the brook I slipped slightly on the mud and Julie, seizing the opportunity, flung herself at me. She knocked the bow from my hand and landed on top of me as I fell forwards. She grabbed my head in both her hands from behind and slammed it into the earth. I was lucky that the ground was soft, my forehead left a dent in the earth and fortunately I was not badly hurt, however, she was making it difficult for me to breathe.

"Right, let's get the food out of that bag then," she said as I lay face down beneath her. She sat astride me in the mud with her legs pinning my arms down and, pausing first to punch me twice on the back of my head, she began to search me for food. "Try getting rid of me now, Badger," she said with venom.

Slightly dazed by her blows I struggled underneath her, trying to twist and turn to shake her off. My bow was now a hindrance to me, as its strap was wrapped around my left wrist, making it awkward for me to roll over. She reached for my pack and I heard her begin to undo it.

I felt her fingers knit into my hair as I struggled underneath her and she slammed my head into the soft mud twice more. Again I was not hurt by that but I tried feigning unconsciousness for a few seconds, to see if she would let her guard down if she thought she had knocked me out.

"Let's see what you've got hidden in 'ere then," she snarled as she started rummaging in the top of my pack.

A moment later, while she was distracted by her looting and as I recovered from her earlier two blows to the back of my head, I got my right hand free of her, more by brute force than anything else. I reached down and drew my knife from its scabbard, I do not think she had noticed that it was there and as it came free I drew the blade sharply along the inside of her thigh as it held me down. She screamed in pain, instinct causing her to move away from the source of it and I used the momentum of that movement to roll her off me. I quickly scrambled upright and while she clutched at her bleeding leg I punched her hard on the nose. My knife was still clutched in my hand as I hit her, adding its weight to the impact. I clearly heard her nose breaking and blood began to stream from that too. I climbed out of the ditch that the brook ran through, pausing momentarily to collect the arrow that had fallen off the bow string and put it back in place.

"I'm sorry, Badger," she groaned. "I'm hungry and you've got food. I didn't want to hurt you. Don't kill me. Please don't kill me, Badger."

I said nothing, brushing what I could of the thick mud from my face and clothes.

"Help me," she moaned, looking down at her wound. "I think you got the artery, I'm gonna die, I don't wanna die. Please help me."

I looked down at her kneeling in the mud. Her leg

was bleeding but not too badly. She had her hands over the wound and it oozed between her fingers. Blood also ran freely from her nose and, sniffing repulsively, she coughed some up and spat it out into the brook.

I checked my stuff to make sure nothing was missing. I was really enraged by her now, she had been nothing but a nuisance to me. "Maybe I should have killed her when I first saw her," I thought to myself, but I was not that sort of person. I was certainly furious enough with her to do it now, but knew that was no reason to; it would have made me no better than the mainlanders we held in such contempt. How dare she attack me like that, she had given me no choice but to sink to her level and hurt her.

"Listen to me, Julie. It's not down to the artery, it would come out in spurts if I'd cut that." I felt the back of my head and the two large lumps that were forming, as I tried to rationalise both with her and with my own conscience. "I want you to know something," I told her. "If I ever see you again, I *will* kill you. Do you understand me?"

She did not answer me.

"Do you understand, Julie? If you follow me or if I see you again I will shoot you and I will kill you," I repeated firmly.

"I'm just so hungry," she said. "I'm sorry, Badger."

That was how I left her, bleeding in the ditch; I could not afford to show any weakness if I was to make sure she understood that she had no chance with me. Her sobbing faded into the distance as I went on my way. For a while afterwards I turned regularly to look out for her, I did not see her or indeed anyone else. I was glad, though I found her unpleasant and I would not have hesitated, I really did not want to have to shoot her.

I felt again at the twinned lumps on the back of my head. If the ground she had slammed my head into had been harder, she would probably have succeeded in knocking me out. I wondered what state she would have left me in if her robbery had been successful, what lengths would she have gone to?

My anger at her slowly faded as I tried to concentrate on the present. I walked on, underneath one of the pylons. Small birds seemed to almost cover the top of it, ignoring me as I went on towards the road again.

It did not take long after that to come to the road I was looking for across the fields. According to my map, if I followed it south for about a mile I would come to the East Lancashire Road. I did not walk on the road; I was still concerned that I might stand out too much, particularly after my latest experience. I kept it to my left, still trying to be careful and to keep out of sight. I also remembered the hunters of earlier, wondering again what their prey was.

I found the crossroad I was looking for and I turned left, going over to the other side of the road for better protection amongst the trees. The extinct traffic lights stood there stiffly, as the wind swayed the trees and long grasses around them. I walked to the right of the large dual carriageway, through a wood that had once been a cemetery. The markers for the deceased, now long forgotten, lay spread around me as I walked on.

Soon there were more buildings around than before. Then the road entered a long shallow cutting, almost appearing to have worn a valley with the erosion of all those wheels, like a river, so many years ago. I walked over the top of the hill, thinking warily that the valley would have made a good place for an ambush.

For a while my route took me up a long hill and as usual I walked while looking around me continually for any movement. There seemed to be very little activity or wildlife, just ruins, yet more rusty cars and chaos wherever I looked. I walked on down the other side of the hill across the barren ground. The land beyond the road dropped away and to my right through the trees I saw a truly astonishing site. My map had indicated that I should be walking past a place called St Helens, but the town was no longer there. It had been literally wiped from the face of the earth. It looked as if it had been torn up from the ground like an enormous plant with deep roots.

Most of the destruction twenty years ago had been caused by nuclear bombs air bursting above their targets. St Helens had apparently been hit, whether by accident or design, by a ground burst with the weapon detonating on the floor. I thought it must have been a multi-megaton device because the resulting crater was so huge. I could see the rim of it stretching out to either side in front of me. I would estimate it was several hundred metres deep and so wide I could not see anything on the other side of it.

I decided to sit for a while, to have something to eat and take in the overwhelming sight of it. The trees and grass grew poorly around the vast indent in the surface of the earth and I wondered if it was due to the radiation or whether some other effect of the blast had caused it. I knew that an explosion like that could turn the ground underneath to glass if the soil contained enough sand.

Everything surrounding the site leaned away from it, the devastation worse the closer to the blast site I looked. A lot of objects, some quite large, had clearly been thrown a long distance by the shock wave. Off to one side I could see a large badly damaged transport container, resting on top of a crushed house.

Any brickwork and buildings that remained were badly scorched on the sides that had faced towards the flash. I had read a book once about the Hiroshima and Nagasaki bombs of nearly seventy years ago and I knew that some of the scorching would have the outline of the previous residents etched into them.

Although it felt wrong to do so, I could not help myself from taking out my binoculars for a closer look, but the walls were too far away and at the wrong angle for me to really see. I looked into the middle of it all and tried to imagine how anything could be powerful enough to do so much damage and I could not understand how anyone could unleash that on hundreds of thousands of fellow human beings. Despite having known deep down that I should not have been surprised to come across the crater, strangely the reality of it seemed almost surreal.

After I had eaten a few of my biscuits, I got up to leave. Something sparkled in the grass and I bent down to see what was there. I picked up a woman's shoe, covered in tiny shiny circles, a ridiculously high heel stuck out from the rear of it. I wondered how anyone could wear such a stupidly impractical item and I threw it back where it had come from.

I thought back to the Island where we rooted through all of the old houses. There are only a few thousand of us living there now, a fraction of the seventy thousand that had been resident before the war, so there was an abundance of unused properties. All useful items were removed from the empty dwellings and put into storage: clothes, fabrics, footwear, books, furniture, tools. The list was almost endless, anything at all that could ever be useful. Even the plumbing fittings, the sinks and toilets were removed from those houses, all catalogued and warehoused with the rest. Everything will break down eventually and there is no point leaving an empty house still fitted out with serviceable goods before abandoning it to rot to pieces. One of the few things that we left were shoes like those.

As kids we would go and play around in the abandoned buildings. We were not supposed to, but children rarely follow all of the rules. We ran around the derelict housing estates and played in the rooms. We sometimes vandalised them, writing our names on the walls, at the time not realising how foolish it was to write your own name somewhere that you were not supposed to go.

A lot of the Island's old buildings are starting to fall down now. The rain got in where the wind had blown off a tile and then the roof joists quickly succumbed to mould and rot. They would slump down, slowly crumbling to pieces if nobody took the time to repair them. Most of Ramsey was like that; we only had enough people to occupy the centre of the town.

I remembered sneaking into one of those collapsing properties when I was about ten years old. Bracket fungi had stuck out from the walls like thick rough shelving. The carpet had not been removed and it squelched underfoot as I walked. Every surface was slimy and a bubble of rank smelling gas had risen through the puddle at the other end of the room, forcing me to run out of the building as the smell was so bad. There was no time to dwell on that then though, I dragged myself back to the present and set off again.

# CHAPTER 9

I kept going along the road for another half an hour, as always carefully trying to avoid being spotted by anyone who might be in the area. Picking my way past an area of rubble where houses had once stood, I came upon a large freshwater lake and refilled my water bottles. I was still covered in mud from my recent encounter and I paused for a while longer, to wash in it and cool off from the early afternoon sun.

Between the road and the lake were the ruins of a pub or restaurant. I kept it behind my back, letting it shield me from sight, and for a few minutes after I had washed I lay in the sun letting its warmth dry me. I listened intently for anyone nearby as I lay there, but heard only the wind rustling the trees.

A short while after I had arrived I was off again, still heading east towards Manchester. As I set off, to my right a pair of figures caught my eye, their movement stimulating my peripheral vision as they approached the road from the south.

They had obviously seen me and were looking directly at me. A surge of adrenaline ran through my body. After my recent brush with a local I was not going to hesitate to aggressively defend myself again.

I saw them turn to follow me, although they tried to look innocuous. They were stalking me, albeit somewhat inexpertly; they kept their distance, but not too far, close enough to see what I would do and how I might react. Two men, furtive, shambolic and dishevelled. I was in no doubt that they were dangerous, the way they followed me showed clear intention. Somehow they had survived out there for years. That would not have been easy and after my experience with Julie I tried not to think of the things that they must have done to subsist. I passed under a large bridge with them still behind me.

For half an hour I did nothing but keep walking - what else was there to do? Sooner or later they would try to catch up with me, that much was obvious. They were certain to be looking for food or anything else they could steal. *Anything* else.

I was feeling very nervous. My training back on the Island had prepared me for that sort of situation, but it was only then that I was going to find out how well prepared I really was. I was not going to give these men the benefit of the doubt or the opportunity that I had given to Julie earlier. This time I had to be on the offensive. There was no room for error, no chance to try again if things went wrong. I put my fear aside; I had no time to think about how it might go wrong, this was going to be a time for action.

Looking back occasionally, I tried to make out as much detail as I could. One of them was tall, about six feet I judged. He carried a staff or pike of some sort. His shorter companion carried what looked like a home made crossbow. I let the wrappings on my own bow loosen a little; if they saw that they would either back off and wait for night, or be much more hesitant in their attack. I knew that they would certainly try to take it from me at some point. I did not unwrap it all of the way, I needed them to be rash.

They stayed together at first, but as I approached an open section of plain they separated, not yet trying to come after me, just taking advantage of their ability to outflank me. In the distance was the shell of a farmhouse, off to the left away from the road. It was little more than a single doorway and a section of wall, but there was nothing else around and so that was where I chose to make my stand. It was unlikely that they would just follow me indefinitely, so my best option was to ensure that the confrontation was on my terms.

My heart was racing, but again I swallowed any fear, channelling it into determination and drawing strength from it. I had made up my mind; I would have to seize the initiative.

About two hundred metres from the farm, I suddenly started my run. They sped up after me, but not fast enough to gain on me, either unable to catch me or still just keeping pace. I went through the doorway into the ruins and, hoping I was out of their sight, I unwrapped my bow. An arrow was already nocked, waiting on the string, but I knew I would be needing more than one and that I would require them in very quick succession. I took another six arrows from my quiver and stuck them point first into the ground at my feet, within easy reach of my right hand. Then I drew the bowstring back. I did not have to wait for long.

The first of the two to reach me was the crossbowman. He appeared over the wall to my left and I saw the look of horror on his face as he saw my already drawn back compound bow, pointing towards him. He swung his crossbow up quickly, and with little aiming or chance of hitting anything, he let his bolt fly, missing me by a long way. Then, as he tried to get back to cover, he slipped on the loose bricks and tumbled down the pile of rubble on the inside of the wall. My first arrow was still waiting on the drawn string.

His companion with the pike then rushed through the doorway, roaring at the top of his voice in what must have been an attempt to intimidate me. It seemed that their intention had been to shoot me and then storm in. I swung the bow round and his roar was cut short as my arrow hit him at the base of his throat. At that short range it went right through his neck, leaving only a few inches protruding from the front. He fell, gurgling and flailing and as he hit the floor he kicked up a cloud of dust. He was thrashing around with blood gushing from the wound in spurts. I knew he did not have long to suffer and could not allow myself to feel any sympathy. What would he have done to me?

All that had happened in an instant and I immediately turned my attention back to his companion, who then made his second mistake: he clumsily tried to reload his weapon, fumbling as he knelt there on the floor. He never had a chance of having that crude crossbow ready before I shot him; I was much quicker preparing my bow. If he had come at me physically he might have stood better odds, but reloading he had none. My arrow hit his left shoulder and went through into the wooden door frame behind him, pinning him there. The crossbow fell from his hands as he shouted out in agonising pain. I quickly nocked another arrow and walked towards him, past his companion who was now motionless on the floor as he lay there dying.

I felt a huge wash of relief come over me. I had done it, stood the test of it, fought them off and won. I felt more than a little proud of myself, a little less vulnerable to fate and circumstance.

"You've got a problem now," I said to the impaled man as I kicked his crossbow aside. "I can't put down this bow while you're still a threat to me, but I'm going to need *all* of my arrows back." He was shaking with terror, no doubt thinking that I was about to kill him as swiftly as I had just killed his partner.

"So there's two ways this can happen," I said and paused to let him think. "Would you like to collect them all for me?" I asked him. "Then, maybe I can let you live."

Leaving him unable to move was the least of my concerns. There was no way I was going to leave those arrows behind, they were far too precious in a world where replacements would be almost impossible to come by. It took him an hour, with the arrow of my drawn bow aimed at him for all of that time. Firstly he had to unscrew the shaft of the arrow from the barbed head that was still pinning him to the door frame. Even if he could have pulled the arrow's head loose from the wood without, he would not have wanted to pull the head back through the wound. To unscrew it, he had to turn the shaft of the arrow with his right hand. Once the head was unscrewed he pulled the shaft out with a cry.

I then made him screw the shaft back onto the arrow head and pull it out of the door frame. The second was easier for him to get. He showed no grief over his dead comrade, as he kicked the body over onto its side and knelt down to retrieve the other arrow from his neck, and I wondered how long they had been allied.

I was shaking a little by then, coming down from the rush of adrenaline that had kept me going.

"How do you get by out here?" I asked him.

"Same way as everyone else, getting food and things where we can." I saw the rotten stumps of his teeth as he spoke and his breath was foul.

"You ever eat people?" I asked him, curiously.

"Eat meat, people're just meat, can't afford to waste it once they're dead," he said matter-of-factly.

I looked down at him, still kneeling on the floor.

"Will you eat him?"

"You not taking him yourself?" he asked.

I was filled with revulsion at the suggestion. I could not even contemplate eating another human being and I could smell the unwashed sweaty corpse from where I stood. The thought of it, along with the drop in adrenaline made me feel slightly nauseous.

"No, just bring me my arrows back, okay."

"And then you won't kill me too, right? he asked.

"I'm still thinking about it."

He reached over and put the arrows down on the ground in front of me.

"Would you have eaten me?" I asked, already suspecting I knew the answer.

He had the sense not to answer my question.

"Where you from?" he asked angrily.

I ignored his question too.

"If you 'ave enough to squander where you're from, don't go and think you got some right to look down on me for me stayin' alive." It was a brave statement, given that he was looking the wrong way along my arrow. He stood up defiantly, the bleeding from his shoulder was slowing and a large wet red stain covered most of his shirt.

"Let me 'ave it then if you're gonna kill me. Let's just get all this over with. Ain't much of a life any more anyway," he said despondently, as if suddenly resigned to whatever fate brought, the fight in him evaporating.

"Do you want me to kill you?" I asked him. He looked at me as if I was naive and stupid, after he answered me I felt it too.

"Look at me," he said, "I'll do anything I've gotta do to stay alive. You can sneer if you want. Do you think I'd be doin' all this if there was any other way for me to get by. If I'd wanted to end it all, well, there's plenty of bridges to jump off. Those as wanted to check themselves out after the war 'ave all managed it long ago." He looked at me in bold resignation. "So I'll ask again, let me 'ave it, or let me go."

After that I did let him to go, nursing his shoulder. I tried not to wonder what might happen to him. If the wound got infected he could still die from it. I had left him defenceless and injured, but I could not let my conscience bother me. I had only killed another human once before his partner, then too out of necessity, during a raid on the Island by some pirates.

My attacker's crossbow came with me, along with his four bolts; it was of no use to me and a hindrance to carry, but I could not let him keep it. I watched him until he disappeared from view. He did not look round so I hoped he had no further interest in seeing which way I would go. Despite the time of day it suddenly grew almost dark and ominous thick black clouds covered the sun as I left the farmhouse ruins, but I walked on for as long as I dared to gain as safe a distance as possible. I could not stay there in case he came back with reinforcements.

An hour and several miles later the rain came down heavily, almost like a monsoon, bouncing off every hard surface, so I sheltered a short while in a small copse surrounded by thick trees. While I waited for the rain to stop I spotted a birds' nest in one of the trees, and anticipating a meal, I scaled it and shooed away its inhabitant to retrieve three eggs. I risked a small fire since the trees were dense enough to shield me from sight and to protect some of the drier wood from the downpour. I was very glad of my precious gas lighter. As the fire grew I cupped each egg in my hands, letting the light from the flames shine through, and was happy to see that they were quite freshly laid. I boiled the eggs and nearly scalded myself peeling and eating them as soon as they were cooked, not wanting to wait around anywhere for longer than necessary.

I shivered a little, freezing cold despite the small fire I had lit. The rain had caught me without my poncho on and had come down so fast and with such force that I was soaked to the skin before I had time to react. Most of my clothing would dry quickly enough though once I started to move on.

Once I had finished the eggs I set off again, leaving the cumbersome crossbow behind me hidden in the undergrowth. With the rain easing, I headed back to the road I was following, finding it again at a crossroad, near a short strip of burned out houses. There was another cutting ahead which I skirted around without incident. Shortly afterwards there was a huge embankment, built up for the road to run along for a number of miles. I did not want to walk along on top of that, as again I would be vulnerable and visible for a good distance around. That part of my journey was hard going, the bottom of the banking was very thickly forested and the ground between the trees was strewn with ruined brickwork from destroyed houses. I had to move slowly, regularly stopping to listen for any signs of movement other than my own.

My earlier victory over the two aggressors had restored some of my confidence. I hoped I really was tough and competent enough to make it through that blighted landscape. I walked, arrow nocked as usual feeling rather more self assured, though still as cautious as before.

Later that evening I found a gap in the bank alongside me as the road traversed a bridge. Underneath was an obvious camp site where smoke still drifted from the embers of what had been a large fire. I hurried on, hoping that the residents were no longer around. I might have felt a little more secure in my own capability, but it would have been foolish to allow myself to become complacent.

"Drop the bow." It was not a request.

From five metres in front of me a tall man moved away from a tree that he had been leant against. His camouflage had been perfect; he wore the greenery of the woodland, threaded through netting and I think I would have walked straight past him if he had remained silent and not deliberately made himself known. He held a stubby looking green rifle, also dotted with camouflage. The barrel was pointed directly at my head. I lowered my bow slowly to the ground, bending at the knees to do so. I stood straight again, raising my arms unbidden, hoping that he was not an acquaintance of the last two men I had met.

My new found confidence drained away as I tried

not to think of what might come next. The man had me completely at his mercy and there was nothing I could do. I thought back to my recent experiences, of Julie and the two men I had shot that afternoon and I hoped my own death would be swift.

"Who are you, what do you want here?" he whispered to me.

"I'm nobody, I'm just passing through," I whispered back, wondering who we were keeping our voices low from.

"You don't walk like a nobody; you walk like you know what you're doing." I took that as a compliment from someone who was clearly so proficient himself. "Where are you from? Have I seen you somewhere before?"

"Have you ever been to the Isle of Man?" I asked. "If not, then you must be thinking of somebody else."

I wondered what the man wanted, his tone seemed far more conversational than I would have expected. His manner was not hostile, but not welcoming either. His gun dropped to waist level, no longer pointing directly at me although that could have been remedied in a second. The threat was still implied but was beginning to feel like less of a certainty.

"You remind me of somebody, maybe someone I used to know." He paused. "Anyway, round here, this is my land, mine and my family's. There's nothing for you here."

"I'm just passing through," I reiterated. "I swear I won't touch anything, I won't even pick any fruit."

"Good, then be on your way. I'll be watching you for the next mile or so, don't walk too slowly."

"What about my bow?" I asked him, looking towards it.

"It's okay, I won't leave you defenceless, I might as well shoot you in the head myself as take that off you." I nodded, in a mixture of relief and gratitude, while he continued. "I'm going to trust you. Pick it up in a few minutes. Then be off, okay?" he told me, as he disappeared into the background. Seconds later he was gone from sight and I waited there for the few minutes I had been instructed, before I picked up the bow and moved off myself.

I could not believe my lucky escape; he had had me right in his sights and had let me go. There was a lot I did not know about the world out there and although his actions had seemed honourable, my paranoia hoped that he had not let me go as part of a larger plan.

Soon after, the ruined buildings that had been swallowed by the forest disappeared and the floor of the woodland became easier to walk over. My progress was faster and I made better time. The light was fading and I could ignore the impending dusk no more.

I came to the end of the bank of earth and the road came back down to meet me. Ahead was a vast traffic island surrounded by trees. Above it was an enormous and still complete, concrete and steel structure, a bridge held aloft on a row of huge thick wedge shaped supports. It was another motorway, but this time suspended in the air over my head, crossing the road I followed, as I walked beneath. Its uprights rose out of the ground, getting wider as they went higher until they met the underside of the road, about ten metres above me. From that angle it felt like it was even larger than the other motorway I had seen. On the Isle of Man there is nothing of that magnitude, although I think what I found more awe inspiring was what it represented in terms of the sheer scale of the life that used to be, to actually see it for real rather than in books. I wondered afresh what the city would be like when I reached it, how big the structures there would be and how much would remain.

I decided to stay there that night, the area looked quiet enough and I sheltered at the base of one of the wedges. I spent a while gathering some berries from around the area and uncovered some potatoes that were growing wild inside the circle of road. Since the area was densely wooded, I risked lighting my stove and heated one of my jars of spiced mince over it. I boiled two of the potatoes and stashed into my bag the others that I had dug up.

It had been a very eventful day, in particularly sharp contrast with the one before. I was still making good enough progress to achieve my three day target, but I hoped that the next day would be calmer.

The last of the sun was setting as I sat eating and

reading through the book that Shiel had given to me. To my right, a glint of reflected sunlight caught my eye through the twilight. I marked its direction by laying out a straight stick on the floor. It was not very far away but it was too late to investigate it then, I decided to have a look in the morning; rationalising that anything of concern would have made itself known to me already.

I huddled up in my poncho and curled myself around my bow, for a feeling of security and as I tried to get to sleep I thought back to my archery training. Earlier that day it had saved my life. Shiel's dad had been an excellent teacher and I remembered my first lessons with the compound clearly.

"Okay," he had said, "hold it like you would any other bow." I did as he bid me. "Right, now pull back the string just a little. It will be harder than you're used to." I had pulled on it with my right hand and for the first inch it had indeed moved quite freely, then it seemed almost solid.

"That's it, keep drawing and it will get easier," he encouraged me. I drew the string further back and it did start to take less force. Once the string approached my chin it took almost no effort at all to hold it there. I could have held it back with my smallest finger quite comfortably.

"Right, so that's on about thirty pounds of draw weight," he explained, "but we'll soon have you up to fifty or more. Let it down slowly and carefully, it will seem to try and pull your arm off as it gets off the cam, then we'll try it with an arrow."

I think that was one of the hardest parts of the training. As the arrow was pulled backwards on the string it would shake and fall off the arrow rest. It could be held onto the rest with the index finger of the left hand, and indeed I did do that sometimes if I walked along with it drawn. However, if the arrow is shot while you are still holding it on there, then the fletchings would cut through your finger and the arrow would go badly askew. Worst of all, if the string is drawn back and let go without an arrow on it, then with no other outlet for the potential energy, the bow could break.

Eventually I got the technique of it right and he congratulated me.

"Well done, Badge, I wish my Tim was that good with one of those. Aim through the peep sight on the string there and through the lens. You'll see it magnify the target."

It did indeed make the target larger and the front lens had a small pin in front of it as a sight. I trained it on the centre of the circles.

"Right," he said, "don't worry about where it hits, we still need to set the sight up for you. Take aim, release the arrow and we will see where it ends up." Almost instantaneously the arrow disappeared from the bow and reappeared quivering in the target forty metres away.

I remember being surprised at the potency of it in comparison with a traditional bow and I wondered what it would be like at full power and range. I hoped I would be strong enough to pull its string back.

"Okay, five more and we will see if they all go to the same point on the target. If they do we can set the sights up and I can leave you to practise for a while," he told me.

I nocked up another arrow and drew again. I aimed and again the arrow seemed to vanish as I released, it thudded into the target not much more than a centimetre away from the first.

"That's my star pupil," he said. "I knew you'd be good with that bow, it could have been made for you."

The next four arrows also hit the target in almost the same place as the first, with two even touching each other, and as he adjusted the sights for me I went to collect them. They were stuck fast, like they were nailed into the very heavily compressed straw boss. I struggled to pull them free, even with the palm sized rubber mat he had given me to aid my grip. I had thought it might be a good idea to stand a way further back from the target for the next six shots.

"I've set your sight. I think it will be right for this distance and we'll adjust it as we get further away," he said unfurling a large piece of paper. It had six much smaller target faces drawn on it, one for each arrow. "Use this target now while you practice. With your accuracy, your arrows will hit the backs of one another otherwise and we can't afford to have you breaking too many."

Back under my poncho on the mainland, I eventually drifted off to sleep and the happy memories merged into dreams of home.

# CHAPTER 10

"Good morning," said a voice as I stirred the next dawn. As soon as I heard it I opened my eyes and immediately pulled out my knife with a start. I tried to untangle myself from my poncho, keeping my eyes on the stranger kneeling a few feet from me. He did not move, he just sat there watching me.

"Relax," he said. "If I'd wanted to hurt you, I'd hardly have waited till you had woken up first would I?"

"So you want me alive? Am I supposed to thank you for that?" I could think of several reasons why he might want me alive and I had no evidence yet that I was able to trust him. "What *do* you want then?" I asked him.

"I don't '*want*' anything and I could have tied you up, no?" He stood slowly. I could see that he was old and rather too slim, what remained of his thinning hair was wispy and grey. He seemed to be unarmed as far as I could tell.

"If you like," he continued, "pack up your stuff and I'll make some breakfast for us, nothing fancy mind, potato cakes and dandelion tea. Over there," he motioned with his hand in the direction of the previous night's reflection. "There's an old petrol station. I live in it now. My name's Frank. Make up your own mind and maybe I'll see you over there, once you've got your stuff together."

He walked off in the direction he had indicated,

whistling at first.

"Don't worry, I live quite alone," he called back. "Quite alone."

I felt less wary of him but was annoyed at having allowed myself to be caught out again. I saw the logic in his argument; asleep I had been helpless. I remembered the crossbow man and his accomplice from the day before. Right then I was more concerned about the man I had not killed, it had been a merciful act, but possibly naive and foolish too. I was worried that he might be following me and planning some sort of revenge. I looked briefly around the small clearing, relieved to see that for now at least, there was no one there.

I checked my belongings and nothing was missing but that was still no reason to fully trust Frank. I started to assemble my things, getting ready to move on quickly. Ten minutes later I caught scent of his cooking, wafting through the trees. It was too tempting and I decided I would move a little closer, thinking that if anything appeared to be suspicious I could turn back immediately. After picking up my pack I put an arrow on the string of my bow, drew it back, and trod lightly through the forest towards his home.

As I got closer, I noticed that some of the 'trees' in this particular forest were in fact tall metal lamp posts and as I crossed the crumbling road surface itself, I could see that nature would reclaim that area soon too. Small saplings speared upwards through the old cracked tarmac and grass grew deeply wherever it had taken hold. On the other side there was a thin strip of trees and vegetation, shielding from view a clearing containing the remains of the large metal weather shield that had once covered the forecourt of the petrol station. The canopy had been broken up over the years and the stumps of the pumps stuck through it.

Frank sat outside at a table, some distance away from the buildings, almost at the edge of the clearing near to where I emerged.

"I thought you might prefer to be over here, in case all the imaginary men that I haven't got hidden anywhere, decided to jump out at you from inside," he said, as if he had read my mind, smiling at his own joke. "Sit down and eat before it gets cold. I'm sure you could overcome a feeble old bloke like me if you had to."

The food was already laid out on the table and it smelled good. I relaxed my bow and moved slightly towards him.

"Why should I trust you?" I asked.

"You've no reason to but potato cakes and tea," he told me honestly. "And there's the fact that I could have done all those evil things in your imagination to you already, but I didn't."

Again he had a point. I sat down and sipped at the tea. It was rather good, as was the food.

"Sorry, but you know how it is."

"Sadly yes," he agreed. "What's your name?"

"People call me Badger. How do you get by out here alone?" I asked him.

"Ah, I choose my guests with *great* care." He emphasised the word 'great', stretching it out almost comically. "Everyone else, I hide from." He flashed his gappy smile at me before resuming his meal.

"Nice tea," I said by way of thanking him, holding up the chipped cup.

"Where are you from?" he asked. "I can't place the accent."

There was no reason to lie to him and I was starting to feel more trusting, so I told him. As I did so he looked more than a little surprised.

"I'm from the Isle of Man. There's a ship moored up near Ramsey that my parents were on during the war. It's an aircraft carrier, nuclear powered, the electricity is still on and we have a decent enough way of life over there. It's not like the mainland these days, we have a proper community and everyone is relatively safe."

"So they've got a little haven out there by the sounds of it," Frank said. "If I was younger I'd take a look myself. So how have you come to be passing my little corner?" he asked. Then conspiratorially he added, "What mission is this lone Manx with the unusual name on? Have you come to spy on the mainland? Are you the spearhead of an invasion?"

I laughed, genuinely warming to the old man.

"No," I told him, in the same whispering fashion, "it's a rescue mission! I've come to get my Dad back from Manchester. I think he might be being held in The Castle at Trafford."

His face fell and immediately his demeanour changed.

"Oh, child," he said. "Don't go there, please don't go there."

"I have to," I told him, "my Dad could be in there." I mentally added him to the list of people who had tried to change my mind. At home I had hoped that the negativity towards the mainland was partially due to an exaggerated fear of the unknown, but I was starting to realise that this was probably not the case.

"Do you know what's there? What's inside that castle? What those animals living there are like, child? Do you? No, you can't or you wouldn't be fool enough to go. Listen to me, its enormous for a start and heavily fortified. How will you get into it? They'll slice you up in a heartbeat. They'll have sliced him up already anyway. It used to be a football stadium, they used to get seventy five thousand people in there and all of them needed a ticket. You can't just go and ask for him back you know," he said all in one go, rambling slightly, giving me no time to interrupt or answer his questions.

"He sent a radio message," I told him, "so I know he is still alive and I have to find him."

There was no way that old man who I had met just minutes before was going to change my mind. He did not know how determined I was.

"Oh, child, if he sent you a radio message he won't be in The Castle, he can't be! Can't be!"

"Perhaps he's escaped!" I felt hope springing once more.

"No, nobody escapes from in there. Nobody." He looked adamant, then added, "I hope you can find him, but don't delude yourself. I beg of you, don't end up in that place. I saw it maybe ten years ago, floated by it on the canal leaving the centre of the city. It already had a reputation back then."

There was a lull in our conversation. Frank rolled up his sleeves as we carried on eating together and I saw that the skin on his left arm was a mass of raised scar tissue. He noticed me glancing at it.

"Got a bit of sunburn from a flash back in the day," he told me. I felt embarrassed to have stared at his injury and hastily changed the subject.

"So who's the camouflage expert in the woods back there?" I asked him quickly, nodding my head in the direction I had arrived from. "I bumped into him last night, almost literally I should add. He could have taken everything I have but he just warned me off his patch."

Frank smiled again, "Don't worry about him. He looks after our little neighbourhood around here, you know, the helpless ones like me. If anyone too unpleasant comes hanging around, well he...." Frank paused. "You know the rest already," he said and he pointed his first two fingers to make a gun shape. "Bang."

"Where did he come from?" I asked, intrigued.

"He's from around here originally, but he wasn't here right after the war, he came home afterwards. I think he was in the special forces, posted abroad somewhere," he told me. "When you get to know him he's full of old stories about his journey home. Bores the pants of me sometimes," he added with a smile, "but he's a good enough bloke really."

"I don't think I'd like to get on the wrong side of him," I said.

"I very much doubt he'd have anything to fall out with you over, you seem nice enough."

"Thank you and I hope you are right," I said to him.

Frank and I finished our meal together quietly after that. He really had not wanted to do me any harm and I was glad that I had made an effort to trust him. He had managed to find a place where he could live relatively peacefully and had showed me that not everyone on the mainland was as savage as I had been led to believe. He had shared his food with me only for the company and to hear news of the world around him.

"Do you manage to get enough to eat around here?" I asked him after we had finished.

"Well I'm up to my knees in potatoes at the right time of year," he joked. "I don't know why, but potatoes love it round here. They sprout up everywhere."

"Yes, I found some last night," I said.

"There's rabbits, cats and dogs, I set up snares here and there. I can get by well enough."

"You have a good place here," I said as I looked around the clearing, "I hope you manage to keep it to yourself."

"Nobody bothers about the old potato man. If anyone unsavoury ever drops in, I have my places to hide till they're gone and frankly, they can take all the potatoes they can carry for all I care. There's more here than I need." He paused looking wistful. "Never seemed to work out why though, funny isn't it."

"Maybe there was a lorry hauling a load of potatoes that somehow spilled its cargo and they took root," I postulated.

"As good a theory as any. I've often wondered, don't suppose I'll ever know. I've looked around the area for the remains of any lorries." He smiled at me again and added, "When you eat as many of the things as I do, well you know, maybe I'm going a little strange. Too much time on my own with too much time to think." His index finger drew circles around his temple. "Potatoes aren't that important are they?"

I liked Frank, he seemed like a genuinely nice old fellow.

"Oh I don't know about that," I said, "maybe where they came from doesn't matter, but what you do with them certainly does."

As I left him, it was already approaching mid-morning. I promised him too that I would call in on my way past, if ever I was in the area again and we parted as friends. I was glad to know that if I did have to walk back to the coast on my return journey to the Island, then I would have two safe places to stop and rest during the night along with two men that I could trust to help me on my way back home.

As I strode out, continuing on my route towards Manchester, I wondered just where on earth my Dad was if escape from The Castle was indeed so difficult. Still, where else was there to look? Shiel had been absolutely certain that the signal had originated from Manchester. I supposed I would find out when I got there.

My route east ran straight for a while and the going was easy, through the woodland at the side of the road. Every now and again I would glance back at the motorway fly over; getting smaller each time I looked.

I wondered if I ever would come back that way, or if I would ever see Frank again. He had survived the twenty years since the war, so I supposed I did not need to worry about him but he was the kind of man that you could not help but warm to, a caring grandfatherly figure.

I had lingered over my breakfast with him for far too long and it was already mid-morning. The sky was overcast, threatening rain and the atmosphere was warm and humid, making the air feel thick after I emerged from the trees. I walked for a meagre ten minutes before my progress was halted again.

Across the fields I saw five men on horseback to the south of my position, heading towards me at speed. Looking around quickly for the nearest cover, I flung myself into a roadside ditch, anxious that they were likely to be trouble. I could see that these people had a brazen confidence and no intention of trying to hide from others. I was concerned in case their fearless attitude might not have been because it was a safe area, but more likely because they were the ones who others feared.

I watched them from where I lay; I could not risk moving while they might see me across the open land. They watered their horses at a large pond and one of them dismounted briefly to fill his bottle. A few moments later they set off again towards the road I was following and the ditch that I was hiding in.

It did not take them long to arrive at the road and I watched them warily as they spread out from each other and surveyed along its length. The closest was approximately fifty metres from me and I could see that he carried a bow, a pre-war compound like mine. They wore thick trousers which were caked in dirt and their tack was old, repaired in many places but still serviceable. The rider nearest to me had decorated the rear of his saddle with three skulls, hanging from the leather, stripped of flesh and painted in garish colours. They handled the horses with such expertise that they almost looked as though they were conjoined with them; the animals under the total control of their masters.

I ducked back down as the rider I was watching turned his steed towards me. I heard him clip-clop closer to me. There was nothing I could do but try and stay hidden. I might be able to take one or two of them down if they saw me, but they had equal weaponry, coupled with the multiple advantages of numbers, speed and height. I knew that I would not stand a chance in a fight and so discretion was called for.

I sank to the earth as low as I could, hoping that the long grass would keep my proximity concealed from them. In the distance one of the other riders called out, but I could not make out what he said.

"Yeah, al' right," this rider called back, adding quietly afterwards, "I know, I know."

He turned his mount away from me and urged it forward. I could clearly see his spurs, hand forged by the look of them, not sharp enough to really hurt the horse, but enough to encourage it on when necessary.

He clicked with his tongue and the horse moved away, back towards his fellow riders, the decorative skulls knocking together with a hollow sound.

They moved on, out onto the field behind me. I did not turn to look in case the grass around me moved, betraying my presence. I heard more horses then, the sound was coming from the pond where I had first noticed the five riders. I risked lifting my head slightly to peek over the edge of the ditch. I could see then why the first party moved so openly across country. They were a scouting party for the rest of their much larger tribe, who then surrounded the pond, letting their own animals drink.

There must have been at least a hundred people there, along with what looked like all of their possessions, loaded onto carts, or dragged along on crude sleds made of poles strapped to the sides of animals. Cattle and horses were tethered to anything that could be pulled along. Children ran around the edges of the gathering shouting and jeering at one another. Goats tied to the carts bleated loudly adding to the noise. Most of the men and women were armed, mainly with bows and mounted on horseback, a few older people and the smaller children rode on the carts.

They set off from the pond as I watched, the drivers whipping at the dray animals, moving in a long caravan with well practiced ease. The noise they made felt cacophonous after my few days of creeping across the quiet countryside. Still I could not have moved without being seen so I remained confined to the ditch, hoping that they would pass without noticing me hiding there.

Soon they reached the road, about twenty metres ahead from my position. As they did so a small group of children ran up and down a short section of it near to me. They looked to be fed well enough and I wondered how they could manage to live so well, especially with so many animals to keep. I realised that they were probably nomadic, in the same way as our early ancestors, travelling between feeding grounds and moving on each time their livestock had finished off the greenery. They reminded me of Mongolian tribesmen I had read about some years earlier.

The children did not spot me in my hiding place and I was able to get a better look at them. They wore clothing that was either patched together or poorly woven post-war and their young bodies already had tribal tattoos on them. Each one bore blue markings of a symbol I did not recognise emblazoned on their biceps, all identical. Some of the larger children had additional tattoos that I could not distinguish the shape of either. The children ran round each other playing tag, ignoring the adults' calls, only returning to the tribe when threatened with beatings.

As the main body of the procession crossed the road a little way from me I could clearly hear the poles being dragged along as they scraped across its surface. After what felt like an age, the tribe was gone and I was left there alone and very relieved to be so. If they had found me, even if they had left me alive, I was sure I would have at least been robbed of my weapons.

I stayed still for a while longer, in case there were

any stragglers or a rear guard; leaving them enough time to move further away and for me to be out of their sight. When I was sure I would not be spotted I emerged and resumed my journey. I mentally scolded myself for staying too long with Frank and his breakfast. Added to the latest hindrance I had ended up wasting nearly half a day of travelling time.

It rained again as I walked along that straight, open section. I paused momentarily to look at the swathe of tracks the tribe had left behind, almost as wide as one of the motorways I had seen, crossing the road and heading off through the fields. The ground underneath my feet was sticky clay and caked my boots, I could have caught up some time if I had walked on the hard surface of the road that remained but I still preferred the security of the tree cover. After what I had recently seen I felt better near to cover.

I put on the poncho, having left it a little late, wondering if it was wetter on the inside or the outside and feeling rather soggy as I tramped onwards.

On my left I saw a row of houses coming up. The first was now just a mound of ivy with the silhouette of the building just recognisable. They were large, grandiose properties, with their own tributary road running parallel to the main. I continued past without incident. In the distance I could see another traffic island where two roads crossed each other. This time the junction was much smaller than the motorway crossing had been, but I still wondered about that past age, a time so chaotic and busy that all of that was necessary. I reached the crossroads by midday and continued on, pausing only to unpack my other map from my bag and put away the one that I had been using up until then. I had crossed their join and despite the morning's delays that still gave me a sense of achievement.

It would have been easy to feel sorry for myself, walking alone through the rain soaked countryside but I could not allow myself the self-indulgence. I thought of my Father and wondered how he had felt out there alone. I had always remembered him as a very positive man and hoped that was not just the brave face a parent naturally puts on for their child, but hoped that he had a genuine resilience too. I put my momentary melancholy aside and cheered myself with the thought that I should with any luck be back at the ship with my Father soon enough.

The rain subsided and I took my poncho off again. Shortly afterwards the road ran over a bridge, crossing a railway cutting, so I detoured to my right. As I went around I was glad to find a small stream, where I took the opportunity to refill my water bottle and to wash in it. The water was cold, but refreshing. On the other side of the stream was a small copse of trees where I stopped to eat a quick snack when I saw a variety of berry bearing plants growing in close proximity to each other.

When I set off again, I altered my course to the left, across the densely covered grassland to converge once more with the road and the rain resumed. That afternoon felt like a long hard slog, but I was glad that it was so uneventful compared to the previous day. The late afternoon saw me making my way gingerly through the remains of a small town. A road sign still stood, confirming my location with that gleaned from my map and once I was free of the remains of Lowton, I started to look out for somewhere in the distance where I could spend the night.

Since I had left the old man's place that morning, apart from the nomadic tribe, I had seen nobody else, nor any indications of recent human life. However, as the path I followed crossed a bridge above another railway cutting, I saw just off to the side, a dead rabbit caught in a snare. I deviated just enough to pick up its small body. After sniffing at it to make sure it was still fresh, I took it with me, hoping that I would not run into the owner of the trap.

The rain stopped once again and I packed up my poncho as the sun came out. My mood had lifted a little with the return of a clear sky and the prospect of fresh meat to eat. I liked rabbit very much and as I walked onwards I looked forward to cooking and eating it later that evening.

The road turned to the left slightly and ahead I could see that it climbed to the summit of a long, low hill, carrying on straight once more. I took out my map and noticing the pencil scrawling on it from the priest at Ormskirk, I remembered what he had told me. It would not be a long detour so I decided to walk around the hill instead of over it, keeping off the skyline as the priest had said. I walked down off the road onto the fields again. It looked as if in the pre-apocalypse world this had all been open farmland. Walking through that was easy; I did not have to be too careful of my footings as there was no stray brickwork to twist an ankle on.

I was getting hungry again and the cover around me was good. I lay down my pack and sat in the long grass, eating a small amount from my provisions, saving the rabbit until later when I stopped to camp for the night. The breeze moved the grass around me in waves as I looked out across it, with the tops of the stalks at my eye level. It looked like a calm green sea around me. I finished eating and went on my way, it was warm as I walked along and I could not help letting my mind wander a little.

I remembered my Father and I walking along on a similar day, eleven years before. I used to love spending time with him and had wanted to be just like him when I grew up. He had believed that I was never too young to learn, although I had needed no encouragement from him. He had taken me on my first hunting trip at only six years old and we were gone for two full days in the mountains at the centre of the Island.

"There's a café at the top," he had told me as we climbed. "We'll get you a cold drink."

"No there's not, Dad, you always say that. Stop teasing," I remembered saying to him.

"There is," he insisted. "And an old train. We can walk back down along the railway."

"Stop teasing me." I had shouted at him insistently. He just smiled back down at me, so I had pushed his leg as hard as a six year-old could.

"You little horror!" he had shouted and pretending to be angry he had chased me round in circles. I had laughed hysterically as I ran as fast as I could to escape his feigned attempts to catch me.

I remembered the day clearly. Later we had stalked a hare near to the top of the mountain. He had let me take a shot at it with my new first small bow. I was surprised at how easy it had been to hit the animal and he had finished it off with his knife for me. He had looked very proud of me indeed. We had roasted it that night as we camped and he told me stories of the world before. This was not spoken of often and I sat, listening to him intently. As the fire crackled in front of us, I hung on his every word.

He had described flying in his plane, one of the fast fighter jets – an F14 Tomcat, that was still in the hangar deck back home.

"It's better than being a bird, it's more like being a missile. Imagine being an arrow shot from a bow, but never slowing down. Going faster and faster, but able to turn, up, down, left, right so fast your brain can hardly keep up," he said, staring into the fire that licked up at the hare, dripping fat from its improvised spit. "I'll tell you what, I'll smuggle you onto that little Cessna the next chance I get. We'll go for a fly round the next time I get to go up, and I'll show you what I mean." He had looked at me then and winked. "It won't be as fast as a fighter jet, but trust me, you'll love it."

Three weeks later he did just that, he took me up

in the light aircraft and we flew over every beach on the Island, making sure that nobody had landed there, doing security sweeps and searching the coastal waters around our home. I had sat silent, overwhelmed with the excitement of flying in the small plane - the same little plane that he had disappeared in less than a year later.

He had done some acrobatic manoeuvres for me, showing off to his only child and making the most of the experience for me. Too young to know any fear, I laughed loudly as he looped a loop and then rolled the small plane around on its centre axis. At one point he had let me hold the stick, controlling the plane myself albeit very briefly and with him operating the pedals and throttle.

For now as I walked, I thought of the hot slices of hare at our camp site accompanied with buttered bread from the ship's canteen that we had taken with us. I thought of sleeping in the shelter of his tent, listening first to the wildlife and later waking up hearing him snoring next to me. I thought of the other trips and all the other things he had taught me during our short time together not realising at the time that he was training my young instincts in preparation for the years ahead, I was just enjoying our adventures together.

As I thought about my Dad, I walked a little faster towards him; I had been missing him for far too long.

# CHAPTER 11

The terrain soon changed, with the appearance of small craters peppering the vicinity. The smallest of them were a metre wide, many much larger. As I advanced they became more numerous. I thought at the time how strange this was, since I could see no buildings and there were no obvious targets; the land would have been ploughed flat, possibly for centuries before the war and those scars were clearly not a feature that had been here for all of that time.

Ahead of me, I could see many short sections of a tall fence standing in a line interspersed with broken sections, like a long piece of Morse code across the landscape. I wondered again why the priest had sent me there and what was significant about that place.

I reached the boundary line where it crossed a stream. I could see from what remained that the fence had once zigzagged out there to cross the water, but that section was gone too. A concrete dam still stood across the stream, built up to allow the fence a path across the top without causing a weak point in the defences. The stream itself emerged through a small pipe, covered with a grill.

Behind the dam was a stagnant pond, dense with reeds and other plant life; the small stream burbled into it on the far side of the thick green water. Bubbles of stinking gas rose to its surface as I passed by.

I wondered what sort of place would need such high security. My curiosity grew, I had always had that in my nature and I could not resist taking a closer look.

I crossed over into the enclosure and to my left I could then see a large mound, over two metres tall. Like the field, it was covered in long grass and plants growing wild, but I could see that it was flat and angular, as if man made. I went closer and climbed it to have a look around, crawling to its summit to remain hidden amongst the greenery.

Once I reached the top I could see that this artificial hillock was in fact square shaped and hollow inside. Not ancient like some earthworks, but relatively modern. As I squatted there, facing south, I could see to my right that a road entered the square through a gap in the corner. Other than that, all that the hollow contained was grass and rubble. Looking to my left I could see another similar mound and behind it I thought I could just make out another, though its shape was disguised by the dense vegetation. The craters in the ground were now more common, dotted everywhere: inside the hollows, outside and on the mounds themselves. My curiosity deepened further.

I walked round the base of the square banking, caution once more had me moving very slowly and my bow was held ready. On the other side of the earthworking ran another road, connecting this mound to the next and repeating into the distance, in what turned out to be a network of interconnected mounds. I walked back up the side of the bank, not to the top but just enough to get a look round with my field glasses. There were at least five more mounds to the south of me, running east-west, parallel with the first row. Some of them were hard to distinguish due to the trees growing on them. There was no sign of any recent human activity that I could see.

Beyond those five were more, smaller mounds, maybe eight or ten. Closest to my position on the south side, I could see along the entrance road into another of the hollows. That one contained a building, squat and very solid in appearance. I felt I needed to take a look.

I walked alongside the broken road surface. As I moved across the huge compound towards the building, the landscape visible to me consisted of nothing but flat earth, interspersed with those bunker like lumps and the numerous craters which were obviously a later addition.

I soon reached the entrance of the building and saw a large door which was standing open, to what looked like an empty store of some sort. I walked around the outside of it, once round the outer circumference of the mound, then a second time between the inside of the earth banking and the outside of the building. Satisfied that everything around me was overgrown and that there was no sign of disturbance or occupation anywhere, I went inside, with my bow drawn just in case. The interior was almost completely empty, except for an office structure to my left. I walked over to take a better look, pushing open the door with the tip of the nocked arrow. In front of me there was a broken chair and a filing cabinet on its side. There was paper strewn around and a few items on the floor, including pens long dried up. A closer look at the paperwork instantly revealed the purpose of the buildings to me.

It had been a storage facility for munitions. Huge amounts of explosives had been warehoused there; the manifest I had picked up listed it in tonnes. Tonnes and tonnes of C4 plastic explosives, enough to blow up unimaginably vast areas, maybe even enough to split a mountain in half. I realised that the banked up earth around each one was not to hide or protect the buildings themselves, but it was designed to protect the surrounding area, to deflect any accidental blast upwards.

I went back outside. It seemed obvious with the benefit of hindsight, the layout and structures all made sense: the distance between each one, even the entrance roads did not face each other for safety, but I still did not understand the significance of the place to the priest. I moved across to the next store along. That building was the same, open and empty. Nothing seemed to have moved around there for years.

I walked across to the next storehouse, then a fourth, both were empty. Thinking that the place had obviously been picked clean years before and that whatever the priest had sent me to see was no longer there, I decided then that I should get on with my journey and so I set off back towards the road. As I began to move away I noticed a central building. Again shrouded in earthworks but that one was different from the others in two ways: it had a peaked roof instead of being flat and the doors were shut.

"One more won't hurt, then I'll be on my way," I

thought to myself as I walked towards it.

I struggled to believe and comprehend what I saw when I got there. On the metal door was a message, with the letters having been burned into it. Lying at the bottom of the door was the torch responsible, along with the accompanying rusted oxygen and acetylene tanks. The message, like a tombstone's engraving read: 'DIED AT THE HANDS OF ADMIRAL GILL, MAY THEY REST IN PEACE'.

The door was secured with a hefty chain and padlock, but was not totally sealed; it was slightly open at the top, just a few inches where the metal had warped. Inside I was horrified to see bones, thousands of them, still wearing their clothes. It was a mass-internment in a makeshift mausoleum and it seemed apparent that someone held Gill responsible for it.

That was unquestionably the reason that the priest had suggested this small diversion. I wondered how he knew about it, what involvement he might have had, if he had even burnt that message into those doors himself... and if it was true.

The light was starting to fade fast by then, I had been carried away by my inquisitive nature again. The evening was clear and warm, and stars were starting to show from horizon to horizon. Since there seemed little chance of the weather changing for the worse, I climbed onto the top of one of the other low structures to sleep in the open. If I stayed in the centre of the flat roof it was very unlikely that anyone would be able to see me and it seemed to be the safest place to spend the night. I cooked the rabbit on my small stove, frying the meat in its own meagre fat, then added water and some of Frank's potatoes, leaving it a while to reduce down and cook through. I ate while staring at the beauty of a billion stars above me, enjoying the tranquillity of that isolated spot. Then I wrapped myself in my poncho and tried to sleep.

I kept thinking of the piles of dead bodies in the building nearby. I was not superstitious at all, but I felt differently about the place then. If anywhere deserved to house ghosts it was there. In some way I supposed that it did have a ghost of sorts, in the form of somebody's guilt. I did not know if the words on the door had any basis in reality, but the bodies inside were certainly not a figment of the imagination.

Nevertheless it was an isolated position and whoever was responsible for the tomb did not seem to be around then. While it might have been an unconventional camp site, I actually felt a little more secure sleeping there because of what I had seen, hoping that any locals might give it a wide berth for that very reason.

Later that night I was woken by the sound of drums, it was still dark and I had no idea what time it was. Realising that I had not dreamt it, for a moment I just lay there, scared to make a noise, trying to assess the situation, as the constant slow rhythmic drumming continued. Silently I started to assemble my belongings. The noise of the drums seemed to be getting closer and closer.

I stayed on the rooftop, putting my pack on my back

and an arrow on the bow string. There was nothing to do but wait, just sit and wait as the drums got louder. I could not just run off into the darkness surrounding me. In the inky black of the night, I could not see well enough to navigate the unfamiliar terrain safely without the risk of falling into one of the craters.

It was cloudy overhead, with the stars of the previous evening having been covered. There was no moon visible in the sky, just a very faint glow through a patch of the cloud, but that was not necessarily a bad thing, I could not see but by the same logic, neither could I be seen. As I waited for the inevitable arrival of the drummers, I was becoming increasingly spooked by them. "Who is out there? What are they doing?" I asked myself.

They got closer still. I heard them splashing through the stream and by the sounds of it, there was more than one who fell into it.

I heard some people off to one side of the building I lay atop. Moving quietly but talking as they went past, oblivious to my presence. A parent was trying to hush a whimpering child as they went on their way, the percussive beat chasing them onwards.

"Shush my darling, we don't want the drummers to hear us do we. If you're quiet they won't know where we are and they'll go away. You'd like that wouldn't you, don't cry now." I could clearly hear the voice, whispered in the dark as they hurried away from me.

I reconsidered moving, it would only take me

seconds to jump down off the roof and I did not feel comfortable where I was. I desperately tried to think of anything I had seen, anywhere I could hide, but could not. Again I decided to remain where I was. I had looked around the area in daylight to select my hiding place on the rooftop and, however tempting it was to try, I was unlikely to find a better one by running around in the dark.

Looking in the direction of the noise I could see pin-pricks of light by then. They were bobbing up and down as they were carried towards me. As they got closer I could see they were burning torches, approaching me in the blackness, accompanied by the incessant din of the drums. There was a long line of them stretched out in front of me, getting closer still. It was a thoroughly intimidating experience.

At that point I took my pack back off again, since I had left it too late to try and run away from them by that time. I was worried that if I was found there would undoubtedly be a fight, possibly to my death. I did not know what the drummers' aim was and I was not going to try to find out. The volume of their pounding was becoming unbearable by then. They had entered the perimeter of the munitions facility and were nearly at the building that I lay on the top of.

I spread myself as flat as I could, with my rucksack next to me and holding my bow flat to the roof too, in my left hand, stretched out to keep as low as I could. I could hear voices in between the drums as they drew nearer still.

"Drive 'em all along now, keep up that drumming!" someone shouted in the darkness. "We'll get a few in them pits by the morning."

So that was their plan, herding people through the night towards traps. I was glad that I had decided to keep to my hiding place. In the distance I heard a scream and the drummers heard it too.

"Well that's one joining us for breakfast!" the voice shouted triumphantly and the drumming continued with renewed vigour, accompanied by a few of the others laughing at his cruel joke.

I could see two of them then as they walked along the side of my building. Their heads were almost at the same level as me. One carried a flaming torch, held high as he walked along, and in his other hand was a spear. Behind him the second man carried a large drum made from the top of an oil barrel, with a taut animal hide stretched across the top. A thick strap around his neck supported its weight and he was beating it with a heavy stick which was bound at one end to prevent it from puncturing the membrane.

The clouds cleared for an instant and the light of the moon illuminated the area. For a few seconds I held my breath. I would be clearly visible to them now if they looked in my direction. My night vision was as good as could be after lying in the pitch dark and I silently hoped that theirs would be spoiled by walking along in the torch light.

The cloud passed back over the moon before they

had chance to notice me and plunged me back into the relative safety of the blackness. I would have breathed a sigh of relief if I had thought that they would not hear it. Eventually they passed me by, as I remained motionless on top of the bunker. In between the rhythm of the drums, in the distance I could hear the muted wails of their poor captive as he or she waited for the approach of the tormentors. I had already had a glimpse of how terrifying it was to have to wait as those drums got louder and nearer even though my own presence had not been detected and I pitied them in their ordeal, with their fate sealed and the countdown so terrifyingly pronounced.

Eventually, for me the drums got quieter, but throughout the rest of that night I could hear them somewhere in the distance. Getting a little louder and then quieter again as they combed the area driving people in the chaos and confusion towards their traps. There were further cries for help from the victims as they panicked and screamed in the darkness. I did not know what their fate would be, but it was bound to be unpleasant. It was almost unbearable to listen to them cry out as I lay silent and alone for the rest of that night, but had I tried to intervene I doubted I could have been any help to them. As it was I shivered, worrying that they could return and next time find me where I lay.

I still had no other choice but to stay where I was. I was not going to risk falling into one of the holes myself.

Eventually I must have fallen asleep again, but I dozed fitfully, waking at regular intervals. It was quiet again and I could no longer hear the hunt, neither their pounding nor their victims. I did not think I would see them in daylight, their hunting tactics were obviously better suited to night-time use.

Then in the pre-dawn light I was horrified as I saw them returning. It was time for me to go, the sun was due to rise in a few moments and they would definitely see me then. I grabbed my pack and I ran off the edge of the roof, bow in hand, away from them. I cleared the gap at the side of the building and got a foot onto the surrounding ridge at its peak. I rolled forwards like the assault course training had taught me to, back at home all those years ago.

"Search for any stragglers," I heard the voice from last night order loudly in the distance.

Like a gymnast, I rolled head over heels down the hill and came up at the bottom in a full sprint. There was a time for caution and discretion, but this was not it. The first of the daylight crawled over the landscape as I ran towards the fence. I had to find somewhere better to hide, and quickly. The buildings all had only one door and if they thought to look inside I did not want to risk trapping myself without an alternative exit, so I sprinted on.

I remembered the dam and the pond.

"Ideal," I said to myself and headed towards it, my heart and legs pumping, as fast as I could go under the weight of my possessions. "At least the drums have stopped," I thought. The dam was not the obvious hiding place and that was precisely what gave it the edge over the buildings.

I reached the pond quickly, it was not as big as I had remembered but once I was there it had to do. I wasted no time; if I did not act immediately they would be able to see me at any second. I plunged straight into the water, still running, ignoring the amount of noise the splash made as they would see me before they heard me. I dived towards the reeds on the other side and the weight of the bow and my pack pulled me down below the surface. I slid into the reeds below water level and then surfaced inside them, lying on the muddy bed with only my face protruding from the water, surrounded by the plant life.

It stank, but it was the only hiding place I had been able to think of. Then I kept as still as I could manage, trying not to shiver in the cold water, my gasping for breath subsiding as I regained my composure and waited for their approach.

Minutes later they surrounded me in my watery hiding place. I could not see much but I could hear them.

"Did you say we got three last night?" one of them asked another.

"Two and a kid. He decided to let the kid go. Two's not bad for a night and we don't want to overdo it." I had no idea who 'he' was but presumed that they must have some kind of leader.

"Think he'll trade them with The Castle people again?" asked the first. As they stood at the water's edge I could see fragments of reflections on the ripples blown across in front of me.

Another liquid stream started to enter the water, one that I was not pleased to hear. Although, I did not think I could smell any worse afterwards, the water was so horribly putrid already.

"How would I know what he's going to do with them? So long as I've got enough to eat, I'll work with him either way."

"Didn't your mother tell you not to pee in running water?" scolded the first.

"Nobody is going to drink out of here, it's rancid," said the second voice and I was forced to agree with him. "Come on," he said, "best not make him wait."

I waited for them to move away, it was not pleasant to contemplate what I lay in, but I had no other option but to be patient and try not to worry about it. I had been fortunate to have escaped them for the second time and I could wash myself off upstream once they had gone.

Eventually after I was sure that they had left, I climbed back out onto dry ground. Throwing my pack out first I emerged dripping with the rank, foul smelling water and feeling quite disgusting. I walked upstream as quickly as I could and washed the filthy water of the reed bed off myself and my belongings. Shiel's map of the coastline had been almost ruined, but the other more important map had been in a plastic sleeve and so had been protected. I lubricated my bow, I could not afford for that to seize and I spread myself and my things out on the ground to dry for a short while in the early morning sun.

I thought again about the building with the bodies inside it. I could have wondered all I liked, I would not find out anything lying there. I stood, dressed and walked on, further away from the storage facility. My boots squelched as I went into the long grass and back to my journey to the heart of Salford. I was glad to be able to get away from the area. The dead were poor company and the drummers even worse.

The further away from that place I could get the better, "But who had written those mysterious words?" I asked myself.

# Chapter 12

Leaving that place was not enough to rid my mind of it. Still unnerved by what I had witnessed the previous evening, coupled with my experience of the locals and tired from the broken sleep, I made my way on. I paused momentarily and crouched down in the cover of the grass, it was long enough there to almost engulf me so I knelt and I checked my surroundings against my map. I had made far too little progress the day before and I did not want to let myself waste any more time. I mustered up my determination to continue on regardless and put aside my feelings about the revelations of the preceding evening for another time.

I could see that I would shortly come to a wide brook and I would have the choice of three bridges by which I could cross it: one large and open with little means of concealing myself from any watchful eyes, the other two more discreet. I preferred the look of the smaller one to the right and so turned that way, walking on through the countryside. To my left I could clearly make out the path of the road, as it punctuated the sky with its street lights, and I kept parallel with it as I continued. Once more on my journey and once again feeling that under different circumstances, it could have been a pleasant hike. At least it might have been had my boots and clothes been dry.

I yawned as I walked along, but I could ill afford to let the tiredness eat into my concentration. I went past the remains of a body: a woman, long dead, her shoulder-length hair the same colour as my Mother's. The remains of the corpse lay sprawled on the ground and much of her had been dismembered, as if eaten by dogs or other opportunistic wild animals. Any useful possessions she may once have had were gone, so I left her in the company of her cloud of flies.

As I walked on I remembered more about my Mother, how she had argued with Gill about the search for my Father. Three weeks after he had gone missing, I was sat outside Gill's office, with my legs swinging back and forth under the chair, not yet long enough to reach the floor.

"How can you say you're calling it off? You haven't even found his plane yet. You must be looking in the wrong place!" She was crying again.

"Liz, stop please," he said, trying his best to comfort her. "We can't continue to keep searching forever. He told us himself where we should look."

I heard her sobbing again and I had tried my hardest not cry again myself, because I knew that would upset her even more.

"If he's there, Sir, it will be at that horrendous castle they've built. Those animals will have him and you can't even find his plane."

"I can't keep putting other people's lives in danger indefinitely, Liz. Doug was looking for a missing pilot himself if you recall." His words did not stop her tears. I wanted very much to go in to her, but her reddened eyes had looked into mine when she had sat me on the chair and told me very firmly to stay outside. I had felt like I needed her to see that I was being so well behaved and I think that I had hoped it would somehow help her to cry less.

"Let me go and get him," she pleaded. I could hear them through the door and there was suddenly an angry hiss in her voice. "Send our blasted Cobras in and let me get him back, Gill."

"Would you really have me do that?" he asked her. "Would you really have me risk the lives of more of my pilots – your friends? And then what? They're hardly a friendly bunch are they? Do I barter with guns for his life? Would you let them have more guns if you were me? You know that's what they want and they don't seem interested in anything else. And if I ask them if they have him they will probably lie. If they haven't got him they would certainly go and look for him then."

"Send us to kill them, all of them and then you get my husband back for me, Gill, *I know you can do that*!" She shouted louder towards the end of the sentence. At the time I had not known why she had emphasised those last few words.

"Lieutenant, you are way out of line! Do not presume to speak to me like that." He raised his voice then too. "Get out of my office. You know what decisions I have made and you should understand why I have made them."

Gill's office door rattled in its surround as she slammed it behind her, picking me up as she left.

"Come on, sweetie," she had said, holding me close.

She had gone to the hangar deck straight away and spent an hour with the other pilots, particularly the helicopter proficient ones. She had tried to cajole and persuade them to help her, talking to them about kinship and comrades, duty and compatriots, brothers in arms. She had stayed there until she was sure she had exhausted all chance of starting a mutiny before she took me back to our dormitory; the large room we had occupied, up until three weeks before as a family. She threw herself onto their bed and she cried some more, me joining her then, holding onto her as we shed tears together. I think I was the only reason she had not tried to steal a helicopter and gone off on her own.

Looking back I am sure that Gill knew what she had done and he must have understood why she had tried. Under any other circumstances she would have been severely punished, even executed for her attempted mutiny. Instead he sent the doctor to her, medicine was rare but she refused to accept the offer of those tablets.

"I'm not depressed, I'm justifiably angry! I've lost my husband, not my mind," my Mother had screamed, slamming another door as she threw the doctor out of our room. She had cried again for another fifteen minutes with me, then she stopped and I never saw her cry again. She wiped at my face with her handkerchief.

"Come on then my little Badger," she had said to me. "Laugh and the world laughs with you. Cry and your face just gets wet, doesn't it?" It was not the first or the last time I heard that familiar phrase and I had tried my hardest to smile back up at her.

She had taken me down to the communal canteen after that, not the one on the ship but for a change we went to the one in the centre of Ramsey itself. She had avoided the rest of the Sedbergh's crew as much as she could for a while. The canteen staff all recognised us and they all knew about my missing Father; it is a small town and an even smaller community. They had brought me cake as a treat and I offered to share it with my Mother, she looked at me as she sipped her tea.

"No thank you, sweetheart, you eat it all up," she had said.

As I walked on, trying to put thoughts of my Mother aside, I passed a road that ran north-south across my path and found the small bridge. I crossed quickly, feeling a little exposed as I did so, deprived momentarily of nature's disguise that I had become accustomed to having growing around me. I saw a ruined farmhouse and not wanting to risk any further hostile encounters I chose to skirt around it, before I veered left to meet up once more with the road that was my guide. Once I had rejoined it, I headed off to the right, once more along its route.

I was beginning to think of the road as my friend, I even said 'good morning' to it as I returned to its path. I think the isolation and the stresses of the journey were getting to me that day, since I would not normally have indulged myself with such nonsense.

Shortly afterwards, the road and I crossed another canal together. Though the road was lined with thick forest at that stage and I could see nothing beyond it, I knew from looking at my map that there were towns spread around me close to the road. The increasing possibility of meeting other people curtailed my pace and I took care to stick with my previous methodical habits of caution. Scanning in front of me with my binoculars and stopping to listen intently for anything above nature's background noise. I saw and heard nothing of relevance as I continued onwards.

For a while the road ran arrow straight and traversed a large hump as it crossed a further canal. For once I kept with the road as it went over the rise. The trees on that section were covering my path and I did not want a long detour to find another bridge. At the base of the hill, at a place called Tyldesley according to both my map and the road signs, the road bent right once more.

As noon came I found another motorway intersection. There were three bridges adjacent to each other and the middle span was even bigger than the one where I had met Frank, possibly not as tall but certainly much longer. I walked to one end of the longest, in awe at its size. I found some mushrooms growing in a circle underneath the motorway and I ate them with some of my mince, toasting them over a small fire.

I spent a short time reading the graffiti on that bridge, much of it pre-apocalyptic. Names and dates had been scratched into the surface by people probably long dead, proclaiming 'love 4 eva' amongst other banalities. I found it far too trivial to ponder on for long.

I did wonder about the people, the ones from the world before, and how their lives had been so easy. As usual I felt anger towards them for destroying everything that they had achieved over some stupid war about countries and nations. They had bickered and fought while living in a paradise far better than anything that remained. I looked up at the bridge, trying to imagine the people who could have built something like that. How could the same species that had harnessed science and technology to build that utopian world have blown everything they had made to pieces?

I would never be able to answer that question. I set off again, determined to make it to the centre of Salford by nightfall. The road ahead broadened, as a third lane joined the other two on each side, for the long dead traffic.

To my right, a short while into my resumed walk, I saw a wild beehive hanging from a tree. The honey was too attractive for me to leave, so I rinsed out one of my empty jars and wrapped myself up as much as I could, with my poncho over my jacket and the hood up. I was stung a few times but I felt it was worth the pain since I had gleaned two thirds of a jar of honey for my trouble. Rubbing the itching lumps on the back of my hand as I walked on, every now and then I dipped a finger into my deliciously sweet reward. I felt a lot better after that. It always lifted my spirits to have sweet things to indulge in. They were rare treats to be savoured.

Later I came to a collapsed section of the road. A strip

nearly three metres wide had sunk down, falling into what appeared to have been an old walkway crossing in a tunnel underneath the road surface. I wondered what it must have felt like to walk underneath, with the heavy fast moving traffic thundering overhead and whether people were worried in there as they proceeded through, or if they never even gave a second thought about it. It was not much of an obstacle and simple enough to make my way around it, and I rejoined the road on the other side.

My surroundings were much more urban by then, with most of the plant life confined to areas that had once been gardens. Around mid afternoon I heard a pack of dogs howling in the distance to my left and I paused to check the direction of the wind. It was blowing north to south so I was confident that they would not pick up on my scent. I left nothing to chance though and hurried on as fast as I could safely do so, until I was well away from them.

I stopped for a short while, to stretch out my tired legs on a lushly grassed verge near to another crossroads. The warm weather was particularly taking its toll on a day when I was already tired and I drank from my bottle, hoping that I would find more water soon, since I did not have much left. Down one of the side roads stood the ruins of an old church, the battered sign outside was barely legible any more. Smoke rose from the ashes of a very recently extinguished fire and, though I saw no one, I thought it would be prudent to hasten on my way again.

I soon came to a further crossroads; they were

becoming much more frequent as I got nearer to the city. That one differed from the others only because of the rusty metal foot bridge that stood over it. A few remaining flecks of blue paint were peeling off the badly rusted upright supports where I passed underneath.

After that the terrain became more like woodland again, despite the urban setting. Thick trees and bushes surrounded the road and as I picked my way through these, I looked backwards often, thinking of the smoke I had noticed earlier, worried that I might be being followed through the undergrowth. Although previously on my journey I had usually preferred the comfort of keeping to the vegetation wherever possible, on that occasion I was concerned that it might be obscuring another individual. For once I was a little relieved when the trees petered out and I was back on more open ground.

Late in the afternoon I finished off the honey, scraping the last bits from the bottom of the jar, ramming my hand in as far as it would go. As I sucked my fingers clean, a small bird flew down and landed about ten metres from me, near the middle of the road. A thin, mangy cat immediately emerged from under the central barrier that separated the carriageways. It stalked towards the bird and I noticed a long tail stuck straight out behind the cat instead of the normal stump that I was more used to seeing on our native Manx cats. I considered a shot at it, but would almost certainly have broken an arrow on the hard surface behind it. I decided that there would not be enough meat on the animal to be worth losing an arrow, so I ignored both creatures.

In some ways my surroundings reminded me of the town of Douglas, burnt and lifeless. It was supposed to be a no go area on the Island but Shiel and I had been there once. We had been passing close by anyway, detailed to travel around the whole Island distributing goods and non-perishables from the stores on the ship and collecting anything that needed to go back. Our horse and cart transport around the Island took a few days. It was a multi-functional post and parcel delivery service and at times a one-way taxi service for anyone who happened to be going in the same direction.

Douglas had been burned after the war, deliberately and out of necessity due to a cholera outbreak. There was more than enough housing left on the Island, so the town had simply been abandoned. From the distance it looked like it was sliding off the Island very gradually into the sea, as the ruined buildings collapsed more and more towards the centre of the past conflagration near the shore.

Leaving our horse and cart tied up by the main road, Shiel and I had dared each other on until we were at the outskirts of the town itself. Biohazard signs had been put up at regular intervals and the accompanying warnings advised of a three week quarantine period for anyone who risked venturing further into the restricted zone.

At that time it had been seventeen years since the outbreak, which had happened two years before I was born. We had felt it would almost certainly be safe in there by then and it was not guarded, so we had also been sure that we would not be caught. Looking back it had been a very foolish thing to do. We were putting our whole community at risk, but we did it anyway, we went right into the heart of the town itself.

We had already passed the old abandoned hospital and a cemetery. There were plenty of bones littering the area and that should have been warning enough.

"Come on, Shiel, don't be such a wimp," I said to him in a whisper when he suggested turning back. I did not know why I had whispered when there was no one else there to hear.

"Why do we need to go on, haven't we seen enough? It's all burned down, there's nothing left here now," he whispered back.

"Come on, we've come this far, we might as well have a look around."

We walked on further into the town. It was much bigger than Ramsey. The houses that were not close to others had been burnt separately but as we neared the centre it seemed to have been more like one immense blaze.

We both carried our bows, arrows nocked and ready, I do not know why, it may have made us feel more confident but arrows are useless against the dead. We had stalked around the ruins for a while not speaking much to each other, going slowly into the middle of Douglas while keeping roughly to the riverside so that we could find our way back out again easily enough.

When we reached the shoreline and the piers, we came across the remains of a pyre that had been at Douglas' centre. A circle of asphalt by the shore had been melted by the intensity of the heat. Thousands of blackened bones were still piled up, charred by the huge fire that must have been built to burn so many bodies at once. A scorched skull looked directly at us from the edge of the agglomeration and we stared back open mouthed at the hidden piece of our history that we had uncovered.

"I think we should go, Badger."

"Okay."

We started to walk quickly away, then a jog and shortly after a full on run back up the hillside until we had crossed back over the signs and the warnings, back out to the open countryside.

We sat then, panting like dogs, both utterly out of breath.

"Did you see that skull?" I asked him.

"Which one? There was loads of them!" he said in reply, falling backwards and lying down. He drew up his knees next to me, putting his feet flat on the grass.

"The one that was looking straight at us," I said between my heavy breaths. "Did you see the one staring right back at us? The one that looked like it had a bullet hole in it."

"Yes, I saw more than one of those. I saw lots of skulls. Did you know that lot was there?"

"Of course not, how could I have known that?"

"Shall we not bother going back again?" he suggested. "That place is like one big open grave."

"I can't think of any reason I'll be going back there," I said. "Never again."

"Never again," he repeated like a promise. "Let's go get the cart and find somewhere to camp then."

"Okay. We can just eat what we've brought with us tonight," I said as we went to retrieve our horse and cart from where we had tied it up.

"Yeah, I'm not in the mood to hunt for anything now," he said as we went.

We drove the cart quite a way from Douglas before we made our camp, staying that night near the fairy bridge and saying 'hello' to them as we crossed over it, as tradition demanded. We did not talk much about our excursion afterwards, both wanting to bury what we had seen there. We did discuss our fears of stomach upsets for the next six months however.

I made a deliberate effort to bring myself back to the present. Then was not the time to think of such things, there were plenty of skulls lying around in the open on my journey, without thinking about past ones too.

Moving on again, I was making good time through the debris and detritus of that desolate place. The route I followed bent round to the left and a faded sign at the roadside proffered the invitation to play a round of golf - I silently declined. Walking along the right hand side of the road, I crossed another which ran off the main one due south. The terrain in front of me changed from the cracked paving of the last half mile, becoming wilder again, with nature having enthusiastically reclaimed the open land.

It felt good to have grass under my feet again. The wooded area that ran alongside the road was thick with trees and bushes, but looked like it had once been more open parkland. I had to climb up a steep incline to get to it, so I walked along some metres away from the road to avoid standing out on the skyline of the surrounding areas. I followed the road for only a few minutes before it bent to the left as I had seen it would.

I crawled to the top edge of the slope through the long grass and using my field glasses looked down the section to my right that had been hidden from view. It had been many miles since there had been a cutting through the earth on my path and it felt as if the one that confronted me then was compensating for the previous lack. Huge slabs of concrete lined its sides and a pair of thick road bridges formed a large circle for the traffic of decades ago. Between those roads, parallel to them, were the broken off stumps of a footbridge. The rest of the footbridge lay shattered inside the cutting.

Passing through that cutting would have been

foolish; it would have been another perfect place for someone to ambush me, so instead I decided to cut around it, keeping to the park. I crossed the fields at an angle to the road and into a much thicker, older wood. It was cooler in there, but I realised that I would not be able to see as much of my surroundings, so I elected to proceed at a much more cautious pace. Moving from tree to tree I advanced through the wood, listening for a while every now and then. After a short time I spotted a large building amongst the trees. Flaking white paint peeled off its brickwork and it looked deserted but I gave it a wide berth anyway.

Soon my trail brought me to another area covered largely in rubble. Some walls still stood but few were more than chest high. I turned left along the border, keeping to the trees, still moving slowly, one tree to the next, pausing and listening. I suspected that there might be a lot more people moving around there, so close to the city. I just had not seen them yet. More importantly, I did not want them to notice me.

The route I was taking crested a small hill and bent round slightly to the left. The trees ended and I began to cover the remains of gardens with stumps of ruined houses on both sides. It was late afternoon by then and I was hoping that before night fell, I would get back to the broad road I had been following for days. I needed to find somewhere to hide and sleep before it went dark.

To my right I came upon a ruined church, not an ancient one like at Ormskirk, much more recently built and angular in a modern way. The only way I knew it was definitely a church was from the statue outside. The half naked figure still resolutely spread upon his moulded cross. One of the arms was broken off at the elbow and at some point in the past it had been adorned with a tyre for a necklace and burnt, but it was still clearly recognisable.

As I studied the statue from approximately fifteen metres away, I heard wheels rolling over the uneven surface and the noise of people coming towards me. I ducked away as quietly and as quickly as I dared, just in time as I then saw a large group of people moving brazenly down the centre of the road. Six were tied to the front of a cart, driven by one man sat behind them. It looked like a wagon from the old American west but with the horses replaced by people. The driver whipped at his captives and if one of them seemed to lag, goaded them to pull harder. To both sides of that, walking along next to the piles of rubble, other men walked with the cart, possibly guarding it, I could not tell for sure, but I certainly could not afford for them to see me.

The front sections of the houses I was adjacent to still stood fairly complete. Their garages were conjoined, giving no escape path between them. The doors looked secure and I did not have long before the people coming along the road would see me. I thought that my best option would be to take the risky strategy of scrambling over the top of the garages to get out of their way. It would have been an easy enough climb, less than two metres, as long as the wall did not fall and there was roofing able to hold my weight on the other side. The biggest problem with that plan was that

I would be outlined against the sky in plain view.

I was starting to get very nervous, they were not far away from me and I did not want my endeavours to end then, particularly not when I was so very close to Trafford.

I tried to find another option and wondered if I could try to hide in the long grass. I had to be quick, they were almost on me and getting closer by the second.

Then I noticed the small window, about a foot above floor level, on a section of wall running perpendicular to the garage door. It was almost obscured by the grass growing out of an old drain below it. The glass was already broken in the frame and I could see beyond. There were steps going down into a cellar and it looked like it would be a perfect place to hide. Silently I climbed through and went a few feet inside, onto the first couple of steps leading down. I unwrapped my bow and then turned, drew it and aimed back towards the window, watching to see if they would just pass by.

I stood there anxiously waiting to see if anyone appeared at the window, and I was aware that if they had not seen me then I had missed them by mere moments. I tried desperately to stifle the sudden irresistible urge to sneeze, listening to the cart creak past as it was hauled onwards.

Twenty minutes after they had gone from earshot, I felt it was safe enough to take a look. I went back outside and checked the area around the house. After scouting round briefly and finding nothing noteworthy outside, I returned to explore the underground bolt hole I had found. So close to The Castle, I thought that it might be a useful retreat in the near future. It was getting late, it would soon be time to seek refuge for the night and I thought that this could be as good a place as any other. I was nervous going down the rest of the stairs; I doubted that anyone would be there but I did not like to take any chances, especially in such a confined space. There was no room to use the bow if I needed it, so I put it over my shoulder to free up an extra hand and I drew my knife, lit one of my candles, and went down into the dark.

At the bottom was a short corridor going off to my left and in front of me a door. The door handle was covered in dust and looked like it had not been opened for years, so I turned left just in case there were any more recent signs of activity there. It only took two paces to get to the end of the short hallway. There was a door to my left and one to my right, both were open. In the flickering light of the candle I could see that the rooms beyond were both full of rubble and bricks; their ceiling joists had collapsed, probably when the rest of the house had fallen in. Satisfied that I was alone, I returned to the first room and opened the door, it swung ajar revealing the room beyond still intact.

Looking inside I smiled. "Perfect," I thought.

The room was dry and in the corner was a low wooden fold out sofa bed. It was going to be a comfortable night for a change. In another corner stood a television set and a record player. A guitar lay on the floor next to a box filled with toys. Down there I could risk heating food, as long as I waited until after dark and the door remained closed to stop the smell from permeating too far.

That discovery cheered me no end, I knew that after a good night's sleep and a decent meal I would feel much better. The previous few days had been hectic and extraordinary in so many ways, but I had made it all the way to Salford. The Castle was only a short walk from there and I had proved against all expectation that I could make it. I knew that the next stage of my adventure would be difficult, but after everything I had been through I felt absolutely certain that I would find my Dad and I felt proud of what I had achieved so far, but I could not help wondering how he would feel when I rescued him. I refused to entertain thoughts of other possibilities, I was neither vain, nor arrogant, but I could not think in terms of any other outcome.

I smiled to myself as I lowered my rucksack down onto the carpeted floor and sat down on the comfortable sofa. Leaning back I rubbed my eyes, feeling tired already. The adrenaline of my recent escape from danger had worn off already. The sun had not yet set, but after I had eaten some hot food I decided to take advantage of the darkness of my underground refuge; those short summer nights were far too brief and the night before had been so badly disturbed. I blew out my candle and was asleep almost as soon as I lay down.

# CHAPTER 13

Despite the constant darkness of my hideout, I woke just after dawn the next day feeling refreshed. After lighting a candle, I looked at my map and decided to adjust my route: to leave the road I had previously followed and head through the docklands, towards the place where the priest had told me that The Castle stood.

The early morning sun had not yet broken the misty haze of another humid summer day. I did not want to risk stumbling into trouble in the low visibility, so while I waited for the fog to clear I had a leisurely breakfast in my underground lair. I only had a few miles to walk but I thought it was likely to be my slowest section of the whole trip. I was going to go to the place that I had been advised to leave well alone. That was the day I would reach Castle Trafford.

The satisfaction I had felt the previous night at my success so far had turned to a steely determination to see things through to the end. Since I had made it that far I saw no reason at all why I could not get my Father back and return both of us to our Island. I looked forward to seeing the look on Admiral Gill's face when we returned.

I hoped to set off no later than seven. While I waited, I checked for any of my possessions that might rattle or make any sound as I walked. Then I filled my water bottles to the absolute top by immersing them in a nearby rain butt that looked clean enough, putting the lids on while they were still underwater to ensure that they did not glug. If I opened one during that day, anything I did not drink would have to be poured away. I could not afford to make any noise at all.

I also tried to improve my camouflage to suit the new urban setting, covering my boots, face and the backs of my hands with brick dust. My bow's disguising rags were also re-positioned and rubbed with the same dirt, so that instead of hiding its shape they covered only the limbs and the central solid riser. I did not want to have to remove them before shooting and that way I could use the bow with its wrappings in place. If anyone saw through the compound's camouflage they would know instantly what it was, but by then I hoped that it would not matter - at least not that day, I hoped nobody was going to see me at all that day.

The mist cleared almost on cue and I stole out of my cover, creeping slowly towards my destination. I kept my compass handy after working out from my map which bearing to follow and I picked out pieces of cover as I went. At each one I would recheck my compass, take another bearing and look for my next piece of shelter in that direction. So close to The Castle, precision and vigilance were vital, not only in going forwards, but also if for any reason I needed to retreat back to a safer position.

Every movement around me sparked a pause. Every motion of my own across the desolation was preceded and succeeded with a lengthy examination of my surroundings. It was slow progress, but it was the best way to remain unobtrusive and in control.

I approached The Castle from the north, along the route of a very wide road. I kept this avenue on my left, preferring to keep to the shelter of the rubble and undergrowth. There were more people around this close to The Castle, so I had to be far more cautious as I moved towards it. I surmised from what I had been told of that place that anyone in its vicinity would either already be connected with it in some way or a potential target. As I continued I came to an open space, twenty metres of bare concrete totally devoid of hiding places. I had to cross it and so I waited ten minutes or so, until I was confident that I could sprint over it without being observed.

The trepidation I felt was overwhelming and I knew that my life was on the line. If I was caught, that would be it. Plenty of people had tried to change my mind and it was not that I had ignored them. I had taken all of their warnings on board, I just had not let them deter me.

Continuing south, I was aware of just how much of that area had been picked over for any type of resource; there was very little metal to be seen anywhere. Further down the road I saw gangs of people crudely roped or chained together, being marched along. They were also en route to The Castle. They were herded by men armed with bows, crossbows and other more brutal weapons, machetes, long knives, or crude bayonets bound to long sticks. With those and accompanying outbursts of obscenities, they prodded and urged their wretched charges onward.

They all looked half starved, even the captors. I

made sure none of them caught even a glimpse of me hiding in the rubble waiting for them to pass. Slowly, very slowly I advanced down the road, keeping to the valleys between the mounds of debris. I think that is why I did not see The Castle itself until I was quite close, half a mile away at most.

On the remains of a tall wall that I walked past, written in red spray paint five feet high, were scrawled the words 'The Theatre'. As I looked past that, for the first time, I saw it. It was vast, an immense oval structure and it had few openings that I could see. Huge painted steel works stuck out of the top and looked from that distance as if they might support a roof.

From where I stood, I could see the left hand wall on the city centre side had been badly damaged, possibly in the war, but maybe afterwards. The wide gap had been piled high with rubble to reform as high a barrier as possible; with a gated path through, it also functioned as the only entrance. All other openings had been blocked up with crude brickwork or sheets of metal.

Despite what I had been told, I still had not expected to see anything quite so large. It was not so much a castle as a walled village. I wondered how on earth they could feed so many people. I took a moment to study the building, taking in its size while I pondered how I was going to get inside. I was more than a little overwhelmed by the scale of it but I pressed on anyway. Backing out was not an option I was willing to consider, especially after I had come so far.

I spent a few hours moving slowly around it and eventually completed a full circle of the outside of The Castle. I could not see any viable way in. The going was slower than even before, I had spotted lookouts dotted around the top rim of the walls and had to keep those in mind as I moved. Avoiding being spotted from above meant that I could not get close to the wall in daylight, but coming back at night would be very perilous too and I decided to make that my last resort.

At one point during my inspection I heard the repetitive banging of a drum, accompanied by shouting. Someone inside sounded as if they were begging for their life at the top of their voice. A loud scream ended the gruesome noises and the drum fell quiet.

I was clambering round a jumble of crumbling brickwork when I came across a small child. I guessed at the time that she could not have been more than six or seven years old. Covered in dust and filth, her camouflage against the background ruins was perfect whether intentional or otherwise. She was so dirty that she was practically wearing her surroundings. She had obviously been crying, the tears having left cleaner trails down her face, and she gasped as she saw me. Immediately my left hand indicated silence to her, finger in front of lips, my right hand grasped my knife in a silent threat. She nodded her compliance.

"I won't hurt you, stay quiet," I whispered and again there was a nod of her head.

"Are you from there?" I pointed towards the giant fortress. She gently shook her head.

She flinched as I moved towards her side, but otherwise she did not try to get away.

"Where are you from?" she asked in the quietest of voices. "You're not from here? Will you take me there?"

"Not yet," I whispered back, "but maybe. Do you live nearby?"

She shook her head again, her long lank dirty hair shaking behind it.

"They brought us here, my mum and me. They hurt my dad, then they brought us here."

She was obviously distraught and traumatised by her experience with the people from The Castle. I took her hand and looked at her wrists, they had been bound together recently and the skin was covered in freshly scabbed blood.

"Mummy helped untie me," she told me. "She told me to run away in the night, but now I don't know where to go."

"Where did you live before?" I asked her.

"In the tunnels, with the pilot and his friends," she said and it was my turn to look surprised. I could not believe what she had just said and I wondered if it could be him.

"The pilot, what pilot?" I whispered to her, but she just shrugged. I could not leave her there after that and asking her more questions there was not ideal, so I thought it would be a good idea to go elsewhere to talk.

"Look, you come with me and I'll help you, okay. There's a place I know that we can go to where we'll be safe for now and then I'll try and get you back to your home, alright?" I said quietly to her. "Are there any other people who can look after you there, back at the tunnels?"

"Yes, there's lots of people there," she whispered back.

I decided to take her back with me to the cellar I had slept in the previous night. If my suspicions were correct then there would be no point going further towards The Castle. It took us quite a while, she was malnourished and weak. She was at least proficient in moving while remaining unnoticed, in fact she was probably better at that than I was. However she needed to stop every now and then to rest. Her chest moved with an alarming frequency as she panted. In one of our brief respites I asked her name.

"Alice," she told me.

"Well, Alice, you can call me Badger," I told her. She looked at me quizzically.

"All my friends call me Badger. When I was very young, I was very nosey, especially after dark when no one would tell me to stop. People thought I was like a little badger and so the name stuck." I winked at her in a reassuring manner after I spoke, trying to put her at ease.

"Okay, Badger," she said and for the briefest of instants I thought I might be about to see a smile.

My mind filled for a moment with memories of my own childhood and my Mum. She had often said I was like a nocturnal scavenger - so 'Badger' had stuck, ironic since there have never been any of my name-sake on our Island.

So many people on the Island were introduced to me as 'her little badger' that they always thought of me as that. My Dad was not keen on the nickname and although he tried unsuccessfully to get people to stop using it, he was never able to. I like it; it reminds me of Mum.

"How old are you, Alice?"

"I'm six and a quarter," she told me precisely. "How old are you, Badger?"

"I'm seventeen, Alice." I thought it only fair to answer her question as she had answered mine.

We left the Trafford area, moving back into Salford. The route was exposed and it contained a motorway and a few canal crossings. Sometimes I left her for a minute or two while I scouted ahead, making sure no one was around.

At one point we startled a flock of pigeons and had to move away quickly in case anyone had seen them flee. We hid in the foundations of a large wrecked building on a crossroad. I thought nobody had come to look, so a while later we moved on. It was another mile until we would reach my underground hideaway. Alice did not recognise our surroundings, so I suspected that the tunnels she had referred to were not too close by.

"Stay here for a moment," I said to Alice, "I'm going to look ahead a bit again, I want to be sure there's nobody about."

She was out of breath and I only left her for a few seconds but I heard a voice as I returned.

"Hello again, little girl, your mum's sent me out to look for you," growled a voice from behind her.

I was angered more than I was fearful, wondering what sort of an unscrupulous animal would say that to her when he was so obviously trying to take her back to that place.

There were no coverings on my bow to discard. There was already an arrow on the string and I drew it back, as I lifted it up and pointed it towards him. His expression turned to shock when he saw me emerge. I think he had thought he had found an easy target in the lone child, but then was caught out by my sudden appearance. However he stood his ground three metres away.

"Hello, little boy, see what *your* mum's sent for

you," I snarled at him.

"Whoa, hold on with that thing," he said. "Wait a minute." He raised a hand, palm towards me.

"My mum didn't send *you*." Alice shouted out the words, heavily emphasising the 'you'.

I looked along the arrow at him. He wore what remained of a pair of jeans, heavily patched in many places and smeared in filth, and an old football kit t-shirt. He was around twenty years old, bearded and short haired. He carried a large axe in his left hand, the shaft of which looked crudely hand made for its pre-war, manufactured head. I took an instant dislike to him; his eyes seemed filled with a mocking arrogance, a kind of belligerent self belief. Turning his attention away from Alice, he spoke instead to me.

"You won't shoot me with that thing will you?" he asked with a sneer. "I doubt you've ever shot any*thing*, let alone any*one*."

"Go," I told him. "Now!" Alice moved behind me, trying to hide from him and I could feel her shaking with fright.

"I only want the little girl," he said, "give her to me and I'll let you go on yer way."

"Go back," I said to him again. "I won't tell you a third time. She stays with me."

There was no way I was going to let him take her,

even if she had not been my new hope for finding my Father.

"Why don't you come along with us too then?" he said, ignoring my previous instruction. "You'll like it at The Castle, you'll fit right in you will."

"There's food there," he added. I remained silent for the moment. "Come on, come back with me."

"If you don't leave now, I will kill you. Don't be foolish enough to think I'm bluffing." It was his last warning, but I do not think that he believed me and suddenly he moved towards us.

"Listen you...," he was cut short by my arrow spearing through his chest; at that range it passed clear through him leaving only the three fletchings, in a spreading pool of blood, on the front of his shirt.

He stumbled and grasped at the wound as his ruptured heart stopped beating. Yet he still came towards us, as if on auto-pilot, his brain not having quite caught up with events below it. As he moved nearer still I lowered my bow and I moved towards him. I punched him with all my might with my right hand, striking him hard across the jaw and only then did he sink to the floor. I drew my knife and I pushed it through his throat, just to make absolutely sure.

That time I did not feel the slightest remorse for the man I had just killed. If anything, having learned from my previous experiences, I felt satisfied that he was dead. He had left me with no other choice.

I turned my attention back to Alice.

"You know I didn't want to have to do that don't you?" I asked, crouching down in front of her.

"He was going to hurt me, wasn't he." She didn't say it like it was really a question.

"I think he would have done, yes."

"Thank you for not letting him then," she said.

I was struck by her responses sometimes and this was one of those moments. She was a product of her environment, calmly thanking me for killing him.

"Come on then," I said to her, "let's get on and find somewhere to sleep. It'll be starting to go dark soon." I set about retrieving my arrow and its fletchings for gluing back together later.

I hastily covered his body and the pooled blood around it with a large thick curtain pulled from a crumbling house. Someone or something would find him soon enough, but if he had any friends in the near vicinity, I wanted them to have to waste time searching for him.

We carried on walking, with me rubbing at my bruised right hand as we went. We headed on towards the cellar again and half an hour later we were there. We reached the window entrance and I went in first, knife drawn again, just in case. Alice followed, she seemed glad to be inside and out of sight. I was relieved to be out of danger again too and able to relax with her.

"Is this where you live, Badger?" she asked. I could hear the disappointment in her voice quite clearly.

"No, Alice, no it isn't," I told her, "we are just going to stay here for tonight."

"Okay," she looked brighter at that. "Do you think my mum will be alright?"

That caught me off guard.

"I don't know, Alice, what do you think?"

"I'm scared for her," she said.

"I know, but there's nothing we can do right now, you know that, don't you?" We both knew that her mother was going to be in a lot of danger right then.

"Can't you shoot them with your bow and help her escape? Please, Badger, please," she pleaded with me.

"There's too many of them, Alice. I can't rescue her on my own." The irony of that statement was not lost on me. I was, after all, on a rescue mission already.

"Perhaps she'll sneak away like I did." She didn't look hopeful. "How will she find us here if she does?"

"Well tomorrow, why don't we go to the last place you lived? You can take me to the pilot you mentioned.

If your mother escapes she's bound to look for you there isn't she, or maybe they will have an idea how to help her." I felt a little guilty using the situation she was in for my own ends.

For a second she looked worried. "No, Badger, I can't show you the way in, it's a secret! I was told never to show it to anyone."

"You can show *me*," I told her. "That pilot you told me about, I think he might be my Dad. Surely nobody will mind."

"Can't show you," she said flatly.

"Alice, what about your mum? She will go there and look for you if she can, don't you want to see your mum. And what about your dad, he might be there." I still felt somewhat deceitful with that ploy.

"I can go there because I know where it is already," she said petulantly, "but I was told not to tell and that means to anybody."

I could not blame her, it was what she had been taught and she was right to protect her people.

"Okay," I said, "how about I take you near to it and you go and ask if it's alright for me to come in?"

She thought about it for a couple of seconds then she said, "Alright, Badger, as long as you promise not to follow me in. I do trust you, Badger, but there are rules in the tunnels."

"Of course there are and so there should be. Thank you, Alice, and I promise I won't follow you," I smiled at her reassuringly.

Although she did not complain about her hunger, I realised that she had not eaten since the previous day. I warmed some food for us both and we ate together, my supplies were getting low but would not need to last much longer.

Afterwards she rummaged through the box of toys and found an old Rubik's Cube. She twisted and turned it round for five minutes.

"Badger, what am I supposed to do with this?" she asked me.

"It's a puzzle. You have to match up the colours together on each side," I said. I had tried one once back on the Island, a few years before.

"That sounds easy enough," she said.

The small plastic cube clicked and creaked in her hands for a further few minutes.

"Can you do it?" she asked.

"Nope, not me," I said to her. "I tried to solve one a while ago but I couldn't figure it out."

She tossed it back into the box.

"Well I could if I tried, but I'm bored of it for now," she said as she resumed her investigation of the contents of the box. I had to try very hard indeed to hide my laughter from her, as I sat there gluing the fletchings back onto my arrow.

She selected a small bear next and I noticed that her play was almost silent. She would mouth the words as she pretended the bear spoke to her. When I had been that young I would have spoken the words aloud to myself. She did not put the bear back in the box, he was hers now and he had a name, she had called him Bert.

I felt a strong empathy towards the girl. Her life must have been a challenge every day, I felt responsible for her now and that could cause a problem. I hoped there would be people at the tunnels who could look after her. I was not intending to adopt her but I could not abandon her either, if there was only my Father and a few others at the tunnels I would have to take her back to the orphanage in Ramsey. If I could keep her alive that long.

She and Bert were sat in the middle of the room. She was trying to get a knot out of the string of a yo-yo. I noticed that on the other side of Bert was sat a doll wearing a stained white wedding dress, with a tangled mess of long blond hair. I put the repaired arrow back into my quiver and then went over to Alice and sat opposite her. As long as we were quiet down there we would not be found and I played with her, teasing her new friend whose fuzzy belly stuck out disproportionately.

"Where do you get enough food to maintain this then?" I asked Bert, prodding his tummy.

"Badger," Alice whispered, "he's full of stuffing, not food."

I realised that the young girl must not have developed much in the way of suspension of disbelief.

A little while later I asked her about the pilot and whether she could describe him. She tried, but I could not be sure if it was my Father and I did not want to pressure her. She told me her parents had only learned of the tunnels themselves a few months earlier. Before that they had lived near an old farm elsewhere. Alice was not good on place names.

Then we just sat silently for a while, her cuddling the bear and playing with her hair, twirling it round and round her fingers. I realised too late that I should have kept her mind occupied, as she lay down and then softly, as if she did not want me to notice, she started to cry. I lay beside her and held her, wordlessly trying to comfort her.

As we tried to sleep that evening I thought back again to my own childhood and to the brave twelve year-old, sniffling and trying to pretend it was a cold, stood next the shrouded body of the Mother so recently lost and the open grave that lay waiting for its incumbent.

Admiral Gill had spoken, "We will all miss this heroic woman, we all know of her brave actions and her sacrifices in a time of war and beyond. We will not forget her or those who fought at her side for the peace we now enjoy."

Helen was stood next to me; I think she had been asked to keep an eye on me. Though I was technically considered an adult by that time, few people as young as I was lived alone and I had argued till I was blue in the face that I would be doing just that. Eventually even Gill had given up and a small room on the ship had been allocated to me.

I remembered them lowering her thin body down, wrapped in sheeting. I did not want to remember her as frail, how she was in the end as the cancer took hold and so I had an old photograph of her with me, taken before the war and I looked at that as I pretended I was not crying.

Shiel had put his arm around my shoulder and he wordlessly squeezed it, his sobs as muted as mine were.

Perhaps this was how the girl I comforted felt now, I knew she already missed her mother, but wondered if the uncertainty made it worse for her, or if with her childish optimism she was too young to properly understand the consequences.

There was no uncertainty for me as the bugles played the last post and the soil started to envelop my Mother's wasted body. I remembered how I felt on that rainy afternoon when I had thought I was all alone in the world, orphaned, and as I did so I wiped Alice's tears from her eyes and tried to soothe her sobs. I wrapped us both up as best I could, leaving the bear in her embrace and holding her in my arms as I blew out the single candle.

Many hours later that was how the morning found us.

# CHAPTER 14

The next day we set off to find the tunnel that Alice had told me about and where I hoped I would find my Father. She was carrying the small bear that she had liberated and a bag filled with other toys. Alice's mood improved a little as we walked. We had eaten a light breakfast of blackberries from a thicket of brambles, growing behind the ruins of the house that we had slept underneath. As we picked and ate, Alice had described to me a horseshoe shaped bend in a river, near to the entrance of the tunnel. After looking at my map, I could see exactly which way we should go.

"So where do you live, Badger?" she asked me as we walked along.

"On a big ship, moored up next to an island," I told her. "It's not like here, the people are all friends with one another and everyone has enough to eat."

"How big is the ship then? Has it got lots of rooms in it?"

"It's got hundreds of them, and a runway for aeroplanes," I explained.

"Planes on a ship, what for?"

"To protect it, they've got guns and things on them. And there's helicopters too," I said.

"I'd like to see that," she said, and foolishly I did not get the point she was making.

I decided to head towards the river on the way as my water bottles were running a bit low, particularly now that I was sharing their contents. The route we took was once again down the long road I had been walking along days before. Now it was heading into the centre of Manchester and again we had to detour occasionally as the built up sides made the road too dangerous to go down; we would have been vulnerable to anyone who wanted to sneak up on us from above. Shattered glass, rubble and destroyed brickwork were everywhere. Car shells littered the surroundings, sometimes half buried, but where nature had managed to take hold it had done so with a vengeance. The grass was waist deep on any patch of earth it had claimed and small trees and plants sprouted through gaps in brickwork, forcing the mortar to part.

I felt much more jumpy; having the girl in my care made me responsible for two lives, not just my own. It was dangerous to be out and about in that area. Almost anyone we saw that close to The Castle could be affiliated to it in some way.

Some of the buildings in that area had been taller before the war than any others I had seen on my journey. To the right of the main road, huge slabs of concrete speared through with reinforcing rods, lay like giant bricks. Some still contained a complete window or door frame. The innards of the gigantic buildings spilled out onto the ground around them.

Alice paused, she appeared concerned and was sure that she had heard something ahead. We went to the side of the road and crouched behind one of the few concrete walls left standing. I let the wrappings of my compound bow loosen a little and made sure an arrow was correctly nocked.

Alice looked very nervous as I mouthed to her, "Wait here," and pointed at the ground.

I moved round to the right through the enormous blocks of rubble. I could smell a fire, the smoke wafted on the breeze and sure enough, soon I too could hear voices. I silently moved forwards to take a look and, creeping round a rust streaked wall, I could make out their angry words. There were three people, all arguing with each other, their language littered with expletives.

Once I had moved around the next pile of rubble I could see them. They stood surrounding a car, the interior of which was filled with flames, a fire having been built inside. Through my field glasses, I could make out that on top of its roof was a body and a burnt hand stuck out into the flames. It was cooking. Those around it were debating whether it would be ready to eat yet. Fat ran off the roof of the car, dropping into the fire and sizzling. I was overcome with disgust for the people around that car, I understood that theirs was a desperate existence, compared to ours on the Island, but it was still difficult to witness the stark reality in person. There was nothing I could do though and it was no business of mine anyway. I just had to make my way back to the girl and ignore them. I was confident that if I had needed to I could have shot the trio before they could have got to me, but I doubted that they were alone; they would not have wasted their quarry by cooking more than they needed. The others were probably nearby, possibly collecting more fuel for their barbecue. For that reason I decided to give them a wide berth and I made my way back to Alice. I told her that we would have to detour and I was glad when she accepted without asking any questions.

For the next hour, as we walked, I pondered to myself how anyone could live out there for years without sinking into such depravity. I could not help but wonder whether my Father would still be the man I remembered. For the first time, I realised that I may have been naive in my expectations. I had thought about how he might welcome the person that I had become in those lost years; now I hoped desperately that the man I idolised would still be so deserving, and that he would not have had to sacrifice his morals to survive.

It turned out to be quite a long detour but we made good time. We went round the shattered tower blocks on the other side of the road and past the ruins of an incongruously placed old church; one old building that had once been stood surrounded by the modern high rises. When we rejoined the road we had previously been following, Alice told me that she recognised where she was now and she started to lead the way towards the river.

"It's this way, Badger, come on. We can be at the tunnels in no time," she said.

I followed her over the road, first looking out for anyone who might be further along it. We went down the side of another road, sloping downwards and Alice climbed over a barrier to the right. We went across fields of raw brickwork and aggregate. It was obvious that Alice knew the way and she would stop occasionally to look around. Our surroundings reminded me of the plastic building blocks I had been given as a child, but on a much larger scale, like a box full of half formed structures had been tipped out ready to play, still not entirely dismantled from the previous time.

"Come on! Please keep up with me," she urged me on against my better judgement. She was clearly eager to get there.

We advanced in that manner, keeping to the troughs between the collapsed buildings for a quarter of a mile. Ahead of us I saw a structure still largely intact, looming over the red bricks. It looked as if it had mostly been clad in glass originally and although the frame had survived, almost all of the windows had all been blown out, probably by one of the blasts twenty years previously. As we skirted around it I could see that a large heraldic lion plaque decorated its side, still clearly visible.

We continued on and Alice showed me a route down, underneath the road surface to the left of it. It was supported on pillars, almost like a bridge. The whole road ran along a banked section of earth like a huge shelf, with little growing underneath as it was almost dark down there. As we moved along the bank I walked along a thin pathway that I could only just make out in the soft soil.

"Badger, get off that path!" Alice scolded me in the

way that children do. "Walking along a path makes it bigger and then other people can follow it."

She said it like it was the most obvious thing in the world and she was right.

"Sorry, Alice." I wondered at how different it must be to grow up out there, how hard it must be. That was the kind of trick you only learned by mistake.

It was a very hot day and as we walked we had started to sweat. I was glad when we found the river, we were both thirsty. The water was fresh and cold and I could clearly make out the objects littering the river bed: old tyres, a plastic chair and the usual bones. We drank enthusiastically from it regardless, making the most of it; there was so little fresh water in that urban area. Then we watched out for each other as we quickly took turns to splash our faces and cool down.

Following our brief wash and after I had filled my water bottles, Alice was keen to continue. "We're very close, Badger. Hurry up. I want to see if my mum's got back yet."

She did not sound like she believed it herself and I think that she knew it would not be true, but I said nothing on the subject, I just followed on. She took me further along the banking and we came to the base of a footbridge leading back up onto the road. We climbed up onto it, a rope had been left tied to the railings above. It was not high so I took the chance of letting Alice go first, telling her to wait for me at the top.

We moved up the footpath and lay on the ground looking out onto the main road again. I insisted on spending a while looking down it both ways with the binoculars I carried. Alice gave no show of attempting to cover her frustration. The only thing I saw moving was a crescent shaped sign swinging in the breeze, still attached to the highest part of a collapsed building, with a closed doorway below it.

We moved off to our left, as Alice impatiently mumbled under her breath, "Finally."

We crossed another road and the remnants of a large brick built ruin to our left. Coming up in front of us I could see what was left of a huge church, which turned out to be a cathedral. Alice told me that I would have to wait in there, since the entrance to the tunnels was very nearby. As we got closer I could see the damage to the building, there was no tower or spire left and the roof had collapsed in. I wondered if there would be anything remaining inside.

When we arrived at it, I looked up at the broken off fragments of the once mighty structure. There had been three large windows, I could still see the bottom of the frames in the stonework. I had no idea how tall the windows might have been as little survived above them. Alice swung the door open and boldly led the way inside, I followed her. As we picked our way over the stonework and roofing slates, Alice led me to a room off to one side. I could guess her plan.

"Could you wait in here, Badger?" she asked. "I'll go to the tunnel and ask if you can come in."

"Okay, I'll wait here." We had made a deal and I was faithful to it. "Don't be long and be very careful out there on your own."

I was well aware that after she left, the next people I would see would be heavily armed and not accompanied by a six year-old. In the corridor outside, Alice pressed herself against the wall so she could see me through the door, till the last possible moment before she ran quickly away. I let her go, she was sharp enough to know if I followed. She would almost certainly have been taught to wait a few moments to see if I would come after her. Instead I waited, but not in that room with no escape route; if the people from the tunnel were not friendly that would have been too dangerous.

I wondered where the entrance to the tunnels was and I remember thinking at the time that they might be in catacombs beneath my feet. I waited nervously, hoping it would be him and thinking of ways it might not. Different scenarios ran around my head, how many people might be known as a pilot, how common would it be now? The anticipation was all consuming. I thought at least if it was a different man, not my Father, then at least I had brought a small member of their community safely back to them. It might not necessarily mean they would let me in or help me though.

It was an hour before anyone arrived. Hesitantly they opened the door to the building and came inside, two women and a man. He was limping badly and walking with a stick. The women both carried bows, not compounds like mine but still good solid powerful ones. They carried them fully drawn, advancing one at a time to cover each other. The man followed closely behind and I did not blame them for their caution. He held a pistol in his hand. A fourth person followed them in, but kept his back to the room watching the street outside, he had a pistol crossbow in each hand.

"Keep a sharp eye out," the first man said, "we have no idea who's really in here."

As soon as I heard him speak I knew that I had found my Father and I could not stop myself, I cried out to him instantly.

"Dad! It's me, Dad. It's Jane. I came to find you." As quickly as I could I jumped down from the thick wall I had been hiding on top of, and revealed myself to them.

The four of them looked confused, the women kept their arrows trained on me, the other man turned back to watch the entrance after glancing at me briefly.

"Jane? How did you…?" my Dad's voice trailed off. "How can it be you, you're so grown…. You…. Alice said it was someone called Badger and I thought…."

He looked at me, with bewilderment as his main expression.

"It's really me, Dad. Shiel heard your radio message and I had to come to look for you."

"Put down those damn bows," he ordered and came

towards me. I ran into his arms and he held me for the first time in a decade.

"I thought you were dead." My eyes started to fill with tears.

"I nearly was, once or twice," he told me, as overcome with emotion as I was. "I didn't leave you, Jane, I couldn't get back. I wanted to but I couldn't. You believe me don't you, Jane, I would never desert my daughter."

"I never thought you had, Dad." He had surprised me by saying that. "I never thought for a second you had deserted me."

"What must you think of me, staying out here for ten years," he sobbed. "And your Mother, how's she? What was she thinking letting you come out here?"

I did not think I could cry any harder than I already was, but I did. Naively I had overlooked the fact that I would have to break such terrible news to him. It simply had not occurred to me, but of course he did not know.

"Oh, Dad, I'm so sorry, she died. Five years ago now, it was cancer. I'm so sorry."

"My poor girl," he said, "all alone for those years." And for a while we stayed there, unable to let go, all other thoughts temporarily eradicated.

Once my Father and I had regained our composure,

the five of us left the cathedral and crossed the road. My Father sent the two women ahead to check that the immediate area was clear of people. He had introduced them to me as Faith and Hope, they were twins and had been born during the war. They were twenty-two years old and had managed to survive the final round of the nuclear exchanges as infants. The other man was introduced to me as Vincent. He did not turn to look at me, he kept his eyes trained on watching out for any other people in the vicinity.

We waited by a three story brick building, that was remarkably intact. It was horseshoe shaped and the area inside the 'U' was fenced with very sturdy high metal railings. Inside the fence was what I had initially assumed to be an old electrical substation or telephone exchange. It was a brick built block, about ten feet tall and eight feet across both sides. On the front was a steel plate door.

As the sisters returned at a jog, my Father led me around the gap between the wall and fence. I could then see that there were actually two fences, one inside the other. Long spikes adorned the overhanging top section and they looked to be very high security for just a junction box. I soon realised that I was very wrong to have thought it merely housed utilities.

At the rear of the compound, where it was not visible from the road, the bars of the fence had been forced apart, probably using a car jack or something similar. We squeezed through the gap and made our way around, between the two fences to the front of the second fence. A large steel plate was leaning against this section, concealing a second gap, where the railings had again been forced apart. Once we had gone through, the steel plate was laid back over the gap, covering our entry point. To anyone who did not know it was possible to enter the compound by that route, it would have appeared to be still secured or at least of no obvious interest. When we were in the centre of the second fence, my Father walked up to the door and gave a coded knock, it opened from the inside and we entered.

"Welcome to the Guardian Tunnels," my Father announced. "They were sealed up for nineteen years after the war. It was supposed to be a fallout shelter, but for some reason nobody made it in. I found it and opened it up a few months ago."

"How did you know it was here," I asked as we walked past the door keeper and headed down a long flight of stairs, lit with dim light bulbs.

"From my time in the military. I knew the rough location and I tracked it down easily enough," he told me. "Getting through that door the first time was a bit more of a challenge."

The stairs seemed to go on down forever, twelve steps then a landing, reversing direction to spiral down. The walls were painted grey, flaking here and there with age, the hand rails enamelled. Eventually we reached the bottom, still in semi-darkness with just the weak emergency lights glowing in the ceilings. The tunnel floor was flat, the walls and roof above formed a circular arch. Pipework snaked away along the roof and walls, mounted in trunking on hundreds of brackets, disappearing into the distance as the tunnels curved. I was a little surprised that the bores were not straight and wondered if there was some geological reason. To either side I could see doorways lining the walls and I could see a few people too, walking back and forth.

"Badger!" a familiar high pitched voice rang out. "I wanted to come with them to get you but they wouldn't let me."

"That's okay, Alice, it doesn't matter I'm here now," I told her, as she rushed forwards and threw her arms around my waist. She was still holding the little bear and looking much cleaner.

Another man approached us, who looked to be about forty-five or fifty years old. He seemed to be in a very poor state, having clearly been badly beaten recently.

"He must be Alice's dad." I thought to myself, glad that she still had some family left, especially after my own recent reunion.

"You're the girl who brought my Alice back?" he asked.

I simply nodded.

"Thank you, thank you so much for my daughter's safe return," he said to me with great emotion.

"My pleasure," I told him. "I should be thanking her

though. It was she who led me back here to my own Father."

"So this is your girl then," he said to my Father, before turning back to me.

"I will never forget the great service you have done me." He was very well spoken, almost formal in tone. "I thought I had lost them both."

He picked up his daughter, awkwardly due to his injuries and moved away down the tunnel. I think he was hiding his tears.

"Bye, Badger, see you later!" Alice called out to me over his shoulder, waving.

"Bye bye, see you later, Alice," I replied.

"Come on, 'Badger'," my Father said, with mock disdain in his voice at the nickname he had always hated, "let's get you something to eat and cleaned up a bit."

"Maybe there are some earthworms for you around here somewhere," he added winking and I smiled at the old familiar joke that I had not heard since I was Alice's age.

He led me through the tunnels, which were surprisingly complex and quite extensive. At some points they widened out and were multi-levelled, with the different layers connected by stairways. I could see that it would take some time to learn the layout.

Directions to various locations within had been painted onto the walls at some of the intersections, probably in an effort to help new arrivals like myself.

I noticed that there seemed to be a tide mark around some of the walls in the lower tunnels and my Father explained that some had been flooded when he first opened them up, but the pumps that drained the water away were still in good order.

A short while later we sat in a corner of the bunker's canteen and talked as we ate together, then we carried on talking for hours more. The two sisters sat on the other side of the room, near to a pool table and an empty fish tank. Having accompanied us from the door, they then left us alone to chat. Vincent had left us as soon as we entered the tunnels and I still had not heard him speak. Just the four of us occupied the room at that time.

My Father wanted to know everything that had happened from the day he had last left the Island, so I told him my story. I told him about my Mother, how she had argued with Gill to keep searching for him, about the years that followed and then about how she died, how brave and calm she had been at the end.

I told him all I could remember about the last ten years, the progression of the work to improve Island life, about his friends and colleagues, everything. Most of all though, he wanted to know all about me and how the young child he had left behind had evolved into this fully formed person now before him.

I could see that he was in conflict, his euphoria at having me there, contrasting with his grief for my Mother. He was clearly trying to show me a brave face and I felt so sorry for him. I got the impression that the reason he was asking me so many other questions was to change the subject, so that he could have time to come to terms with the sadness later.

Then he asked about the details of my journey from the Island to Manchester. He laughed out loud when I mentioned the mad old priest at Ormskirk, still watching over his flock; I had not yet mentioned where he had sent me on my detour.

"I'm glad to hear he's still alive, I remember him arriving with that little kid not long before my plane crash," my Father reminisced.

"Edward," I reminded him.

"Yes, that's right. Didn't Helen take to him," he asked.

"Yes, Edward's twelve now and nearly six feet tall," I told him.

"Is he really, you all grow up so fast, just look at you."

As I returned to telling him the story of my journey, he looked horrified as I recanted the more gruesome episodes, of Julie, of the men who had attacked me and the things I had seen. He was clearly uncomfortable when I mentioned the explosives storage compound.

"The priest told you to go there." He said it as a statement not a question. "That's a dark chapter from our past. He would want anyone from the Island to know about that place for sure, but it's not as clear cut as he thinks."

"What happened there?" I asked him. "What did Gill have to do with all those dead?" I almost dreaded hearing his answer, in case knowing the truth might change how I thought about our Island life.

He paused, as if thinking for a moment how best to answer me, and then he said, "I think that was the reason the priest wouldn't stay on the Island, why he went back to his church."

"Go on," I prompted him. Then he told me the rest of the story and I could see that it was not a thing that the admiral would have been happy to be reminded of.

It had happened in the first years after the war, before I had been born. He explained that our people had made many expeditions to the mainland back then to try to find the more useful items that could be salvaged in any great quantity for the Islanders' use, pharmaceuticals, weapons and such like. One of the native Islanders had been a lorry driver and he had known about the existence of the explosives store. Gill had decided it was worthy of investigation.

They had flown in by helicopter and my Father had been part of the mission. When they arrived the fencing was still complete and the site occupied. My

Father told me that the people there were uncivilised, cruel and barbarous, but had access to worryingly large amounts of munitions. He described how they would blow things up for entertainment, not just inanimate objects, but also live cattle or sheep. They would eat what they could find later.

"Ah, that would explain all the craters," I said.

"Of course they thought themselves to be very heavily armed compared to anyone else and so that bred arrogance," he said. "Gill had tried to reason with them by loud speaker, he had offered them a home on our Island with us in exchange for the explosives. They turned him down and nothing would persuade them, but it was too valuable a resource to us and too dangerous left with them. Gill wouldn't leave it, he couldn't. He couldn't risk them expanding their domain and terrorising any other survivors they could find."

He looked guilty, as if haunted by what had happened.

"What did Gill order then?" I chose those words with care, in case what I suspected was accurate.

"A night mission for the Cobras, you know, the attack helicopters."

I simply nodded and he continued. I knew how efficient the Cobras were, out of all our aircraft they were by far the most deadly.

"They used night vision goggles and they just wiped them out with their twenty millimetre cannons.

Massacred them in the dark, them and their children, they didn't stand a chance. They wouldn't even have seen what killed them," he told me. "I found out later, they had tried to fight back, throwing handfuls of explosives at the choppers half a mile away. Pointless. I was part of the ground force that went in afterwards, in the morning. There was no resistance then, I think most of them had died, but anyone else must have fled."

He would not look at me as he told that tale.

"We combed the whole place for anything we could salvage. We didn't move the bodies or write anything on the doors though. We just got the remaining munitions and got back to our Island as quickly as we could. When the priest came to the Island, he knew about it. Maybe it was him who moved all the remains into an improvised tomb, we'll probably never know. He came to the Isle of Man with a sick baby, because there was nowhere else he could have gone, but he wouldn't stay. 'Not after what we had done' was all he'd told us."

"You were ordered," I reassured him and he looked up at me. There were tears in his eyes and he would say no more about it. He already had enough to contemplate that evening and I felt sorry to have caused him any further upset.

I tried then to change the subject. To distract him, I told him about Frank, of his potato obsession, how I had been glad to find not everyone in this new world to be harsh and cruel. He smiled a little, but I knew that in his mind he was back in that compound, sifting through the remains of those they had killed, for their spoils. Perhaps a little piece of him always would be. I hoped not. For the first time, I wondered how much else I did not know about the Island's history or what he had been through during the war, but then was not the time to ask.

It was nice to see a smile on his face again and it took me right back to the Father I knew all those years ago.

Eventually my tales were all told, we had been there for two hours at least.

I was surprised when the main lights came on. My Father smiled as I looked round quizzically, blinking as my eyes adjusted.

"We only turn them on for an hour or two in the evenings," he told me. "We are out for most of the day and fuel reserves for the generators are very limited, but we can't light a fire down here, so we might as well have a few lights on too while we are cooking. Those weak lights that were on before are part of the emergency system that runs on battery back-up, so it gives us chance to charge those too."

# CHAPTER 15

Then it was over to my Father to tell me his story, where he had been and what had happened to him in the previous ten years. The story he told astonished me and gave me renewed respect for the strength of the man and huge pride, coupled with relief that any of my previous concerns were dispelled.

"You remember the little Cessna, the propeller driven one?" he asked me. I nodded, remembering the light aircraft from my childhood.

"You took me up in it once," I said.

"Oh yes, so I did. Well I was in that, searching the countryside for a downed plane myself if you recall." Again I nodded, listening intently to everything he said. "I don't really know how it happened, perhaps the fuel was contaminated or something. I still don't really know to this day," he said. Leaning back in his seat, he stretched his arms behind his back.

"The engine started to splutter and stall out," he continued. "Maybe it was me, maybe something I did in the pre-flights." His voice trailed off.

"Listen," I said, "I'm not going to go back to the Island and start trying to find someone to blame, just tell me what happened."

"Okay, I think it was the fuel, it would explain both crashes. Maybe some contamination at the distillation plant, who knows, it's not relevant now." He paused, looking as if he was trying to remember in more detail. "Yes right, so I'm over a place called Worsley I seem to remember. Both engines have stopped and I'm gliding, I think I was around about twenty thousand feet."

"I came through Worsley," I said to him.

"Hum, didn't look too nice from the air."

"Carry on," I said.

"So I'm at twenty thousand feet and I try to get a bit of speed up, I knew I couldn't glide for long so I tried to restart it, hoping to limp home. But that doesn't work, she wouldn't fire up again. I radioed back my mayday, giving my position and they replied, promised to come look for me too."

"They did come you know. Mum didn't let them stop looking for ages," I told him.

"No, she wouldn't have done knowing her," he said. "She'd have driven Gill nuts. So anyway, I'm at ten thousand feet now and I need somewhere to put it down, at this stage still hoping to get the plane back, you know, eventually once Gill's help arrives. I thought they could guard it while we repaired it. Something like that anyway, so I look for somewhere I can land and where I can take off again."

"Right, I see what you mean," I said.

"There's three options, two motorways, or the road you walked down," he said.

"Too many lamp posts I'd have thought."

"So did I," he said. "The M60 was full of trashed cars, I could see that straight away. So, I opted for the M602, and put it down on a clear section. There was a bridge over it part way down that I'd have to go under, but I just had to take the risk."

"So what happened at the bridge?" I asked.

"I knew the plane would fit under it but I didn't have time to check if the whole motorway was clear. As I came in to land I saw there was the wreck of a van under there, but it was too late by then. I think I hit it at about sixty miles an hour," he said. "The worst bit was waiting to hit, I knew it was coming as soon as the wheels hit the deck."

"That must be why they couldn't find the plane," I said.

"Yeah, it didn't catch fire or anything, which was lucky for me really. I was out cold from the collision. I've no idea how long I was sat in it for. The next thing I knew, I was being pulled out of it, chained to the next slave and dragged off to The Castle. My new career started from there."

"I saw one of their chain gangs heading into The Castle," I told him, "just before I bumped into Alice." Remembering their faces as they had filed past, I tried not to think of him in one of those processions.

"Yes, you can see the poor souls being dragged around from time to time. What your friend Frank told you about The Castle is an understatement of the conditions in there."

"Why, what's it like inside?" I asked, not sure if I wanted to hear the answer. When he spoke again his tone changed; up until then he had tried to make light of the situation, but he could hold up the pretence no longer. I could hear the hatred, anger and frustration in his voice.

He explained that the people of The Castle are ruled by a man called Terrance, not a large man, but very aggressive, perhaps psychopathic. He controls them with fear and would kill any of them without a second thought. Anyone taken there is a resource and Terrance himself decides their fates; most would end up as food once any other usefulness is exhausted. Nobody is there voluntarily, the slaves are watched over constantly by Terrance's hierarchy, who are themselves watched over by their self-appointed lord and master.

"The interior of that place is full of banked rows encircling a wide open field of mud, with huge fires burning at its centre," he described. "People are sometimes thrown alive into the flames for any slightest supposed misdemeanour against the slave keepers, or just as a warning to the others to keep in line. Sometimes I think it's just part of their power play, so they can sadistically watch them burning and screaming."

I thought for a moment he was not going to continue,

but he did.

"The slaves are chained to the railings on the surrounding steps, men, women and children, all wailing and begging for food. All of them are utterly desperate, having to do almost anything to survive." My Father told me of the things he had seen in that place, the dark horrible side of mankind. "It was like hell, stinking of faeces, urine, and death. Constant screams echo off its walls from one place or another, many are just begging for an end to their suffering."

I could hear the hatred of that place in his voice as he told me about his horrifying experiences there. I could not help noticing that he talked about the place as if he was a distant observer; he was obviously uncomfortable talking about his own personal role and fate there.

"Some of them have even set up their own breeding program for the slaves," he told me. "Can you believe that? They go around the slaves, selecting the healthier, stronger men and women and forcing them together, to spawn stronger workers for future generations of the slavers' children to command. Of course sometimes they'll just keep the prettier ones for themselves as well. Nothing is beneath them, nothing. If it's ever a choice between dying and going to that place, you choose the first option, okay. You get seen by anyone from there, you kill them on sight. Have no compassion or mercy because believe me, they will have none for you."

I thought of him living in conditions like that for

years and I silently cursed Gill for not making more of an effort to find him then. Again I thought back to my early years and sitting outside Gill's office, swinging my legs while my Mother argued with the admiral.

"If I ever meet Frank, or see that priest again, I'll thank them for trying to persuade you to stay away from that place and those people," he said to me. "Not that they had a chance of changing your mind, from what you've told me. You should be called Mule, not Badger."

"Sorry, what?" I asked him, not understanding what he meant.

"There's an old expression," he said, "as stubborn as a mule."

"Hey, that's not fair," I told him, putting on a hurt face.

"Well anyway," he said returning to his past, "if I do say so myself I was in pretty good condition for a slave back then, so they chose not to just eat me straight away. They put me to work, on a gang with some others. We'd farm, digging the fields by hand, or in gangs pulling a plough. We'd dig through the piles of rubble too, looking for tinned food some days. There was a lot of digging. For a while I was stuck down the bottom of a hole, digging a well at one end of the old football pitch," he paused to smile wryly. "That was a fun way to spend a week. They worked us for twelve or thirteen hours a day and the pay was rubbish. Don't even ask about the time off."

I could see that he was regaining his composure and trying to put on his usual cheery face again, but I did not and never would ask him what he had been forced to eat and to do in order to stay alive in that place.

"It took me nine and a half years to escape," he said. "Nine and a half long years."

"How did you get out of there?" I asked him. He stood for a moment, stretching out his injured leg and I moved in the hard plastic chair, to get more comfortable.

He described having being sent to live and work at an outpost; a former park about three miles from The Castle at Trafford, it had a large house to accommodate them all and fields that they farmed. The men of The Castle had made their slaves work it for years to produce food.

"Eventually, they put me on a different team, before I keeled over I think," he said. "They sent me out to Buile Hill, that's a farm they run. It's a couple of miles from here."

"Was the work any easier?" I asked him.

"No, still a lot of digging, but you got to sleep inside at night and they looked after us a bit better. See one of the problems, never mind the way *they* treated us, was the other slaves, the competition for survival."

"So it was better there then, or rather less bad?"

"Listen, compared to what went on inside the walls of that castle, it was a paradise." His voice had gone cold again.

"What happened then, at the farm? They didn't just let you go?" I asked.

"No, we were attacked."

"Who by?" I was intrigued to hear about the turn of events.

"I wasn't sure at the time, it was obviously another tribe and I could tell they were having some sort of feud, but I didn't know what it was about. I just thought it was you steal my food and I'll steal yours sort of thing."

He explained that it was not until weeks later, that he had learned more from a traveller he had met, that the men of The Castle at Trafford had been terrorising the Heaton Park people in an attempt to take over their farms and that had driven those that lived there into desperation, which had obviously prompted a retaliation. My Father did not know many details of why and was unsure of the politics between the other tribes in the area, but that was not the time to try and find out if the others were friendly, he was understandably wary of any strangers.

"So anyway, back to that day. I'm working in the fields as usual, trying to dig a furrow while I'm bound to the other slaves. The first I know about it, it's gone loud."

"Gone what?" I interrupted him to ask.

"Sorry, 'gone loud' it's old military terminology for 'the shooting started.'"

"I see, what happened then?" I asked him.

"Well, this is rare you see. Ammunition is a bit scarce these days as you can imagine. Nobody ever seems to discharge a weapon any more and the first time I hear a gunshot in years, I catch the bullet with my leg." He tapped it with his stick. "Typical isn't it?"

I did not answer, but gave him a sympathetic look.

"So as you'd expect after I was shot in the leg, I fall down. But I'm still tied to the others and everyone else tries to run off, away from the shooting," he explained. "So there I am, getting dragged along by my bindings and slowing everyone else down. Until one of the slavers sees me, that is. I'm hindering the progress of the rest of the livestock, so he cuts me free, leaves me there and that's that. I'm back to being a free man from a slave, without even a thank you for all my years of hard service. At least he didn't cut my throat before he cut my ropes. I try to think of that as my retirement gift."

His tone lightened again after that, once his tale did not remind him of his time in The Castle and as he made us both a hot drink, the familiar waft of warm milk filled the room.

As he sat back down he continued his tale. "Where was I, oh yes, so I'm bleeding on the floor with a gunshot wound." He winked at me reassuringly and carried on. "Now things get a little worse for me."

"How could they get any worse?" I asked him.

"Don't worry, I survived, but if you stop interrupting I'll tell you." I was glad to see he was joking with me again. "Right about then I realise that if I'm not bound to a load of other slaves, the guys from Heaton won't know that I'm not with the other side, I could try telling them I was an escaped slave but I think that they might not believe me. So, I start to crawl away. Then the slavers from The Castle arrive and launch their counter attack on the Heaton mob. That was the 'things getting worse' bit."

He described briefly the pitched battle that took place around him as he tried to drag himself to safety, moving only when he thought no one would see him.

Again he smiled. "I manage to get myself to the wall at the edge of the parkland and scramble over it. At this point I'm starting to get more worried about the trail of blood I'm leaving, there seemed to be a lot of it. Then I realise there's someone on the other side of the wall with me."

He paused infuriatingly, tempting me to interrupt him again, but I refrained from doing so. I rolled my hand on my wrist, gesticulating to him to carry on.

Eventually he spoke again. "It was the body of a woman. I didn't recognise her so I presume she was with the other lot. She'd been shot through the head by someone in the battle. I searched her body and I couldn't believe my luck at what I found."

Again he stopped trying the same trick again, this time I gave him 'a look'.

"She had a bottle of water and a nine millimetre pistol with two full clips of ammunition in her pockets," he said. "So I took them both and crawled off as fast as I could. There was an old school or college or something nearby and I hid in that for a while. I was a bit woozy, I'd lost a fair bit of blood I think. I tied a tourniquet round my leg and eventually the bleeding stopped. Thankfully there was no damage to the bone, at least I don't think so. I've been lucky with it, the bullet went clear through, I've kept it clean and it's not got infected."

"What happened to you after that?" I asked him.

"Oh yeah, erm, a dog tried to eat me."

"What! It tried to eat you, how?" I asked incredulously. He reminded me so much of when I was young, I could rarely tell when he was being serious then either.

"I was tucked into my little hideout in the school, under a collapsed bit of roofing and I fell asleep, or passed out, I'm not sure which. Well, anyway when I wake up there's a large black and brown dog lapping at my bloody leg."

"What did you do?"

"What do you think I did? I shot it in the face and then I ate it," he said. "I knew the noise was possibly going to draw attention, but I'd probably have died out there without that dog. Nobody came looking for the source of the gunshot anyway, at least not that I saw."

"The dog meat and the water kept me alive long enough to recover and I headed towards these tunnels. I expected people to be living here already and I was quite surprised to find them still sealed up and unused. I often wonder why they weren't used in the war," he told me.

He had decided to stay in the tunnels since they made an excellent refuge while he worked on trying to contact the Island.

He finished telling his tale with, "I realised it was going to be difficult to survive on my own, so I kept a lookout for any other peaceable people I could find, to try and build an alliance here in the meantime."

He smiled, "I think Alice's dad, John will vouch for your membership here." Then he winked at me. "One day I'll put the full story down in a book, what do you think?"

I just smiled at him and said, "You've had quite a time of it haven't you?"

"Hasn't everybody? I don't think it's as bad as it could have been though, I'm still here after all." He stood up then.

"Right," he said suddenly, "you're getting in a shower, and then a change of clothes."

"What are you trying to say?" I asked him with mock indignation.

"I can smell you from here," he put it bluntly. "In a few hours the rest of our group will be back. We tend to spend the evenings together and I don't want you driving them away."

"How many people live down here?"

"About thirty of us now. Will you be okay if I leave you with Hope and Faith? I'll get them to find you somewhere to sleep and something clean to wear."

"Well if the smell is too off-putting I suppose I better had," I conceded, playing along with him, although in reality I knew he had a fair point. I was really looking forward to being clean and comfortable again.

The two women stood then and guided me towards the door.

"I'll see you in an hour or so," my Father said.

Hope was the taller of the two though not by much. I was relieved that the twins were not identical; it sounded like I was about to have to learn a lot of new names and could do without any added confusion.

"'Badger' is an unusual nickname," Hope said. "Our parents named us a little too optimistically though, so I don't suppose we can comment."

"Something to do with being born during the war?" I asked her.

"Yes, everyone can tell that as soon as they hear our names," Hope said as we walked along a corridor together. "That's a fine weapon you have by the way."

"Thank you," I said, unsure how else to react.

"Have you had to use it much?" her sister asked me.

"I've just walked here from the coast. I've had to use it a lot."

"Were you trained with it? By a professional I mean?" asked Faith.

"Yes, everyone where I live is taught to shoot a bow by an expert."

We reached a doorway, Hope opened it and we stepped through into a small dormitory. There were personal possessions dotted around some of the bunks, marking out the occupied ones and reserving them.

"Perhaps we could compare our archery techniques then sometime?" Hope asked me.

At that point I grasped where their line of questioning had been leading to.

"Sure," I told them, "why not."

"Great," they said together and Hope added, "Select whichever bunk you want from those that aren't being used and the bathroom's over there." She indicated towards a side door.

Faith went across to one of a pair of bunks that had been pushed together and which I assumed belonged to the sisters. Blankets had been hung around it, making it a small cave of privacy. She reached under one and passed me a towel.

"Here, you can have this," she said. "There's soap and everything else in there."

"Thank you, that's very kind of you." I noticed a few cuddly toys were spread amongst their untidy sheets, then I thought I spotted one of them move. A moment later as I questioned how tired I must have been, my observation was confirmed as a kitten yawned, stretched and then stood up. It was tiny and jet black from nose to tail. It mewed quietly at us and its huge green eyes blinked slowly. It walked unsteadily towards us over the bed. Like most young animals, its paws looked as if they were several sizes too large in comparison to the rest of its body, as if it had borrowed them from an older sibling.

"Aw, Snowy, you are just so cute!" Hope said rushing forward and picking it up. She kissed the ironically named kitten on the top of its head. "Who's a lovely puss cat then?" she squealed excitedly. I was very surprised to see that they kept a pet but I did not comment on it as I did not want to offend my new friends.

"We'll have a look through the store rooms and find some clothes for you and then put yours in the laundry. I'm afraid we haven't got that much to choose from, only old uniforms, but I'm guessing you won't mind that too much," Faith told me.

"I'm sure I'll be fine, thank you," I said, and then jokingly added, "Maybe the three of us could go and rummage through those shops I saw round the back together some time."

"We could have a look, but I think they'll have been picked clean long ago," said Faith sardonically, looking confused. I realised she had missed my joke when she added, "You'd have more luck in what's left of those flats. We'll leave you to get cleaned up. Come back to the canteen when you're ready."

Hope was still cuddling their kitten, talking nonsense to it.

"Right, okay. Thanks again for your help, I'll see you in a short while," I said gratefully and I went into the bathroom, looking forward to being free of the last few days worth of sweat, blood, grime, filth and the last of the manky pond water still in my hair.

I was happy to discover that there was hot water

and half an hour later I emerged, wrapped in a towel and pulling the last knots from my long hair with my fingers before tying it back still damp. There was a small selection of clothes spread out on the bed and I pulled on a pair of khaki pants along with a baggy shirt, they felt crisp and new, which was not something I had ever experienced before. There were also some fresh socks and I pulled my own boots on over those before heading back to the canteen.

As I walked into the bustling, busy room all eyes seemed to turn and look at me. I saw my Father stand and I walked towards his table. It was clear that everyone wanted to see the new arrival.

Alice waved frantically, as I walked past her and her father and I gave her a little wave back, accompanied with a smile and a wink. I saw Faith sat with her sister, feeding titbits to the tiny cat. They were right, it really was a very cute kitten but I was surprised there was space in their world for such sentimentality. I pulled up a seat at my Father's table and the paused conversations restarted as I sat.

"The sisters tell me you've said you will help them brush up on their archery skills," he said, leaning back.

"Well they did ask me to." I did not want him to think that I thought his friends were not as skilled as they ought to be.

"They're pretty good," he said, "but I seemed to recall you showed a lot of promise."

"Top of my class," I said simply.

"Did old Fred Shiel pick out that bow for you himself?" he looked proud.

"Called me his star pupil more than once." I smiled, happy to see that he looked so pleased.

"Maybe you can show them one or two things then," he said. "Now, let me introduce you to everyone, show off my little girl."

The majority of the bunker's inhabitants had all returned from their daily duties and my Dad took me around to each table in turn, letting people know who the stranger in their midst was, although I think rumour had already run round the room five times before we even stood up. It did not take long to get round them all. There was a mix of men and women and a whole range of ages, but Alice was the only child present. I saw a man sat in a battered wheelchair, with his leg bound to a metal pole to keep it stretched out.

"Fell off a top step and tumbled down the flight of them," he said as he saw me looking. "Death sentence usually, breaking a leg out there but thanks to your dad I'll be on my feet again soon enough. He found me and helped me back here. I owe him everything. My name's Jurgen by the way, good to meet you."

"And you, hope you're up and about soon." I grabbed and shook his outstretched hand.

My Dad introduced me as Jane but I think everyone

had already been told by Alice, probably more than once, that I was called 'Badger' and it had already stuck. If they asked me a question that was how they addressed me.

A middle aged woman, whom I was told was called Phyllis, gave me a welcoming hug and then she asked me, "Badger, how did you manage to get all the way here on your own? You've walked here from the coast I believe."

"Well, I suppose I was just as careful as I could be," I told her, not wanting to go into all of the details again so soon.

I knew there was no way I would begin to remember everyone's name yet, but at least they all knew me.

"Will you ever give up on that nickname?" my Father asked me as we returned to the table.

"I'm just so used to it from everyone back home. I think it's already caught on here now too," I told him. "Besides, Mum used to use it."

"Your Mother coined it," he said.

He fell silent for a while then, staring off into a distance that was really the past. I knew exactly who he was thinking of and I could not help but join in. The news of her death was still all too fresh for him.

I was very glad to be back in a proper bed again that night, albeit in a dormitory rather than a room of my own. The exertions of the last few days, the lack of rest stops and the disturbed nights had exhausted me and I fell asleep with no difficulty. I was dead to the world and the others who shared the room did not disturb me as they went to their own beds later on.

In the early hours of the morning I was awoken by something thudding onto my bunk. I was disorientated at first and my base instincts took over. My hand slid out from the covers and I reached under my pillow, towards my knife, as I came into full consciousness. Whoever was touching my bunk, they were moving now, upwards towards my head. My hand found the hilt as the depression on the bed passed my waist. There was a thin scrape as the blade started to emerge from the scabbard. I looked up, as my eyes became accustomed to the low level emergency lighting that was left on overnight; I could see no one but still felt the pressure of their touch. Thinking that they must be hiding down the other side of my bed, I swung round.

"Meow," said Snowy over the top of my blankets.

I let go of the knife and reached over to the young cat, I picked it up by the scruff of its neck and put it back down on the floor.

"You scared me, you daft puss," I whispered to it, feeling a mixture of relief and annoyance. "Go back to your own bed." I pushed it away from me, but it remained stubbornly seated as I slid it across the floor.

I saw movement across the room as Faith emerged from the two pushed together bunks. She scurried across the floor towards me, in a t-shirt, shorts and thick socks.

"You naughty boy," she whispered as she picked up the kitten. "You shouldn't wake people up. You little terror!" She hugged it to herself.

She looked down at me and apologised quietly, "Sorry he disturbed you."

"That's okay, goodnight." Without waiting for a reply I rolled over and as I went back to sleep, I heard a little 'mew' sound repeating but getting fainter as it disappeared back towards their bed.

# CHAPTER 16

The next morning I woke early; back on the Island we always rose at dawn to make the most of the natural light, so despite the gloom of the bunker it still came naturally. I dressed in the clothes given to me the day before and I crept off, walking in my socks to avoid waking anyone and carrying my boots with me. For once I left my bow behind under my bed; it would not be far away and I felt safe enough down there.

I left the dormitory and walked along the corridors of the complex, towards the canteen. I was hoping that I would not be the only one awake. The dim battery powered emergency lamps glowed just enough to light my way and so I managed to avoid walking into anything. I reached the canteen and before I came to the door I could hear the hushed voices inside.

I pushed the door open and walked inside. There were candles burning in there, supplementing the dim lighting. My Father was there, along with Vincent.

"Good morning," said Dad, rising to his feet as I approached their table. He kissed my cheek and pulled out a seat for me.

"We were planning the day's activities," Vincent said gruffly. "We are very busy around here you know."

"Don't be unfriendly, she *is* my daughter," Vincent was told firmly.

"Good morning," I said to Vincent. "Perhaps I could

help?"

He ignored me, turning pointedly towards my Father.

"We should try and get out to Swinton again, there could be decent scavenging to be had even now," he said to my Father.

"Vince, we know it's just slag now, I saw the town with my own eyes only three weeks ago. They got hit just to the north west with a ground burst, there's nothing there now I promise you. What about Ancoats, at least that's a bit closer?"

"St Helens got a ground burst too, I saw it on my way past," I said, trying to join in.

"It's a bit too far to walk to, sweetie." My Dad had said it as a joke but it still irritated me. I had only been trying to take part in the conversation; I decided not to bother again for a while. I sat and laced my boots, resting each foot on the edge of their table, purposely marking out my existence.

"Doug, we know there was a tribe around Ancoats for years, they'll have picked up everything there was to find there long ago." Vincent was still making a point of ignoring me. "It's only the edges of the craters that will have anything left any more. People have stayed away from them. We have to go and get a close up look."

"I'm still not sure the rim of the craters will have anything worth finding."

"They're the only part of the country that haven't been picked over for the last twenty years. I'm convinced they could still hold some stuff of use," Vincent said, almost enthusiastically for him.

"Okay then, here's the plan: two parties today, you take a small group to look at the area around the Swinton crater, check it out and see if it's worth sending a bigger group. I'll see about Ancoats again. Maybe one of us will get lucky."

"Right then," Vincent said, starting to get up. "I'll take Faith and Hope with me if that's okay. I'll leave 'Sweetie' here," he nodded towards me, "for you to take with you if that's what you've decided. Have a good day." Without waiting for a response he walked across the floor of the canteen, flung open the door and strode out.

"What's his problem? I should have said something to him! What have I done to annoy him?" I said loudly when he had gone. I was half hoping he was waiting on the other side of the door. I knew that I was probably overreacting, but after everything I had been through I found his dismissive manner just too much.

"Don't take him on, he's like that with everyone."

"He wants to be told," I said, "before he meets someone with less patience." I was incensed at the way the man had spoken to me.

"What, less patience than you?" He smiled at me

and sniggered. "Look it's nothing personal, he can't help himself. He doesn't waste words and he can be a little abrasive, but he doesn't mean anything by it. It's just the way he is I'm afraid."

"There's no excuse for that."

"I know," he said, "but really, don't take offence. Deep down he's a decent chap, he's loyal and brave, and he knows his way around very well. We've just got used to his manner."

"He'd do well to keep away from me, I don't like to be spoken to like that."

"Jane, look, trust me on this. He's a good bloke really, just a bit of a pain, you know what I mean? Give him a second chance, for your old Dad." He paused, waiting for my reaction. "I'll make you some breakfast," he offered, "we've tinned sausage and beans from the past world?"

"All right," I said, "but I'm only doing it for you." I was doing it for the food really and he knew it.

It had been a very long time since I had eaten anything from before the war and I was looking forward to it as he heated it through. The smell took me back to my childhood when such tinned food was more readily available. I was salivating in anticipation by the time he brought it over to the table complete with knives and forks. As it turned out the memory was better than the actual taste, and when I ate it, I found it was far saltier than I had remembered.

"What are you planning on doing today?" he asked. "Want to take a walk to Ancoats with me?"

"Don't forget I want to have a look at your radio, see if I can get a signal to the ship. Perhaps after that I'll come with you."

"It's broken, trust me on that."

"Indulge me," I said around my last mouthful of beans.

"Well okay, I'll show you where it is, but it definitely won't send anything. Finish your drink and I'll take you down there."

"This coffee tastes funny," I told him.

"That's because it's real," he said. "You've never had the proper stuff before. We found a whole crate full of freeze dried coffee in the stores. You'll be climbing the walls on a caffeine rush in ten minutes."

"Oh dear," I said in slight disbelief. "What's with the twins and that cat, I was surprised that you let them keep that down here?"

"Don't try to suggest they shouldn't have that kitten," he advised me in a cautionary tone. "They won't let it go, trust me we've tried."

"What about the name?" I asked him. "It's black, surely it should be called Sooty not Snowy."

"That was John's idea, he's got a wicked sense of irony. He nearly persuaded them to call it 'Rover' at one point."

"Really?" I laughed.

"Oh yes, but on a serious note, you look out for those two girls. They may come across as sweet and harmless, with their fluffy toys and their even fluffier kitten, but in a fight? Well, I'd back them against anyone," he told me. "I'm really glad they are on our side and not against us."

"They're that good are they?"

"They've had to be," he said. "Anyway, I think that kitten is probably good for them, it gives them something to care about, calms them down."

My Father and I left the canteen and we walked through the labyrinth of tunnels to the communications room. I was surprised I had not noticed the smell before down the length of the corridors. A nasty odour like burnt plastic enveloped us as he opened the door. The room was blackened by smoke on the inside.

The radio equipment itself was a complete wreck; the fire had clearly started inside it and had destroyed it quickly. On the floor next to it stood an exhausted fire extinguisher and a fire blanket was scrunched up and abandoned next to that. The wall behind the radio was soot stained and a black trail led up and across the ceiling. The casing was covered in the inert white powder from the extinguisher that also covered the innards of the apparatus' scorched remains.

"I'm not completely sure what's wrong with it now," my Father told me humorously. "I would have thought that down here it should have been shielded from the EMP from the blasts, especially seeing as we did get it going briefly. I think it's got more to do with the mouse nest. Judging by the mess they'd been living in there a while, but it looks like one of them finally chewed through something fatal."

"Frankly," I said, "I'm astonished you got it to send anything."

"It hadn't been quite so 'on fire' before the message was sent," he said dryly. "Who'd have thought mice and electricity where such a flammable combination?"

I had noticed he still liked to joke a lot.

"Roast mice don't smell too nice," he added, smiling at his own rhyme.

"How's the radio antenna?" I asked him hopefully.

"That's fine, good as new."

"Okay," I said, "how about making one of these then." I showed him the book that Shiel had given me and he flicked through it.

"This looks a bit...," he paused, seeming to search for as fitting description, "Frankenstein?"

"I have no idea what that word means," I told him.

"No, of course not," he looked thoughtful, "I keep forgetting all the little things you youngsters missed out on." He left that point and instead he asked, "So, how does it receive a signal?"

"It doesn't receive, it just broadcasts. You set it up with a wheel or something to switch it at the right intervals so you can send a signal with Morse code."

"Like a piano that plays itself you mean?" he asked.

"Will you be serious for a minute, please," I asked him.

He looked confused for a moment, but I did not know why.

"Never mind," he said. "You mean set it up so it's driven by mechanical switches to send a message automatically."

"Yes, exactly." I was glad that he had stopped fooling around and was taking me seriously.

"That would be a good idea," he said, "because it says here you'll need about twenty thousand volts. I wouldn't want you to end up like that mouse."

"There's a derelict university nearby isn't there?" I asked him.

"Yeah, just up the road, you and Alice will have walked past it. There's a plaque of a lion on the outside of it."

"That's right, I saw it. I don't think I'll find everything I need down here, so I'll go there today and look around for anything that I might be able to salvage from the ruins there."

"Okay," he said, "give me a few minutes to find John. He can lead the trip to Ancoats if he's feeling any better this morning and I'll come with you. Show you around the charming city of Salford, spend the day together. I might even take you somewhere nice for lunch, somewhere posh."

"That would be lovely," I said, joining his joke and looking forward to spending the day with him. "I'll wear something really special."

"See you by the door," he suggested.

"Right, I'll have a quick look round the tunnels first and see what we'll need from outside and I'll see you there." I walked off to the dorm to get my bow and quiver then I looked through the stores for anything we could use for the radio.

An hour later the two of us arrived at the university, or rather the remains of it.

"Look up before you go into or out of the buildings," my Dad told me. "There's sometimes a shard of glass lodged into a window frame that falls when you disturb the surroundings."

"Ooh, that would hurt, I'll watch out for anything like that."

He pulled his collar off to one side showing a relatively fresh scar that was about four inches long.

"I was lucky it stayed in one piece. Vincent pulled it out for me," he said. "That was the part that hurt the most I think."

"Nasty." I screwed up my face as I spoke.

"That's how you learn out here, trial and error."

"Painful lessons though."

"Yeah, but you learn fast." He wore a resigned expression.

For the rest of that day we searched around for electrical items in the ruins, collecting anything that looked like it might be vaguely useful, not sure if the components would work, but taking plenty to choose from. We ate tinned peaches for lunch; Dad had brought them along as a surprise for me. I had never eaten a peach before and was unlikely to again. The sticky sweet syrup they were suspended in was heavenly.

"Have you got any more of them?" I asked him after we had finished. "Back in the tunnels I mean." We were sat in the long grass of what was once a park, looking out over the river, where I had stopped off with Alice the day before.

"Nope, last ones we've got. Possibly the last ones in the whole country. I've been saving them for a special occasion."

"Well thanks for sharing them, they're fantastic."

"When's going to be more special?" he asked. "It's just a shame we might not see any ever again. I remember before the war when you could have had as many as you wanted, every day if you liked."

"I think I would, if I could. I might have to ask Gill to move the ship and go somewhere they grow. You know, when we get back."

"You might struggle with that, tinned peaches don't grow on trees you know." He laughed and then looked more thoughtful. "Do you think he *will* come for us?" he asked me.

"Yes, if he knows for certain we're alive he will," I said. "If he doesn't I guess we'll just have to walk back and give him a piece of our minds."

"I know you would, too," he said with a laugh. "Come on, let's try and find some more of the stuff you'll need for your transmitter. Then we'll find out if you need to walk back to see the admiral or not."

"You know he'll be glad to see you. Really glad Dad, more than you think," I said.

"How's that then?"

"We ran out of proper toilet paper years ago, and you've uncovered a treasure trove here." I smiled at him.

"Right, so I live in a toilet paper mine do I?"

"Come off it," I said to him, "I've seen how many rolls there are in the store rooms, there's millions of them."

"And they're mine, all mine!" he said it like a madman and I don't think I fully understood his joke at the time.

"Are there other things down there? You know, like the peaches? Things that I missed out on?"

"I wish you hadn't," he said, sad again. "Did you ever get to try chocolate?"

"Yeah, I had that once, someone in Port Erin unearthed a box of chocolate caramels, Gill gave all the post war kids one each. What else have you got here?"

He did not answer at first, he was thinking.

"That's not what you missed. You didn't just miss out on some food. That's nothing. You missed a carefree life, being a child. You missed cartoons and fair grounds. You missed going shopping with your friends and hanging out just for the sake of hanging out, with no responsibilities. That's what you missed,

Jane, peaches just taste nice, that's all." He did not look at me as he spoke. "It's a different world now kiddo. The old one is dead and that's that. Best not to think of it any more, it won't bring it back." He stood quickly. "Come on then, let's find what we need and get back to the Island. It's as close to the old world as we'll get any more. Gill will be waiting to wipe his bum and you wouldn't want the admiral to have his legs go numb would you?"

"That's no way to talk about your commanding officer," I said as I grinned at him and stood up too.

"Perhaps the past is better off being left," I thought to myself.

For the next few days I worked on the radio transmitter. It was fortunate that the old university buildings were so nearby, since picking through the leftovers of that institution yielded several useful parts that we could not scavenge from the bunker itself. With the transformer out of an old instrument panel and some heavy duty wiring ripped out of a ring main, it was never going to be a pretty device, but it was function that mattered.

While I was out scavenging on the second day I came across another very useful, albeit unrelated find, in the university laboratories: a bottle of nitric acid. I took an hour off from the radio and I boiled down the liquid contents of a couple of sealed lead acid car batteries. I had been shown this trick in 'improvised munitions' classes back home. While the newly concentrated sulphuric acid cooled, I rummaged around the tunnels until I found some cotton wool in a first aid cabinet and with that I had everything I needed to make nitrocellulose.

Once prepared, I gathered it up carefully and put it in a metal tin, out of the way in part of the bunker we did not use. I knew the substance was volatile and unstable, but so was this world and it paid to be prepared; finding the chance to make the explosive wadding was too good an opportunity to miss out on.

I went back to my other work then, putting the radio transmitter together.

# CHAPTER 17

The days I spent in the tunnels were easy after my travels. They were dry, comfortable, relatively safe and my Father had chosen who to share them with very carefully. There was a reasonable supply of tinned food stored from before the war, though we never did work out why it seemed not to have fulfilled its purpose as a bunker previously. They did not rely solely on the reserves, fruit was picked from the surrounding area and they caught what meat they could too. There was even a plentiful supply of fresh water, as the tunnel had its own artesian well.

I took a little time out in the evenings to spend with the others and it was as we finished eating, late one afternoon, that the twins reminded me about my promise to them of an archery lesson.

There were still a few hours of daylight left and so the three of us walked out to a patch of open ground nearby where they sometimes practiced. As we walked, they told me the story of their past. They had survived the bombings as they had been in the far north of Scotland, on a short family holiday. Their parents could not have found a better protected spot if they had been able to plan it, but as it was those final few apocalyptic days had taken everyone by surprise.

"Of course we don't remember anything of it, we were too young," Faith said. "We might as well have been born after. Our family stayed up there for years after that. We lived with a group of crofters, growing just enough food to feed us all. It wasn't a bad life up there."

"Until the raiders," said Hope with angry passion.

"Yeah," Faith added. "They came from what was left of the cities, but it's the same story everywhere."

Hope carried on with the tale as we walked. They moved with feline grace across the rubble, stalking almost. Their movements were sleek, slow and considered.

"The raiders came and killed them all. We were the only two to escape. We were only thirteen then. Our parents were killed and everyone else we knew, all for the harvest we had just helped to bring in."

It would be hard to convey the cold hatred and the venomous tone she spoke with.

"We saw them from where we had hidden and we had to wait. Just sit an' wait till they took what they wanted and left. We were scared to stay there after that, in case they came back so we headed south towards the better climate when we were sure they had gone."

I began to realise then why I had never seen the two girls separately. I do not think they ever parted.

"We had a tough time for the next few years, scrabbling in the rubbish like everyone else. We never gave up though and never will. We look out for each other and now we look out for the people living in the tunnels who took us in too."

"Which includes you now, Badger," Faith then added more cheerily.

I thought then that even if I pressed them I would never learn more about their experiences. Going from the tone in which they spoke of them, I did not want to know.

"How did you meet the people from here?" I asked.

"Through your dad and John," said Faith. "We were out hunting for food as usual and they saw us." She paused for a moment. "They saw us and so we put up our bows to kill them before they could kill us and that was when they did something strange."

"What?" I asked.

"They put down their own weapons and invited us for a hot meal," said Hope. "Of course we didn't trust them at first, it was rather unusual behaviour and we'd fallen into that sort of trap before."

"But they did, they gave us some food and talked to us for a while and didn't try to get anything from us in return. We must have looked like wild animals to them. Then, after a while they told us about this place and invited us to come in," Faith told me. "We turned it down at first, wasn't going to make that sort of mistake again, but we stayed in the area. We stalked around for two days and if they saw us they would wave and offer food. We saw others coming and going too and we realised they weren't like most people. Eventually we came to trust them."

Again I thought of cats but I said nothing for a moment.

"Where did Snowy come from?" I asked Hope a short time later.

"We found him a couple of weeks ago. He was just wondering about, he was so tiny his eyes had barely opened and he was all alone, so helpless the poor thing. Well I just thought he was the cutest thing I had ever seen and we took him in there and then," she said. "One or two people said they didn't want a cat around but when we said it's us and Snowy or we'd leave, they soon changed their minds."

"There was a bit more to the argument than that," interrupted Faith. "Like the part where you punched Vincent on the jaw."

"Well he shouldn't be mean to a defenceless little kitten should he? We're here, Badger. Faith, you keep an eye out and I'll practice first."

I watched them, shooting in turn, while the other looked out over the landscape for any sign of danger or anyone's approach. I helped each of them to improve a little. Hope kept too firm a grip on her bow while Faith did not always pull the string back to the same point for each shot. It did not take long to correct those small bad habits.

The sun was starting to get lower in the sky and I

was stood with Faith. Her last seven arrows had all hit the centre of their makeshift mattress target and she was about to shoot again. Hope came scurrying down the pile of rubble that she had been on look out from.

"We need to go, I think they saw me. Five of them," she said in a whisper.

The three of us reacted as one, following Hope's lead, nocking arrows and following her at a run.

"Hello there, ladies," a man's deep voice called after us, "don't run off."

Nevertheless, run we did, through the wreckage of the dead world, as quickly as we could. There was no time for caution or to pay much attention to our surroundings. Stumps of walls flickered past us or were leapt over, as we attempted to outpace our adversaries. We headed away from the tunnels and down a slight hill. Covering an open area, I could hear the thunder of feet behind us; they were moving faster than us. It was inevitable that they would catch up soon if we carried on as we were and I think that the sisters realised this too.

Just ahead of me Faith abruptly turned around and her feet slid across the dust as she ground to a halt. Her bow was up before she had even stopped moving and I ran on past her before I had time to react. I heard the twang of her bow right next to me and then a scream from further behind me.

Hope did the same as her sister, who was now

starting to move again and I realised it would be my turn next. With my heart pounding I fought against the instinct to keep running from our pursuers. I too slid to a halt and sunk down onto one knee. My bow was drawn back as I turned and I selected the target closest to me, a heavy set man. His face had been tattooed in spirals of blue ink and I saw it contort in shock and pain as he ran onto the arrow I had loosed at him.

He fell in a heap right in front of me and I could see then that there had indeed been five of them chasing us. Two others had also been hit by arrows. One, a woman, had been impaled through the eye socket and she was most definitely dead. A thin balding man was on his knees, bleeding badly from his chest, the arrow still lodged in him.

Two remained standing: a tall woman with a hooked nose and a scar across her forehead and a stocky man, armed with a Japanese style sword. Things had happened so quickly that they had not yet had chance to come to a complete halt and as they caught up with us, I saw Hope swinging her bow by one end. She hit the man across the throat with it, probably closing his windpipe. Faith stood in front of the woman, who looked scared once the odds were reversed and it was she who was outnumbered. I recognised her from the barbecue I had detoured around with Alice and I reached for another arrow.

Hope roared as she once again went for the man who was now clutching his throat. She was a savage force, flinging herself at him. She kicked him repeatedly in his groin until he collapsed onto the ground before she started to do the same to his head.

Faith was similarly brutal; by the time I looked across at her, the older woman's nose was little more than a smear across her face. I watched as she stumbled, clutching at her face, while Faith kicked at her until she too fell to the floor. Faith's foot then continued to pound into the prone body. The intensity of my comrades' attacks was astounding and I stood open mouthed as they frantically tried anything to inflict as much damage to their opponents as they could. Their brutality seemingly knew no bounds.

Hope finally managed to crush the man's skull by stamping on it repeatedly with the heel of her boot. I could clearly hear the bones shattering each time her foot was slammed down onto his head, until the crunching became squelching. She did not stop until she was absolutely sure that he could not be alive. She then turned her attention to the man with the arrow stuck deep in his chest. He looked up at her, with eyes wide in prescient fear and I think at that point his heart gave out on him and he slumped over backwards, turning blue.

Faith had the woman face down now and she sat astride her, strangling her with a garrotte made from the sleeve of her shabby clothing. As I watched, Faith put her knee on the back of the woman's neck, getting more leverage as she hauled on both ends of the sleeve, leaning backwards to add her body weight to the strangulation. The woman's legs raised a cloud of dust as she thrashed underneath her and moments later I heard the crack as her spine broke and she became still.

Hope had pulled her arrow out of the dying man's chest with a heave and now used it as a stiletto dagger. She stabbed first him and then the others that we had taken down with that same arrow. She plunged it repeatedly into each of their necks, before tearing it back out again once their jugular veins had been severed. She was still on her knees, covered in the mixed blood of the five, smeared in their gore, with a wild look in her eyes when she looked up at me.

"We *never* give up, Badger! *Never*! And we *always* look out for one another, don't we?" She yelled it out like a victory call.

We both looked round as we heard more feet, thundering towards us. Vincent came sprinting around a corner towards us. One of his pistol crossbows in his left hand and a baseball bat in his right. He slowed as he saw us, surrounded by the bodies.

"Anyone hurt?" he asked between his heavy breaths.

"No, at least none of us," I told him.

"Hope, no more shouting from you, okay. I've told you that before, it doesn't help to draw unnecessary attention to ourselves." He bent in half, out of breath but still managing to be curt. Behind him I could see others from our group arriving.

"I heard them call out to you not to run," Vincent said. "We weren't too far away."

I thought at the time that this was out of character for Vincent, but soon realised that I had unfairly misjudged him. He had come running to our aid, outpaced his friends and arrived ready to fight, without knowing what sort of odds he would face. He might have been brash and annoying, but he had proved himself to be a brave and dependable man.

Without saying anything else Vincent simply walked away, back towards whatever he had been doing. He did not wait for a thank you or to see if anyone needed further help, he could see that the fight was over and knew that there was nothing else for him to do there.

Hope took the dead man's sword as a trophy, telling me that it was called a katana, a word I had not heard before. We went back to the tunnels to clean the blood off them and attend to Faith's cut knuckles. The five attackers had carried little else of any use to us.

After that I think I understood more about the life that Hope and Faith had experienced after losing their parents than they could ever have put into words.

"You fight well," Hope said to me as she washed.

"Not as well as you two," I said. "You were incredible."

"Listen, Badger, you have to be aggressive at a time like that. It really is them or us, we learned that long ago," Hope told me. "You don't always just run, sometimes you have to turn and you fight, but if you do that, then you need to be capable of doing anything you can to bring down your opponent.”

“And when they are down, you make sure they stay down forever,” added Faith as if it was their motto. Her back was towards me as she washed her hands. Her voice was calm and unemotional. “There’s never any room for error now, Badger.”

They were right. It was not bravery or heroism. It was not a celebration and nor was there any sort of pleasure found in the acts of violence. It was just a cold fact of life. Whatever needed to be done, these two young women had learned to do well, first time and every time. Go in hard and do not falter, give no quarter, it was the only way to deal with situations like that.

“I think I’ve got a lot learn from you two. More than I can teach you about archery anyway,” I replied.

“Don’t worry,” Hope said, “we’ll be watching your back.”

I was very glad to hear it.

# CHAPTER 18

Finally the transmitter I had been working on for days was finished. The small switch used to fire the spark was solidly fixed onto a table and above it was mounted a vertical wooden wheel, found in the wreckage of a pub. This was driven round by a variable speed drill set to run very slowly. Around the circumference of the wheel small pegs were carefully inserted into the outside edge, their purpose to depress the switch and activate the signal.

"Please be careful when you plug that thing in," my Dad said to me when he saw it assembled for the first time.

"Volts just jolt, amps kill," I told him, quoting Shiel without really understanding what it meant but hoping to sound like I did.

"Right," he said, looking uncertain, "but just you be a bit careful, okay?"

The placement of the pegs was critical; in those gaps was the message itself and I had worked for hours to make sure that once decoded it would be correct.

It read 'badger and dad alive in salford look for smoke.' Or rather '-... --- -.. --. . .-. .- -. -.. -.. .- -.. .-.-.. .. ...- . .. -. ... .- .-.. ..-. --- .-. -.. .-.. --- --- -.- ..-. --- .-. ... -- --- -.- . .-.-.-' Each turn of the wheel took around ninety seconds. The fat sparks jumping across the gap had quite an audience in its flickering glare for a while after we had turned it on.

I did feel the slight swell of a proud sense of achievement as it started to turn, it had not been easy to make and for it to seemingly start running straight away caused me a momentary smile of relief. Unfortunately we still had no idea if it was actually transmitting anything or not.

I had intended then to try and find a small radio and see if I could receive my own signal. I wanted to make sure conclusively that we were really broadcasting. I knew the chances of finding something that would work were slim but I tried to keep an eye open for anything that might. In the meantime I prepared a large fire, ready to be lit and produce the smoke signal as soon as any rescue planes or helicopters were spotted. I put it together right next to the cathedral where I had first found my Dad again. Locating it there had been an easy decision, it was close enough to our tunnels, but also right next to an ideal position for a lookout to be posted and watch for any rescue on top of the ruins of the building itself.

The signal was to come from a beacon built to give as much smoke as we could manage to produce. A nest of paper and dry grass surrounded by kindling, designed to light as swiftly and easily as possible, was topped by larger pieces of wood and then tyres, some of which had been cut into smaller chunks to increase the surface area in anticipation of a thick black smoke. An old but still serviceable gas lighter, similar to my own, and a can of our precious diesel oil was hidden next to it. The whole arrangement was covered by a tarpaulin to keep everything dry. It would take mere seconds for one of us set light to it and the column of smoke I hoped it would produce should be easily visible for quite some distance.

While we waited to find out if Gill's men would come to our aid, we carried on with the normal routine. It was a very labour intensive existence and we did not know how long it might take for rescue to arrive, so we could not afford to be complacent.

Around midday I saw Vincent walking towards me down one of the corridors.

"Thank you for yesterday," I called out to him as he got closer.

"What for?" he wore his usual perturbed frown but with an added hint of bemusement.

"You came to help when the three of us were attacked," I reminded him.

"So?" he said curtly.

"Well, I wanted to thank you," I said. He looked at me like I was wasting his time.

"You would do the same as me if our positions had been reversed?"

"Yes, of course."

"Yes, well that's because you are part of this community now, the duty to help one another is implicit in the agreement to be here. You don't need to thank me for yesterday, it wasn't anything I wouldn't have done for anybody else," he said and continued on his way.

For a while I thought about what he had said and his words played on my mind. He certainly had an unusual demeanour, but overall I could see that my Dad had been right about him.

In the afternoon of that day, several of us set out to hunt for fresh meat. Even with the hope of an imminent rescue we could not rely solely on the reserves of food in the bunker. After all we did not know how long they would need to last or if there might come a time in the future when we would have only those reserves on which to survive. It would have been foolish to rest on our laurels and do nothing; there was still a chance that the signal we were sending might not reach the ship and also a chance that it might be ignored. We split up into groups of two or three and since I was unfamiliar with the terrain, John had volunteered to accompany me since he knew the area well.

The two of us took the north-west quadrant and set off towards it, with John walking in the same way that he had taught his daughter Alice to; he had been out there for years and he prowled the ground like a well armed predator. His bow was powerful, not as complex as mine, but at least a sixty pound draw. He was an expert with it, my Father had told me, not trained formally like I and the other Islanders, he had been self taught. That was no reason for concern though; I had already seen how proficient people could be even if they had taught themselves. I thought back to Hope and Faith's capabilities, both with a bow and without.

We followed roughly the reverse of the route that Alice and I had taken to the tunnels. This time however, we did not need to detour around the site of the burnt car; it was not in use at that time. We came to the ruins of a shopping centre and from within could hear animal noises, it sounded like a sheep in distress. The layout of the buildings was like a concrete maze, which meant that tactically it was a hazardous venture, but the possibility of a substantial quantity of fresh meat was too tempting an opportunity to forgo.

"We should have a bit of a scout around the place first I think," John said. "It's probably best to make sure nobody else is about before we make any noise. If it *is* an escaped sheep, somebody is bound to be looking for it."

"That's fine," I said in reply, "you lead the way if you know where you are going."

We walked around the remains of the shopping precinct. It was badly damaged on the side furthest from us; there had been a large residential tower in the middle of the shops and it had collapsed onto that area, destroying anything below its fall.

After we had checked around the circumference we moved inside the remaining half. There was no roof over the spaces between the shops and it looked like there never had been, since it was not too strewn with building wreckage in there. However it had obviously suffered from some severe looting, all the windows were broken and various contents discarded around the place. John and I proceeded, with our bows drawn, scanning around ourselves and listening intently. A rat ran across between the shops in front of us and we both almost shot it on instinct.

I did not like being in that kind of environment, it would take only a few people to trap us in there and I knew that John would be wary of that too.

John indicated with the tip of the arrow he held ready across his bow. He was silently instructing me to move around a corner as we came to our first intersection. I looked out briefly and having seen nothing out of the ordinary I moved around the edge of the shop. John scurried over to the other side of the passage and we took it in turns to move along one after the other, advancing along the rows of shops on either side.

We made another turn, that time to our left after about fifty metres. The place felt like a giant rabbit warren that had been peeled open. I desperately hoped we would not encounter anyone that morning, it could end up being difficult to make our way back out. We continued our searches and I had to rely on John's memory of the layout. He directed me to turn again through the ruins and when I saw a path outside I was glad to be able to emerge.

We made two further sweeps through those passageways before John was satisfied that there was nobody else inside. I was glad then to be able to start searching for the animal. John chose the first shop to search inside. It was a large store, with doors to the outside at one end and another escape route at the back, near to a second entrance to the complex. The contents had been stripped bare years ago.

He stood guard while I went in. John had chosen the shop well, the noises were louder there and trapped under some fallen shelving I found a goat. I still have no idea where it had come from or how it had managed to find its way into that shop. Advancing towards it I drew my knife and its bleatings started to become louder and more panicky.

Five minutes later we were already heading back towards the tunnels, John laden with the heavy goat. He had insisted on carrying it all on his own. I walked along next to him, my hands still sticky with the animal's blood.

"I hope you realise, I'm only letting you get away with that because I've had a very hard week," I said to him, smiling as I semi-admonished him.

"I know," he replied, "and I would hope you know that I don't mean to imply you are in any way weak. I know you are just as capable as the next person, but on one level I can't help it, it's just the way I was educated to behave I'm afraid."

"Hmm," I grunted, not wanting to offend his good intentions, but still feeling ill at ease with his old fashioned values.

"So, tell me about the island that you're from then,

Badger? What is your home like?" he asked, deftly changing the subject.

"Well it's just an island," I responded. "It used to be like here but now it's safer and a bit less ruined by the war."

"Do you think they'll come for you then, when they get your signal I mean?"

"Yes, I really hope so. I've got a friend who'll make absolutely sure that someone comes. All they need is to receive a proper signal," I told him. "I've just got to let them know that Dad and me are still alive and where we are."

We walked along under the main road once again, nearing the tunnels, next to the faded pathway that Alice had told me off for walking on a few days before.

"What about us, me and Alice for instance? Or even just Alice, could you take her with you to live safely on the Isle of Man?" he asked. He sounded hopeful and pleading at the same time. "You'd look after her wouldn't you?"

I stopped walking, realising how thoughtless I had been not to tell people that which was obvious to me. I had just assumed that they would know and my Father had obviously been equally remiss. I had not even told Alice.

"Of course Alice will be coming to the Island. You all will if you want to. We've easily got room to accommodate a group the size of this one." I could see the look on his face, relieved and elated. Sarcastically I added, "But not you, 'cause you don't think that girls are strong enough to help you to carry goats." I put my head on one side as I spoke, looking at him with as much mock disdain as I could muster.

A cloud of dust rose up as our catch hit the floor.

"Okay fine, so I won't be a gentleman then, open all of your own doors too if you wish. Bare all of your own loads." He used a resigned tone as he spoke to me.

"That's better, thank you and that's how we do things back at home too," I said to him as I started to pick it up again.

"I shall keep that in mind then," he said. "No offence was intended, you know?"

"Of course not," I said, forgiving him.

We carried on back to the tunnels together. He was smiling contentedly and I assumed it must be at the thought of going to The Isle of Man with his daughter.

I was feeling slightly self-righteous, happy about my small moral victory. I knew I should not have been so ungracious, but after losing both my parents at such an early age, I had fought to prove I was strong and resilient, that I did not need anyone and could look after myself. As a result, even now that I was older I often found it difficult to let my guard down, or to show any vulnerability or weakness.

"How did you survive the war?" I asked him as we resumed our walk.

"I was in a reserved occupation, so when they started conscription I didn't get my call up papers," he told me.

"What was it you did?" I asked.

"I was an engineer. I worked in a nuclear plant, on the coast in Cumbria. I was part of the maintenance team on the core. We made electricity and distributed it to the national grid."

"Admiral Gill will be over the moon when he finds out about that, he'll have you in our reactors as soon as your feet have hit the deck!"

"Well I'd be pleased to help him out where I can, seems the very least I could do in exchange for our new home."

"Didn't most of the reactors get targeted by the nukes though? I thought all the old sites had been checked out by Gill's pilots in the first few years after the war."

"Yes, it was hit, but mercifully I wasn't at work at the time. I lived in a small cottage, an hour's drive away, up into the hills," he told me. "I was riding in on my motorcycle one day through a valley and I saw the mushroom over the plant, I turned around and headed right back into the mountains straight away."

"Was life really as hard as I imagine afterwards?"

"No, it was not as hard as you could ever imagine. It was far worse than that."

We walked together in silence for a while after that. I felt naive in the assumption that I could ever really appreciate the aftermath of the war for those left on the mainland.

"John, I'm sorry if I sounded insensitive about the war and what went on afterwards."

"Don't worry, Badger, after everything you have done for Alice and me, it would be rather petulant of me to take offence over any sort of comment." He stopped and turned to me, his expression was the most sincere I had ever seen. "I want to really thank you sincerely for Alice's safety. I know I've said it before, when you first arrived, but she has had time to tell me more about your time together since then."

"You don't have to say...."

"Please, Badger," he interrupted me. "Alice has told me about the man with the axe you had to kill to save her, but she also told me of the time you spent playing with her in the cellar. That you took the time to talk to 'Bert' with her and to comfort her when she thought she had no one else left. That's what I want to thank you for, do you understand what I mean?"

"I understand," I said, "but you still don't need to thank me."

"Just because you don't need to hear it, that doesn't mean I don't want to say it to you. Thank you, Badger. Thank you from the bottom of my heart."

**CHAPTER 19**

That evening Alice took me to see what she called her favourite place. It was hard for her, being a child out there. My own childhood had been difficult, although not in comparison to hers. There were no other children in the tunnels and she obviously was not allowed out alone. The others tried their best with her but she got bored a lot and had to make up games to play on her own, so I gave her a little of my time when I could. We had become good friends quickly, so I went with her when she asked me to.

Her father's words from earlier still rang in my ears. I was very attached to the little girl, more like an adopted sister than a friend, I realised. I knew that when we got back to the Island we would have much more time to spend together and I looked forward to it. I had never had any siblings, but I was enjoying the experience. I wondered for a moment how Shiel would react to my new 'sister'.

Alice's 'favourite place' was not far from the tunnel entrance, down near the place she had left me to go and ask for my admittance. Over the road from the now familiar red brick ruins of the hospital, there stood an iron bridge across the river. We crossed over it after I had scanned the other side with my binoculars and I noticed as we did so, a weir off to my left that I had not spotted before. Alice hurried me on and we turned left with her leading me by the hand.

Her impulsiveness surprised me at times. She was so good at moving unobserved in unfamiliar surroundings but she was worryingly complacent in locations that she was more accustomed to.

"Alice, take care there could be bad people around here too. Just because you walk round here often doesn't mean it's safe," I reminded her.

"Sorry, Badger," she said cheerfully.

"Listen, Alice, I really mean it. There could be people from The Castle around here. I might not be able to fight them if there's lots of them."

She took things a little more solemnly then, looking apprehensive. I had not wanted to scare her, but I was trying to avoid her learning another lesson the hard way.

A short walk later we came to a small wood, surrounded on three sides by the river and she pronounced this to be her favourite place in the whole world. I recognised it as being just a little way from the spot where we had rested a few days earlier, when she had first led me to the tunnels.

"What do you think? Isn't it lovely?" she asked.

"It's very nice here," I confirmed, as I sat down on the ground. She sat too, right next to me.

Around us the city was almost invisible and the only sound I could hear was the water of the river passing by us. It really was a pleasant place to sit in the fading light of that day, but however superficially pleasant the surroundings were, I knew it was not a place to relax too much.

"What's it like where you come from, Badger?" she asked.

"Well, it's just a little town by the sea I suppose," I told her. "But I live in a huge ship just off shore."

"What type of ship?" she wanted to know.

"It's a very big grey one, it's got a runway on the top so that planes and helicopters can land on it."

"That's right, I remember you told me that before. And you live inside it?"

"Yes, I've got a room in it, near to the hangars."

"What's a hangar, Badger?"

"It's a very big room for keeping planes inside, sort of like a big garage," I explained.

"I've never seen anything flying. Did your planes really used to fly in the sky?"

"They still do," I told her, "sometimes."

"Really? Can you fly them, Badger?" she asked excitedly.

"No, at least not yet. I'm hoping to learn to fly sooner or later. The man in charge on the Island said that when I'm twenty one he'll think about it."

"That would be amazing!" she said.

"You'd like it, my Dad took me up in his plane once, when I was your age," I told her. "He rolled us upside down like this." I showed her a loop the loop manoeuvre using my hand. "Then he barrel rolled like this." Again I demonstrated.

"That sounds fun!" she enthused.

"Yes, I've always wanted to fire down the runway and launch up out over the sea, flying for myself."

"I've never been to the sea," she said. "Is it really as big as people say?"

"Yes, it's pretty big. You can't see to the other side anyway."

"Why not?" she asked.

"Because it's too far away, silly."

"But I can see the sun and the moon and the stars. Does it go further away than them?"

"Well," I said, wondering what she had been taught and whether she was just playing games with me. "I'll tell you what, if my friend Shiel picks up the signal we are sending out, I'll take you back to Ramsey with me. Your dad can come too. Then you can have a look for yourself."

"Okay, I'd like that." Her attention fluttered like a butterfly sometimes. "Could you teach me to shoot your bow and arrows?"

"Not this one, no," I said. "It's too strong for you to pull back, you'd need a much smaller one at first."

"Will you get a smaller one for me then? Then you could show me," she persisted.

I looked around before answering and spotted a few likely looking saplings. Then I saw a small yew tree over by the water.

"Come on, there's one over here," I said to her, standing and moving towards it.

"Where, Badger?" she called after me, getting up. "I can't see what you mean."

I found a straight section of the yew and cut it down with my knife, I was quite expert at that from my own youth. I split the wood and pointed the top and bottom thirds, tapering them down slowly. I cut her an arrow from a straight branch and a feather, which she found herself after my prompting, provided a rudimentary fletching. Half an hour later I strung her new bow with a short length of string I had in my pocket. She watched entranced the whole time, saying nothing until I was checking the draw weight for her small frame.

"Where did you learn to do all that?" she asked me.

"At home in Ramsey," I told her. "We have lessons on it with our teachers at school."

I passed the small bow to her and she held it out with reverence.

"Now," I said to her, "you're right handed so hold it in your left, no, not out front, to your left side. Move your head round to look at the bow, but keep your arm straight."

I paused the lesson for a moment to shorten her arrow to the right length, measuring it against her arm.

"Hold the bow gently, like you would hold a tiny baby bird if you didn't want to hurt it," I told her. "Now, move it out at a right angle to your feet." She did exactly as I instructed. "Good, now without the arrow, use three fingers and grab the string with your fingertips."

"You only use two fingers, Badger," she said correctly and I was impressed by her observational skills.

"You can use two as well, once you're used to doing things the proper way," I told her and she obediently grabbed the string with three. I took her arrow and put it on the string between the two appropriate fingers.

"The front of it rests on top of your hand. Now, tilt the top of the bow to the right if you think it will fall off, but the more upright it is the better. Always put your arrow on the same bit of the string, we'll put a mark on it when we get back to the tunnels later.”

“Okay. Should I pull it towards me now?”

“Not yet, let me make a mark on the bow.” I cut a notch in the side, the same distance above her hand as her eye was from her chin. “When you pull it back, the arrow will point at where the notch is. Do you see what I mean?”

“Yes, Badger, if I hold the bow so the notch is on top of something then that’s where the arrow should go,” she repeated.

“That’s right, now when you pull the string back, pull it all the way to your chin and try to make the string cover the notch at the same time so the arrow doesn’t go off to the side too much. Every time you pull it back, try to pull it back to the same place.”

“Okay, I think I understand,” she said.

“Well off you go then,” I said. “Shoot it, Alice!”

A few moments later she shot her first arrow and it was nearly dark by the time we found it again.

She was so excited when we got back to the tunnels and I wondered how often she smiled so widely as she did when she showed her father her new favourite toy. John thanked me for my time, but I assured him that it had been my pleasure.

I enjoyed being in the company of Alice’s playful innocence, but unavoidably tainted by this world, she also had a vulnerability that reminded me of myself at that age. Of all the things I saw and did on the mainland, only finding my own Father had been more precious to me.

I had a late dinner with John in the canteen at the tunnels, after he had put Alice to bed, and we chatted as we ate.

"You're really good with Alice, she looks up to you," he told me.

"I like her too, she's a good kid and she can't have had an easy time of it out here," I replied.

"That's why I'm so grateful when you make her happy. Although she will probably get splinters from sleeping with that bow."

I looked at him and laughed, "You couldn't get it off her then?"

"No, just the arrow so it wouldn't stab her in her sleep," he said. "I told her she might accidentally shoot her bear while she dreams."

"How did you get here? Meet my Father I mean and come to live in the tunnels?" I asked him. "Alice told me you lived near to a farm somewhere before here."

"I think 'farm' is wishful thinking," he said. "It was more like a hovel amongst a few allotments really."

"Where was it?"

"It was located by the side of the River Irwell at a place called Clifton. The same river that runs by here. It's a secluded little valley towards the north," he told me. He had seemed rather ill at ease that day but everyone had troubles that haunted them and I did not pry.

"We managed to live, the usual way I suppose, trapping, hunting, scavenging, and growing what we could. Hiding of course, whenever we saw anyone else, particularly the patrols from The Castle. Maybe we should have stayed there, then the three of us might still be together."

I did not say anything, leaving him to reflect. He looked distant and I presumed he was thinking of his wife. She had not returned to the tunnels as Alice had hoped and he knew as well as anyone else that any attempt at a rescue would be unlikely to end well.

"I met your father down by the river here. I came into the city sometimes. I would usually be searching for things such as shoes, or books and toys for Alice. I had stayed out a bit too late that day and I was going to follow the river back home so I wouldn't get lost if it went dark. Your father saw me and called out to me, he's a good judge of character that man and he could see I was not one of 'them'. He was correct of course, but also rightfully cautious and once he knew we would not try to fight him or steal from him, he eventually offered the three of us a home here. It sounded much safer at the time, I know he isn't to blame, however I think I shall come to regret meeting him." He went back to eating briefly before continuing.

"The men of The Castle found the three of us near to the city centre, during one of their excursions to round up anyone they can find. We didn't often take Alice along with us, but it wasn't fair to keep her cooped up down here *every* day," he explained. "As you know, we fought them and they eventually left me there, after the six of them had beaten me to within an inch of my life. I couldn't stop them taking Alice and my wife. As they left I could hear them discussing taking me back as meat, so they must have believed I was dead I suppose. I think it was too early in the morning for them to return to base and I suppose it would have been impractical to carry me round all day, so they planned to come back for me later."

"How did you get back here?"I asked him.

"One of our own scavenging parties found me at around noon and they helped me to get back. I had only just regained full consciousness when you brought Alice back to me. I can still never thank you enough for that."

"As I've said before, she helped me to find my Father too," I said.

"Yes I know. She'll be well looked after on the Island when your helicopters get here I believe. Keep looking out for her won't you, Badger, she thinks a lot of you."

"I'll be around to see you both regularly, she's like a sister now," I told him, not thinking at the time that his words had any other meaning.

"Well," he said, "I think our evening is over, if you will forgive me I shall bid you goodnight."

"Goodnight, John," I said to him as he stood and made his way towards the room he shared now with only his daughter.

I lingered a little, thinking of Alice and how she would like our Island home, how she and her father would settle in after this world that they had endured. I started to think of Alice's mother's fate, but struck the thought from my mind immediately; after my Father's tales the possibilities were too harrowing and I wanted to be able to get to sleep.

# CHAPTER 20

"Badger! Badger! Wake up!" Alice shook me vigorously a few hours later.

"What is it?" I asked her, as I rubbed the sleep from my eyes. Suddenly a glimmer of hope welled. "Has someone come?"

"No," she said, "nobody's come. It's my dad, he's gone."

Five minutes later almost everyone was in the canteen, despite it being only four in the morning. My Father was asking Alice what she knew of her father's disappearance.

"I don't know where he is," she said in answer to his questions. "I woke up with a bad dream, so I went to his bed and he wasn't there."

"Okay, child," my Dad said, and then spoke louder to everyone. "He's probably going to The Castle for his wife. We'll split up into groups of two to go and look for him. Five minutes till the first pair leave, which will be me and my daughter. Each other group at five minute intervals."

I crouched down. "Alice!" I hissed, beckoning her over to me, and then whispered, "You had a bad dream?"

She looked at me a little uneasily.

"Yes," she said, squirming.

"You once said you trusted me, Alice. You know you *can* trust me don't you?"

"Yes." She seemed uncomfortable and would not look me in the eye.

"Alice, tell me what else you know and I can help you," I told the girl, hoping that she would know I meant what I said and not think it was a verbal trap. I could tell there was something more and that she was trying hard not to say it.

"Do you promise not to tell anyone else? He made me promise not to tell anyone, Badger."

I knew that was a promise I could not make, instead I said to her, "You wouldn't have woken me if you hadn't wanted me to help, would you? But I can't help unless I know what the problem is, can I? I can't promise not to tell anyone else. Not unless I know what I'm promising not to tell."

"No." She looked guilty, as if she was trying to balance up her conscience. I waited briefly for her to think it through.

"Are you worried for him?" I asked her.

"Yes, he's going to try to get my mum back," she blurted out suddenly. "I didn't have a bad dream. I woke up when I heard him getting his stuff. He said he saw her at Buile Hill yesterday morning, in chains and he said he was going to get her back. I do want my mum back, but I'm afraid I might lose them both."

"Alice, I promise I'll do everything I can to get them back." Her face brightened. "But I can't do it on my own, so thank you for not making me promise."

Without waiting to see the look of confused betrayal on her face, I stood again and as loud as I could I shouted, "Stop! I know where John's gone!" I waited for the noise of those around me to die down.

"He's gone to Buile Hill. He saw his wife there and he's gone to get her back. I've promised Alice that I'll go and help him do just that and I'll take any assistance I can get. So who's going to come with me and make a stand for their friends?"

I could tell from the instant cheer that they were with me. I could also see my Father on the other side of the room. He looked at me, smiled and winked. At the same time, to my left, a small hand took mine and squeezed it gently.

"Thank you," her small voice could just be made out.

"Okay," said my Father, "we'll send out three scouts to have a quick look round, then we'll leave en masse. Time is of the essence if we're going to catch up with him."

I took Alice toward Jurgen in his battered wheelchair. He had entered with the others as the crowd had formed.

"Will you watch Alice?" I asked him. "We can't have her trying to follow us."

"Course I will, Badger, of course I will." Then turning towards Alice, he said, "You, me and Bert will have a fun time, while this lot go running off for your mum and dad won't we, Alice?"

I looked down at Alice who said nothing at first, she did not look as if she was in the mood for fun. Her bear hung limply by her side, her hand clasped round his paw.

"Be good, Alice, we'll be back with them both soon enough," I said.

She looked up at me. "You could all get hurt, I'm going to be very worried till you all come back."

I knelt beside her. "We've got to go though, we've got to get them back for you, Alice. I'm going for you and that's that. Do you remember our night in the cellar when I said I couldn't shoot them all on my own?" She nodded. "Well now I've got some help."

"Be careful, Badger." She gave me a brief hug and then let me go.

I felt a surge of nervous energy and, after leaving Alice with Jurgen, I rushed off to hastily prepare. I was back in my own clothes, the ones I had been wearing when I left the Island and I ran down the corridor to the dormitory. As I ran I was flanked by Hope and

Faith; I knew they would be with me. I collected my bow, arrows and one or two other items I felt I might need. Hope was kissing Snowy goodbye as I sprinted off down the corridor, alone this time. I collected my nitrocellulose before rejoining the others, I had a feeling it might come in very handy that morning.

A few minutes later a group of twenty of our strongest were moving swiftly through a light pre-dawn mist towards the park. Although it was unlikely that we would encounter anyone else at that time of day, experience had at some point taught each of them the folly of assumption. Around my Father and I, they scouted around, ducking down, listening and running past each other in perfect synergy. I saw the sisters, moving together as I would expect, feline again through the mist. Vincent had taken point, running a little ahead of the pack, listening and looking intently out into the thin fog.

This gave my Father and I the rare opportunity to simply walk together in the midst of a moving shield, with me helping him along on his recovering leg, without the constant worry of a stranger's approach. For once my bow was over my shoulder instead of in my hand. That morning, for the first time, that tribe was on the offensive. We felt it as a group, not as individuals, there were no words needed between us. We were no longer passive victims of circumstance; we were empowered by choice, fuelled by the adrenaline of 'fight' rather than 'flight'. Hope and Faith were in their element.

"Do you think we can catch up with him?" I asked

my Father.

"I hope so, one person can't move cautiously as fast as a team, but my leg will slow us down."

"And if they catch him?" I asked.

"They'll kill him straight away, or keep him as a slave. Either way, it won't end well," he said. I felt a twinge of apprehension for John and suddenly realised the implication of our discussion the night before.

"I spoke to him last night and now I think that maybe he was asking me to look after Alice," I told him.

"You, a godmother, who'd have thought it?" He looked amused at the prospect.

"I'm serious," I said. "He asked me to look out for her on the Island. I didn't know he'd do this!"

"He is a devoted father, but he's also a devoted husband. I was going to ask Gill to help with a rescue if his helicopters come. I didn't think John'd go off alone to try and get her back."

"Gill would have said no." I told him, feeling a rush of anger towards the admiral again on being reminded of what I perceived as his betrayal.

"How can you be so sure?" he asked.

"He wouldn't come for you."

He paused for a moment, thinking, then pragmatic as ever, "We'll just have to get her ourselves then won't we. You were right to say what you said at the tunnels. We should help our friends." I said nothing and tried to harness all of my animosity for Gill, focusing it into aggression; after all, we were going into battle that morning.

We found John, creeping towards the park carrying his recurve bow. A pack of our size could not have approached him unnoticed and so, to avoid any unnecessary casualties, it was vital to ensure that he recognised we were on his side. Following the usual coded exchange of whistles to establish identity, we reached his position. I was glad we had caught up with him before he had done anything rash, or been seen by those we intended to challenge.

"You should have told us," my Father said to him.

"I know, Doug," replied John. "I just didn't know how to. I couldn't ask you to put yourselves in danger like this - and I couldn't risk you trying to stop me."

"Well we're here now, so let's get this done," my Father reassured him. John's initial surprise at our arrival turned to relief, once he realised that we were not going to halt his plan and try to take him back with us, but help him to see it through.

I gave John a light slap of encouragement on his back. "Come on, let's go and get her back," I said.

We swallowed him into our party. There was no

time for debate, the time for explanations and gratitude would come later. We continued on our way, covering the ground fast, moving like a flood through the wastelands. As we approached the park my Father had us stop, form a circle and listen while he spoke.

"Right, there will be about fifteen of them, so we've got the greater numbers and the element of surprise," he told us all. "Not long after dawn, probably in half an hour or so from now, they'll get up but they won't go upstairs to unchain anyone immediately. First thing they'll do is open up the building. They bolt and bar the doors and windows overnight." His eyes flicked around the circle, making sure we all understood. "They throw back the bars and the next thing they'll do after that is to have a swift survey of the area, to make sure there's no one about. They're usually a bit complacent, especially first thing in the morning so we'll hit them then, as soon as they've started to look around. You all know what these people are like, give them no chances, you'll get none back."

His eyes locked on John's for a moment and he added, "They keep them all upstairs, chained up for the night. Whoever's first in should go up there and stop them taking hostages. We won't have time for negotiations."

He paused, giving everyone a chance to think.

"Any questions?" He was left in silence. "Right, small groups, spread out and keep hidden, it's vital. Everyone attacks on my first gunshot."

The group moved immediately, disappearing into what remained of the mist. John, Vince and two others went straight in the direction of the front door, stooping to keep as low as they could. I needed no second guesses of what they planned to do when they heard my Father's signal. He grabbed my arm as I set off to back them up.

"Projectile weapons at the rear?" he said hopefully.

"Not in a mist, you know that," then I winked at him. "I love you, Dad." I kissed his forehead quickly and went out into the thin fog.

We moved silently through the trees surrounding the house. It loomed up out of the haze, the doors and windows still shuttered up as my Father had described. The house was in remarkably good condition, I could even make out the signs of recent repair work to its roof. From behind them, I could see John's small band directly opposite the door of the hall, hiding behind the thick trunks of a pair of oak trees. They were ready, waiting for the signal and I moved round to their right finding a large hawthorn bush that was ideally placed to conceal me whilst enabling me to aim a shot at the front door. Ignoring the sharp thorns, I climbed almost right into it to get as much cover as possible.

I checked my knife was still in place, briefly grabbing its handle, before I started to prepare the bow. I hunted through my pocket and I took out my release aid. Most of the time I shot the bow using just my fingers, out of necessity for the faster, more responsive, method. This time however, I wanted to take a considered and well aimed shot and the release aid always improved my accuracy. I made a well educated guess on the distance and I set my sight to it. Next I stuck an arrow into the ground by my feet in readiness for my second shot. Then with the release aid strapped to my wrist, I hooked its clasping jaws around the bowstring, the arrow already in place.

I drew back the string and making ready to let loose, I peered through the rear sight mounted in the string itself and rested my index finger on the trigger. I was ready then, all I had left to do was wait for our targets' morning routine to begin. I spotted a few others of our party taking up their positions on the other side of the house, along with Faith and Hope who moved fleetly together into a covered spot behind some bushes.

I tried to mentally prepare myself. These were the people that had kept my Father from me and who also had my friend Alice's mother against her will, the people that caused so much pain, torment and death to others. That morning it was their turn to suffer. Calculated wrath replaced apprehension.

The wind moved the trees slightly, rustling the leaves. It was remarkably peaceful for a while as I stood there in that park, ready for the storm that was to follow the calm. Sure enough, just as my Father had predicted, they soon started to open up the house. One of them came out of the front door and had a quick look round, then after spending barely any time at all on his observations he wandered back inside. The window shutters then dropped down, one at a time, as he worked his way around the house, in readiness for the arrival of daylight.

Another of them came out through the front door, then a third. The pair of them moved five metres away from the house, making the briefest of cursory searches. The last man to have come out of the house started to relieve himself openly, facing towards us; thinking he was unobserved, his back to the house was as much of a gesture to dignity as he considered to be necessary.

The last of the lower floor windows opened as a fourth figure emerged. Suddenly her head flicked to the right, she had seen something. She raised her arm to point and opened her mouth, starting to shout. I heard the loud report of my Father's pistol clearly. The woman at the door immediately grasped her stomach with both hands and seemed to sit, falling backwards onto her behind.

My first arrow hit the man who was hurriedly trying to put himself away, urine spurting all over him, as his bladder refused to stop in response to the turn of events unfolding around him. My arrow punctured the centre of his chest and the puddle on the floor in front of him turned red, as he crumpled into it. I picked up the arrow that I had stuck in the ground, placed it on the string and drew again, back to using my fingers for quickness, with the release aid hanging from its strap on my wrist.

In front of me I saw that John had shot at the other of the men outside the house and hit him, but not killed him outright; John's familiar brown fletchings stuck out of the man's left shoulder. Others of our group had already leapt forwards by then to tackle the remaining targets outside of the building. I noticed John and his small contingent, including Vincent, had already dashed towards the house through the pillars at its once grand entrance, impatient to advance. I saw them kick the injured woman aside, to get through the front door as fast as they could. As they were about to enter, the man with the arrow through his shoulder roared out in pain and anger, as if only just realising his circumstances. He flung back the large overcoat he was wearing and produced a shortened shotgun. As he raised it towards our men in the doorway, my second arrow hit his right temple burying itself six inches into his head. I turned back towards the doorway in time to see Vincent running inside, past John and up the stairs within.

A further member of our makeshift regiment rushed forwards from the trees. After relieving the corpse of the second man I had killed of its weapon, he followed the others into the house. I drew a third arrow from my quiver and followed, bearing a little to the right and keeping my attention directed towards the windows on the closest side of the house. A woman's head rose from beneath the inside of a frame, she was armed with a crossbow which she levelled towards me and aimed. I did not have time to draw my own bow and so threw myself to the ground to try to avoid her weapon's bolt. As I did so, I heard my Father's pistol fire a second time and the woman at the window fell backwards through a cloud of her own vaporized blood.

As I got to my feet again, I looked round to see my Father limping towards me, outlined with a cloud of gun smoke, pistol still raised towards the house.

"Imagine her thinking of shooting my little Badger," he quipped to me, perhaps inappropriately, but I knew that deep down he was all too well aware of the gravity of the situation and that his humour was merely a coping mechanism. I understood that it was not easy for him to show that side of himself to me, the cold killer. Although I had obviously grown up in the last ten years and had just killed two men myself, it was clear he could not help but think of the little girl that I once was. It would take us both some time to adjust to our new roles within the relationship. I remember desperately hoping that we would have that time.

I saw Faith covering Hope's advance as she climbed in through a window, sword in hand. Faith's arrow flew past her sister's head, at her target inside the house. Hope yelled out in fury again and she flung herself at someone inside, with Faith diving in after to assist her. Whoever was inside that room would have had their hands full with the sisters coming in for them.

The fight was already over as my Father and I entered the house together. There were slaves bound together at the top of the stairs, visible on the landings from below. They were illuminated by the occasional flickering oil lamps which had not yet been extinguished after the disruption to the morning routine. We found John upstairs, held in the loving arms of his ecstatically grateful wife and I was happy not to interrupt their reunion.

We also found Vincent. He was dead, lying at the top

of the stairs. Someone had nearly decapitated him. It looked as if his attacker had hidden around the corner and swung a heavy blade at the first person to come up the stairs.

"Vince always was first in," my Dad said, looking down at him. "Goodbye my friend."

Others gathered around his body now, taking a moment to pay their respects. I could not think of any words to say, so instead I silently went back outside to retrieve my arrows. As I walked down the stairs I could hear John speak to the others.

"I'm sorry, it wasn't supposed to be like this," he said.

"It's always like this, Vince knew that," my Dad said back to him.

My Mother's words echoed in my head, "Cry and your face just gets wet."

There had been thirteen people guarding the house and now nine of those were dead. Three had fled and one, our first victim writhed in agony outside the front door. One of our group went to look at her and it immediately became obvious that even if we tried, with our limited medical resources she would not survive. Instead, he did the only thing he could under the circumstance and pushed a knife through her throat. It was a kindness that some of our party had difficulty in coming to terms with once they found out later, especially John. They were not normally violent or aggressive people and once it was over, they could not help but feel some remorse for the deaths they were responsible for; despite the fact that they had been instrumental in freeing the slaves and saving countless future lives. Killer was a role that did not sit easily with them.

I found Faith bandaging a cut on Hope's arm. She had been slashed at, but the wound was superficial, neither deep nor serious. The room that they had entered through the window of now held two of the dead slave keepers. Both had been stabbed in the throat with the sword to finish them off. I did not want to ask the details of their fight in there.

"Anyone hurt?" asked Hope.

"Vince is dead, other than him there's only you," I told her.

She looked down at her arm, obviously upset at the news, but hiding her expression from me. "This isn't hurt," she said simply.

# CHAPTER 21

Freeing the slaves took longer than we had anticipated. By the time we had them all untied we were in serious danger. There had been survivors of our attack and we knew for certain that they would be back with reinforcements and that there would be an overwhelming counter offensive. The people from The Castle would not know or stop to ponder who had attacked, they would care only for the reserves of people and food. They would likely think it was another raid by the Heaton Park tribe. There was no possibility they would not try to regain control; politics and egos aside, those from The Castle would starve without it.

My Father hobbled round the house, trying to rush people. I closed the downstairs shutters again, hoping it would help with defence if we were still there when they arrived. Some of the freed people took off immediately; others did not seem to know what to do with their new found liberty.

"Take anyone who wants to go with us back to the tunnels," my Father told John, shouting down the stairs to him. "Lead them near there straight away, but hide them under the road, near the river until you're sure you can get them inside unseen." John just nodded; it was clear that he and his wife wanted to be reunited with Alice as soon as they could get there.

John had started to lead them all away from the house when I heard another gunshot. I ran swiftly upstairs towards the sound. My Father stood at a rear window, gun in hand, looking out over the farmed parkland. I could see people from The Castle sheltering from any more potential fire, far out of range of my bow. They were at the bottom of a large hill leading down in the direction of Trafford.

We still had a few minutes before they could reach us, but under the threat of gunfire they seemed reluctant to advance. I hoped that would give us time to escape and thought that a distraction might help.

"I can keep them at bay for a while," my Father said. "You get the rest of those people out of here before they can see which way you're heading."

I moved away to follow his order when he added, "Jane, don't you dare forget to go with them." I ignored him and carried on down the stairs. I knew his 9mm was unlikely to hit anyone at the range he was shooting, but it would certainly slow down their advance towards the house.

"Come on, move, move, move," I shouted to the last of the people wandering around the reception area of the house still dazed by the turn of events. "Get out now while you can, follow the others, quickly, come on." Hope and Faith helped me to usher the last of them out, following them through the door.

I pushed the last one of the stragglers through the door and shut it. There was no way that I would be leaving my Father alone and, despite his best intentions for me, he knew that. I barred the door using the heavy swinging beam that the previous residents had installed and ran back upstairs. The loud cracks of my Father's gunshots hurt my ears as I went past the room he was shooting from. I found the rope that I was looking for quickly and I kicked open a shuttered window on the other side of the house from my Father's position. Finding the middle of the rope I hooked it around both the inside and outside handles of the open door, hoping that would be secure enough. I threw the two ends of it through the window. At the same time I looked out to see if the others had managed to escape yet. I could not see anyone.

I heard my Father eject an empty magazine from his gun and slam in the next - his last. The spent one rattled on the floor as he reloaded and resumed firing.

I went through to another of the upstairs rooms and found that one was filled with supplies. Finding some lamp oil they had left, I doused the place in it. I also found a small box of shotgun cartridges, it was yellowed and old but still held three unfired and I put them inside the empty oil can. I reached into my pocket for my home-made explosives and I rammed that into the tin too; that would add a little zest to my distraction when it got hot enough. I secured the lid of the can back in place and I put it at the bottom of the piled up provisions, to maximise its effect. Next I dipped a small piece of rag into the oil and I lit it with my lighter.

"Dad," I shouted, "time we were somewhere else."

He came away from the window and quickly hid behind its frame, as a volley of bullets came at him from outside, peppering the ceiling of the room and filling it with plaster dust.

"What on earth are you still doing here? I told you to go," he shouted back to me.

"No time. Let's go, now." I pointed at the rope and threw the burning rag into the other room. The lamp oil caught with a whoomph. Slinging my bow over my shoulder and grabbing both sections of the rope in my hands, I jumped out through the window and slid down, my hands burning from the friction. My Father followed me, first easing the hammer of his pistol down to avoid it going off accidentally. He climbed down and pulled the rope through and round the door handles above, obscuring our escape route. Gathering the rope up, we left the house together hoping that our pursuers would think we were still inside.

We moved away as fast as my Father's leg would allow, we were in real jeopardy of them seeing us as we left the house and if they did we knew that we would almost certainly be caught.

My Father did not move as fast as I would have liked due to his limp, but it was fast enough. We threw the rope into a bush two hundred metres from the house. Looking back I could then see the people surrounding the house, trying to batter down the door. The upper floor was billowing smoke and as I watched there was a deep bass boom as my improvised explosive blew, pushing out the window of the fiercely burning store room. Burning embers and debris showered those below.

My Father and I went north, out of the park and into the rubble and remains of a housing estate, following the outline of a road to the side of the school he had once hidden in.

"You should have gone with the others," he admonished me.

"I only got you back a week ago, I'm not going to lose you again so soon," I said. "No desperate last stands without me until at least week two, okay?" I joked.

He gave a low snort of laughter. We followed the road as it turned to the right and we moved as fast as we could. The burning house was no longer visible but behind us we could hear the castle dwellers, shouting and yelling angrily. They had broken into the house and found it empty. They were searching for us and had worked out that we must have gone north. Judging by their calls to one another they had just found the rope that we had left behind and that was leading them in our direction. They wanted their slaves back and we knew where they were.

"You're going to have to leave me soon anyway," my Father said. "You'll be fast enough to get away from them on your own."

"I've told you, I'm not going to leave you. We just need to find a place to hide, I don't think this lot will be too hard to outsmart." As I said that, I moved the bow from over my shoulder to my hand, perhaps subconsciously.

"Listen to me, I want you to run. I can hold them back again for a while, we don't both have to die."

"You're not allowed to die, that wasn't what I came here for," I told him firmly. We moved on as fast as I could drag him along. We came to a squat low building on our right and another road ran away from it to our left, northwards again. We took off down that road, the buildings were quite complete on either side and there was a junction at its head, about fifty metres up the road. I was planning to try to confuse our path while we looked for somewhere to hide.

Just as we reached the junction I heard one of them shout from behind us.

"They're here!" a woman called to the others. I turned round towards her and calmly I shot her, my arrow vibrating as it lodged in her chest. She sank to her knees before falling backwards.

I knew then that it was too late and we were going to be caught; I would never leave my Dad behind and they would soon catch up with us now that they knew where we were. As we went to the top of the road there was a further disappointment. It was a dead end, there were no gaps between the houses or the garages and there was no way out of that end of the road. I turned again to see a crowd of our pursuers forming at the bottom of the cul-de-sac, around the body of the dying woman I had just shot. They were all looking in our direction.

We were trapped. There was nowhere left for us to go.

# CHAPTER 22

So that was it, we were cornered. It really looked like it would then be just a case of how many of them and how long it would take to bring us both down. Undeterred I nocked an arrow and heard Dad's Glock click as he cocked it again. Slowly they crept closer towards us, knowing that they had us, but each not wanting to be the first to rush at us. They knew that we were armed and it was only a matter of time before they used firearms too. For now it was better for each of them as individuals to wait for one of the others to get to us first.

"Cowards," I hissed at them, drawing back the string of my bow.

I knew that I had twenty-one arrows left and I was determined to make good use of each and every one of them. One of the mob rushed out from behind a wall, towards us, about fifty metres away and my arrow speared through the top of his leg, near to his groin. He dropped to the ground screaming, then dragged himself slowly behind the safety of an old burned out car. Dad's gun came up to shoulder level, grasped in both of his hands. He was covering me as I took out another arrow and drew back the bowstring again. I knew that he only had a few rounds left, but if he did not hold them back with the threat of the gun, they would waste no time in taking us down.

"Make each arrow count, okay. Don't let them get close," he whispered, "and look out for any of them trying to go round the sides of us."

"How many shots have you got left?"

"Four," he answered. "Last two for us?"

"Okay," I nodded to him, "but I'm not going down without a fight."

"I wouldn't expect anything less."

Letting go of his gun with one hand, he grabbed my shoulder and squeezed it briefly before gripping the automatic with both hands again.

"You shouldn't have come," he said.

"Gill should have," I replied. "He shouldn't have left you out here alone for all those years. As soon as he knew you might still be alive, when you called for help, he should have sent a team. When Gill let you down, I had to come."

"He could have at least left his radio switched on to listen out for your signal," he laughed half-heartedly. "Maybe he's still annoyed about me crashing his plane."

I tried to smile at his joke, but I did not have it in me any more. A strange acceptance washed over me, although not enough to stop me putting twenty six inches of aluminium arrow into the chest of the next of them to break cover as he tried to get closer. He fell backwards clawing at the exposed end of the shaft. Blood flecks sprayed out in his breath, as he coughed and sank to the floor.

"Nice shot." My Dad sounded proud of me again, but there was no time to think about that then.

"Thanks," I said, "nineteen left."

In the distance, beyond accurate range and towards the back of their group, stood a short balding man who was dressed rather better than the others. He was carrying two swords strapped to his belt. He shouted out in anger and frustration at the people around him, exercising his authority, scorning their incompetence, ordering them on. He viciously kicked a man near to him who had been hiding behind a car.

"Get at them you imbeciles!" he shouted.

"We're honoured, that's the man himself," my Father said.

"He's Terrance is he?" I asked him.

"The very same," he said.

"Seems like a charming fellow."

"If we killed him we would be doing what's left of the world a favour." It was as close to a request as he could manage. Despite all that we had just been through and trapped as we were, in his head he knew I was his comrade and equal but his heart still had a long way to catch up.

"Don't worry, the very second he comes into my range, Dad," I reassured him.

"He won't do that I don't think, but keep an eye on him anyway," he replied.

Again they started to advance slowly towards us, their autocratic leader ranting at them, calling them all kinds of derogatory names as he compelled them to attack. I think he wanted them to take us alive for all the trouble that we had caused them, to make a more public example of us later. As I realised that I had to try hard not to think of the things they would do if they did manage to capture us, of what they would do to us both if we fell into their hands. A shudder ran through me and I had to push myself back to reality.

"Listen," Dad said in a whisper.

At first I could not hear anything, but after ten seconds or so I could just make it out too. A low throbbing, I could feel it vibrate in my chest. Almost too low to be audible at all, then gradually getting a little louder, then a little louder still - a familiar fast pulsating whoop. Our pursuers could hear it too. They were shouting out to each other, asking each other what it was, where it was. About forty metres away, one of them popped his head up to look and nearly got an arrow through it, as a reward for his curiosity.

"Eighteen," my Dad whispered.

"Is that noise what I think it is?" I asked him.

"Yes, but they'll have to find us. Don't waste your arrows."

He spotted it first. "Look over there," he gesticulated towards the horizon to our right with his pistol. Seconds later the first attack helicopter arrived, a Cobra, one of ours. I shouted and yelled towards it at the top of my voice, even though I knew they had no chance of hearing me. I tried to see who was flying it but I could not make out the face at that distance. The chopper roared over the top of us at about sixty miles an hour, its down wash blowing dust and debris everywhere. The huge, dark green, insectoidal attack helicopter was only thirty feet above us, close enough for me to make out the white tips of its rockets in the fully loaded launch tubes.

Once it had passed over us, it banked hard right and back, spinning around on its own axis as it turned to return. At that moment we realised that they had seen us and we felt such enormous elation at our reprieve. The gun flared and, in the no-man's land between us and our pursuers, dust plumed up in a short line. The twenty millimetre rounds buried themselves deeply into the ground and the noise was deafening.

The second Cobra came in slower, from behind us, advancing towards the men and women from The Castle. Once directly over our heads it hovered, holding us in its downdraft. The huge gun slung underneath moved seeking out targets, pointing directly at them and daring them to respond. They knew there was nothing to stop him wiping them all out if he chose to; all he had to do was pull the trigger.

They did the only thing they could do. They fled, running as quickly as they could. Some zigzagged as they ran, as if they thought that might make a difference. Terrance was once again shouting at them, though I could not make out his words. Again he kicked at one of his men as he ran past. I saw another one of them, half dragging the man with my arrow still impaling his thigh.

I laughed out loud, drunk with relief, resisting an insane temptation to shout out for the return of my arrow. My Father grabbed me in an enormous embrace. The sense of joy was overwhelming. They had come and now we were not going to die out there. I had got him back and the helicopters had come to rescue us both.

"We did it, we did it!" I shouted at the top of my voice.

"No, it was you! You did it! Thank you, thank you so much!" my Father cried.

The Cobras then worked in tandem, herding the men and women of The Castle away from us like well trained dogs moving sheep across a hillside. One of the men foolishly raised a rifle, aiming it towards a pilot and was killed instantly by a short burst of cannon fire. The enormous bullets riddled him, tearing him apart, spreading out his remains over the ground.

After that even Terrance admitted defeat and he retreated too, following his demoralised mob, still shouting insults. I do not know what his crew would have been more intimidated by, our helicopters or the consequences of Terrance's wrath that they would be bound to endure later on. My Father tried to catch a pilot's attention and have them shoot the despot, but neither of them saw his efforts.

A third helicopter arrived, not a Cobra this time, but a load carrying Huey. It circled and landed, near to the body of the woman I had shot after she had given away our location to her own people. The co-pilot opened the door to us as we approached.

"Captain Playton, it's good to see you again, Sir," he said to my Father.

"Max! Please there's no need to be formal. It's so great to see you and just in time too." His smile was the widest I had ever seen it.

"We would have come a bit sooner if we could have." Then he indicated towards me with his head, "Got a feisty little one there, she's the talk of the Island." Then to me he said, "Hello, Badger, fancy seeing you here."

"Hi, thanks for coming," I said to him.

"Oh, you're welcome. Need a lift anywhere?" he asked us both.

"Yes please, but we've got a few friends to pick up, about seventy all told. Is that okay?" my Dad said to him as his hand patted a hand painted badge on the side of the helicopter, the insignia of a horse, stood on its rear legs.

"Right that will be a few trips then." He leaned back in to the pilot, "Get them on the blower, Gary. It seems we've got a small exodus to organise."

I heard the pilot reply to him, "Not until we turn off that transmission we haven't."

"Oh yes," said Max and turned his attention back to us. "We'll have to turn off your signal first, it's blocking everything else out. That'll be easy enough though I suppose. How on earth have you managed to survive out here for so long, Doug?" he asked.

"Trial and error mostly," my Father told him, modestly shrugging his shoulders.

"And you," he said turning to me, "did you enjoy your holiday, 'Miss Special Forces 2011'? How on earth did you get all the way here without someone catching or killing you?"

I was not impressed with his new nickname for me. "Same way I suppose, trial and error, but I also brutally killed everyone who called me a stupid name along the way too... and of course, anyone who didn't take me seriously." I told him in a deadpan voice and then smiled innocently at him.

"Should I stick to calling you Bodger then?" he said, smiling back at me too.

"Bodger?"

"Well that's what you put in your transmission, 'bodger and dad alive in salford'" he could hardly suppress his sniggering. "I think you need to brush up on your Morse, Bodge."

# CHAPTER 23

Later that day we stood, Shiel and I, on the flight deck of my home. We looked out over the sea to the east towards the mainland. Faith and Hope were moving across the deck in front of us, accompanied by Helen who was trying, rather unsuccessfully, to convince them that they did not have to run from one bit of cover to the next to avoid being seen by so many strangers. Of all those being brought over from the mainland I thought that those two might have the hardest time settling in and adjusting. I noticed that Hope had Snowy safely cradled in her arms and I hoped that nobody would ever mistake that cat for a feral animal.

Jurgen had been in the first of the helicopters, with my Father and I. He pushed on the wheels of his chair to propel himself towards them. He caught the sisters' attention and tried to calm them down. They looked far happier for seeing a familiar face.

Other ex-residents of the tunnels and the house stood in small groups around the deck. The helicopters made short work of the journey that had taken me days. All of the new arrivals looked overjoyed at their good fortune. On one side of the deck, one of the two Cobras that had come to our rescue was being lowered down to the hangar deck on the huge lift.

"I think I half wish I'd gone with you," said Shiel.

"It wasn't a lot of fun really. I only told you the highlights, not the bit about sleeping under a bridge or being piddled on while lying in a stinking pond for instance," I told him. "Fights and running around blowing stuff up only sounds like fun afterwards, in the telling of a tale. I was terrified most of the time out there, cold, wet, exhausted and frightened. I was hiding from everything and everybody."

"I suppose so." He sounded unconvinced. "Do you know those two ladies well?" He motioned towards the now slightly more relaxed sisters.

"Do you want an introduction? I'd give them a bit of time to settle in first. They'll eat you alive otherwise. Don't get me wrong, they're good friends, but they have a few trust and anger management issues, they can be a bit... volatile."

"Really, okay, perhaps later on then." He sounded intrigued. "Is that it?" he said, pointing at the horizon.

I lifted up my binoculars, "No, that's a seagull."

"Oh, okay. By the way, I heard your dad talking to Gill as I came up," he told me.

"Did Gill have much to say?" I inquired.

"Say? No he didn't actually *say* anything," he told me. "Shout though? Oh, yes very much so, much loud shouting, yes."

A moment of silence passed and I knew that Shiel was enjoying himself.

"Words like 'wilful', 'disobedient', 'disrespectful' and 'punished' were used, very loudly indeed," he said, with a little too much relish I thought. "Oh and 'headstrong' too, don't forget 'headstrong'," he added. "He shouted that *more* than once."

"I wonder who they were talking, sorry, shouting about," I said rhetorically.

"I think Gill mentioned something about dealing with you later on, Badger," and after a slight pause, "at the top of his voice." Again he paused, then, "I know what it's like when he shouts very loudly at you for something you've just done. Like giving someone a ride in your boat, for instance."

We continued watching the horizon.

"Can't think what the nice admiral would want to discuss with me," I said innocently. Right then I did not care how much trouble I was in, no retribution could outweigh the rewards of my expedition.

"I don't suppose there's any of my beer left at your flat is there?" I asked, changing the subject.

"What beer would that be?" he asked coyly.

"I see," I said to him, "no beer then."

"My hearing's recovered by the way," he told me, also changing the subject deftly.

"What from?" I kept looking through the binoculars.

"Your signal," he said, "you switched it on when I was wearing headphones in the communications room. On full gain I might add."

"Loud was it?" I smiled smugly.

"Well we didn't have any problems tracking its direction; we did however have problems guiding the helicopters towards it," he explained. "We couldn't communicate with them, or they with each other. Your signal interfered with theirs on all the wavelengths. It's a good job you set that building on fire really."

"It all worked out well then," I said passing him the binoculars and pointing. "Look, over there, that's them."

The small dot grew larger and larger and the noise of its rotors soon drowned out any conversation. The helicopter landed on the deck accompanied by the other Cobra and I could see a small excited face pressed to the glass, with eyes wide, as the child and her bear bounced up and down on their seat in anticipation. The pilot switched off the engines and eventually the doors were opened for her.

"Badger!" Alice sprinted towards me as soon as she had disembarked. "That was the best thing ever! The ground just went away and it was so fast!" I picked her up, giving her a big hug, shaking her gently side to side.

"Alice, it's great to see you again," I told her, adding,

"say hello to my friend Shiel."

I put her down and she turned toward to him.

"Pleased to meet you, Miss." Shiel put his hand out to her formally, bending a little so that she could reach and they shook hands.

"Pleased to meet you too, are you the radio man?"

"I am indeed, the radio man. You can call me Shiel," he added with a conspiratorial wink, "but only if I can call you Alice. Welcome to our small Island home."

She giggled at him, overwhelmed by it all.

I saw Alice's parents looking around themselves in awe, totally ecstatic and at the same time struggling to comprehend that it was really happening. I do not think they could believe that a place like ours could really still exist, or that so much had changed since that morning.

Alice's mother walked towards me.

"Hello, it's Badger isn't it?" she asked.

"Yes, I'm Badger," I said and we shook hands too.

"My name is Susan. We haven't been properly introduced, although I saw you at the house. I believe I owe you a huge amount of thanks," she said. "John has told me of everything you have done for us and especially for me."

I blushed a little. "That's okay. You don't need to thank me."

"Well I'm going to say it all the same. Thank you, Badger, and thank you for rescuing Alice from that place and for taking care of her."

"Badger, tell her about the man with the axe, Badger, I forgot about him," interrupted Alice bouncing up and down again.

Her mother smiled at me, then at Alice.

"Don't interrupt, Alice, not even when you're so excited," she gently admonished the girl. Then to me, "You will have to tell me the tale one day."

"One day I will," I said.

"Thank you for persuading everyone to come to John's aid as well," she added. "Alice told me about you sharing her secret this morning and getting help for John." It seemed like a very long time ago already.

"Badger's great, Mum," said Alice. "There was this man with an axe and he wanted to hurt me so I hid behind her and she said I wasn't going with him and he said I was." She didn't pause for breath sometimes, falling silent this time only because her mother had shushed her. She had placed her index finger vertically over Alice's mouth.

"It seems I have to thank you for things I haven't

even heard about yet," Alice's mum said, removing her finger from across her child's mouth.

"Do we not have to hide from other people here, Badger?" asked Alice looking around herself at the people bustling about.

"Only scary people from the mainland like you," I teased her and then ruffled her hair. "No, Alice, we don't need to hide from anyone here, you're safe now."

"Hmm," she said, "when can I go and see the other children?"

"Tomorrow if you like, as soon as you are settled in. You'll see them at school if not before."

"I've never been to school before, what's it like?"

"Well you remember the bow I made for you," I said, "well they'll show you how to do lots of fun stuff like that."

Shiel gave me a look, one that said I was being economical with the truth. Behind Alice's back I returned his look with one that said 'keep your nose out'. I think he knew exactly what I meant and he smiled.

"Oh, I didn't know it would be stuff like that," she said. "I've still got my bow. It's tied to my bag. Will you give me another lesson?"

"Okay, soon," I told the girl as we wandered back

towards her parents, who were looking out across at Ramsey, their new home.

Alice looked then too, off the edge of the ship. She walked to the small fence at the side of the runway and looked, firstly down at the water, then up towards the horizon.

"It really does go on forever doesn't it, Badger."

"You know what, Alice, it doesn't. If you go far enough, really, really far then I believe you just end up back where you started from."

THE END